Readers love *Cupcakes*
by SEAN MICHAEL

By SEAN MICHAEL

Guarding January
The Swag Man Delivers
Cupcakes
Two Tickets to Paradise (Dreamspinner Anthology)

Published By DREAMSPINNER PRESS
http://www.dreamspinnerpress.com

Guarding January

SEAN MICHAEL

Published by
DREAMSPINNER PRESS

5032 Capital Circle SW, Suite 2, PMB# 279, Tallahassee, FL 32305-7886 USA
http://www.dreamspinnerpress.com/

Guarding January
© 2015 Sean Michael.

Cover Art
© 2015 Brooke Albrecht.
http://brookealbrechtstudio.com
Cover content is for illustrative purposes only and any person depicted on the cover is a model.

ISBN: 978-1-63216-816-0
Digital ISBN: 978-1-63216-817-7
Library of Congress Control Number: 2014920697
First Edition March 2015

Printed in the United States of America
∞
This paper meets the requirements of
ANSI/NISO Z39.48-1992 (Permanence of Paper).

PROLOGUE

RYE SAT on the little chair in the waiting room, feeling like some sort of oversized gorilla.

There'd been three other bodyguards waiting when he'd arrived, but two had gone in and come back out in short order. The last guy ahead of him had lasted a minute or two longer. A tired-looking blonde had poked her head out as well, telling him she needed a couple minutes.

He glanced at his watch. He was between jobs and didn't have anywhere to be, so it wasn't like he minded waiting. This chair, though, was a little on the uncomfortable side. He shifted, the whole thing creaking ominously. It was small, and he was worried it wasn't going to hold his weight.

You could say a lot of things about him—he was a solid guy, trustworthy, surefooted, and reliable. One thing you couldn't say? He was small.

He debated getting up and standing over by the window or something, but he didn't want Donna Heard to think he was antsy or getting cold feet. Reg Storm, who'd given him the heads-up on the job after he'd finished a stint keeping the rock star safe from a stalker, had told him Donna was a real stickler.

A ballbuster, even.

And obsessed with keeping her pseudovampire, crazy-assed-fans-sending-blood-in-the-mail singer alive.

It was a good thing he liked a challenge and didn't judge.

He shifted, and the chair creaked alarmingly again. Okay, he was standing. Looking like he was restless had to be better than breaking the damn chair.

The door opened about the same time his ass left the chair. "Sorry for the delay. I had a phone call. Please, come in."

"No worries. I'm sure you're very busy." He held out his hand. "I'm Rye Sommers."

"Donna Heard. Pleased." The office was classy, furnished with heavy, overstuffed furniture, way more solid than the stuff in the waiting area. "Have a seat."

"Thank you." He sat, nothing creaking or shifting in warning. Oh thank God. That was just… ridiculous.

"Sorry about the tiny chairs out there. You're… a big guy."

That had him chuckling. "You did nearly have firewood there. Big is what you need, though, right?" Little guys weren't bodyguards.

"Absolutely. And LJ is… challenging." She leaned back, steepled her fingers, and was completely in control.

"Challenging? I'm good with challenges. Can you be more specific?" He knew LJ stood for Lord January. Lord. January. He'd seen pictures of the guy too. Skinny, tattoos, piercings, and makeup. Lots of makeup.

"First, tell me about you. About your specialties."

"I've been bodyguarding for six years. I've never lost a client. I specialize in twenty-four/seven care."

"And you're comfortable with travel? This is a long-term position."

Long term was good. It would be nice to have something a little more permanent. He was tired of bouncing from job to job.

"I don't even have a goldfish for someone to feed while I'm away."

"I've checked your references. You come highly recommended. LJ needs round-the-clock attention. And I want you working solo. The last thing he needs is two or three strangers coming into his life full-time. As you can imagine, his persona is… not conducive to normal life."

"I googled him. I imagine not everything I read was true, but it seems very, uh, colorful."

The man was apparently in rehab. Of course he also apparently ate live rats every Friday night before having a massive orgy.

"Colorful is one word for it." Donna rolled her eyes. "He's been in rehab—willingly, I might add—and from all reports, he's done well. The doctors say he's stronger than he was when he went in. He's gained thirty-five pounds. He's clean. It'll take seven seconds on the road with all those assholes for it to be ripped apart."

"So you want me to run interference with the groupies, the band, anyone who tries to get him hooked again?"

"I need someone to keep him safe, fed, clean. Keep the pushers away from him, as best you can. Temptations are everywhere, and LJ is… easily tempted. He gets bored, stressed, worried. You have eight weeks before he goes on the road, then a thirty-week world tour."

"How far do I go to keep him clean?"

"His heart stopped twice the night before we admitted him. Twice." Suddenly Donna seemed like an avenging fucking angel. "I'll pull him off the road forever if it saves his life."

"So I won't be fired for sitting on him to keep him from going out and getting a hit?"

"He can't fire you. I do ask that we keep this as private as possible. His image is one thing, his real life another. You work for me, personally."

"I'm not sure what you're saying. Do you mean he won't know you hired me or what for?" Rye wasn't sure about that. The best way to protect a client was to be up front with them.

"No, sir. I mean he can't fire you. He can fuss and bluster, but only I can fire you."

"Okay." He nodded. "I take it his public image is to remain…." He waved his hand.

"January the Vampire Lord." Her voice was dripping with sarcasm.

How did something like that start?

"As long as I don't have to call him 'my lord,' I think this will work."

"LJ is fine."

"I'm licensed to carry a firearm. Do you want me to?" Some clients felt more comfortable if he was armed; others felt just the opposite.

She stopped and gave the matter some thought. "Perhaps keep one locked away. He might… I don't know."

Lord January was rich, famous, with millions of screaming fans, yet it sounded like he wasn't very happy. Hell, her fear of suicide added to the addictions told that story. "You don't want him to have access. I have a lockbox for it. That way it'll be fairly easy for me, but only me, to get to."

"Yes. Oh yes. Please." She looked so relieved.

"How closely do I need to watch him for… self-destructive behavior?"

"I think the only not-destructive thing he's ever done is agree to rehab."

"So at some point this stopped being an interview and started being a game plan. I take it I have the job?" Thinking back to how quickly the other interviews had ended, he had to wonder if he was the only one who hadn't run off screaming. January sounded like a handful, and it was a huge responsibility, taking it on without backup.

"I take it you do."

"I gather from what I've read that… LJ is still in rehab. I'd like to go through the house before he gets out, make sure any threats have been removed, and become familiar with it. I'll also need a list of who else has access to LJ, who I can expect to be in his life on a regular basis. I assume you've kept a file of threats made on his life." He went into work mode, running through a checklist in his head.

"Yes. Yes, he's out on Friday afternoon."

"I can meet him at the door to the rehab center and stay by his side from then on." He'd spend tomorrow wrapping up any loose ends: shut up his apartment, let his sister and mother know he might be slow to answer communication, all that stuff. That would free him up to do the walk-through of LJ's place on Thursday.

"I can get you all the background stuff you need. How much are you asking for your wage?"

"I realize I'll be getting room and board, but I'll be on duty twenty-four/seven, so that also has to be taken into account. A thousand a day."

To her credit, she didn't even blink. "Fine. He uses once, and you're out. No second chances."

"Understood." He came to his feet and held out his hand. "I'll keep him safe, Ms. Heard. Even from himself."

"That's your job. Talk to my secretary about the details. She'll get you what you need."

"Will you let LJ know I'm picking him up, or am I meeting him cold?"

"I'll let him know. He isn't good with surprises at the best of times."

"I'll keep that in mind. Thank you. You won't be disappointed." He gave her a tight smile and headed out.

He was going to have to drop Reg Storm a thank you note for suggesting the job to him and giving him a reference. Looked like this one was going to be a challenge, which was how he liked it.

CHAPTER ONE

"DO I have to go?" Jeff stood at the door of the room he'd been living in for eight months. Eight months he'd been safe and happy in there. Eight months he'd been able to be just Jeff, instead of Lord January. "Jim, can't I just stay?"

"Oh, honey, you know you can't. You have all the tools to do this. You do." His sponsor and the man who had become a friend stared at him, smiled.

"You look like Santa Claus when you do that."

"Shut up."

They looked at each other, and then they cracked up, leaning together, and if he cried a bit, Jim didn't say a word.

"Come on. Donna sent a car for you, to take you home."

"She sent a babysitter."

He couldn't even complain—he probably needed one—but couldn't it be Jim? Couldn't he stay there where he was safe?

"You have my number, Jeff. Use it if you need it, okay? I mean that."

He nodded, wrapped his hoodie around him, iPod in the pocket, put his sunglasses on, and hunched inside the fabric.

Jim gave him a short, hard hug, then walked him out the front door. Out into the world.

He winced away from the sunlight, tugging his hood down farther. "My things?"

"Already in the car, sir." A mountain of a man threw him into shadow, and a huge paw was held out. "I'm Rye."

"I don't shake hands. Sorry." *Jesus, Donna had hired a giant.* "I'll call, Jim, okay? Soon?"

"Anytime, Jeff. I promise."

The giant waited until he started down the walk, then paced him. "We're the dark gray SUV to the right of the gate."

"Okay." He kept his head down, making sure the light and the long-range lenses couldn't get to him.

He had to admit, having the Hulk walking next to him gave him some cover to hide behind, made him feel less exposed. Didn't mean he suddenly wanted the babysitter, mind you.

The walk down the path seemed to take for-fucking-ever, but at last they were at the car, his minder opening the door for him and bundling him in. The door shut with a very final sounding click, and in seconds they were driving away from the one place he knew was safe.

Jeff put his earphones in and turned the music up loud, the noise pounding in his head.

He stayed in his cocoon until the door opened, his new bodyguard's hand touching his arm. Aside from really tall and really built, the guy had short brown hair, like military cut almost, and a square jaw you'd expect some tough bodyguard to have. His new bodyguard's eyes were surprisingly blue, like bright and alive. Jeff slid his gaze from the guy to the house.

Home sweet home. Goodie. He stood, the garage quiet and still. There were two doors down there—one to his rooms, one to the rest of the house where everyone else was. He grabbed his guitar, then headed to the door on the left, heading upstairs without a word.

Rye—that was what the guy had said his name was, right?— kept up with him, right behind him on the stairs like a shadow.

"These are my rooms." He knew Donna would have had them searched, emptied of anything—uppers or downers.

"I know. Hell, the whole house is yours, LJ."

He didn't bother to argue, but he knew better. The guys in the band came and went, the groupies, people who called themselves friends. Technically his money had paid for the house, but it was a part of Lord January's image and had very little to do with him.

Following him right to his bedroom, Rye put his bag from rehab down at the end of his bed.

"So…. Are you hungry?"

7

"No." He moved to sit in the huge overstuffed chair in the corner. "I think I'm just going to sleep. I'm not sure what Donna wants you to do, but I'm going to just rest for a couple of days. I don't want company."

"I'm not company. I'm your bodyguard. Whither thou goest, there shall I go."

"I'm not going anywhere." He was never leaving this room.

Ever.

And even though he knew that was a lie, it was the one he was sticking with right now.

"Then neither am I." Rye, the giant, smiled down at him. "Except maybe to make you a sandwich. Are you sure you're not hungry?"

"I'm not hungry. Make yourself at home. I assume someone got you a room?"

"Somebody who? It's just you and me." Rye sat on his bed.

"There's staff—a cook, housekeeper, all the people. Someone let you in."

"The housekeeper comes in once a week now, and everyone else has been sent away. Ms. Heard didn't feel you needed the distractions." Rye dug into his pocket and pulled out a little ring of keys. "I let myself in."

"Oh." Jeff pulled the hoodie down farther, found another playlist on his phone, and put the earphones in, the music battering him, drowning out the world.

He wanted to go back to rehab.

He wanted to be safe.

"I'm going to make a sandwich and bring a chair in to sit with you. I won't be long."

He nodded and waited for Rye to leave. Then he went to the closet, took his shoes off, and grabbed a blanket. His stashbox was in the safe, right there, and he didn't look at it. He just needed to have it in case.

He curled up in his chair, hid under his blanket, and went to sleep.

Once today was over, he could work on tomorrow being over too. One day at a time, and all that bullshit. Still, it was all he had.

GOD, RYE was bored.

Fucking bored.

Four days of bodyguarding January, lord of the fucking vampires, and all they'd done was sit in this room. There was only so much Candy Crush a man could play without feeling demasculinized.

LJ was still and silent. He'd eaten once in four days, had one huge bottle of water a day, taken a few bathroom breaks, and mostly stayed in that chair, hidden under a blanket.

It was creepy.

Hell, the kid was creepy. Big dark eyes, long dark hair, skin pale as milk except where the ink covered him.

Rye wanted to feed him the world's biggest ham and cheese sandwich, slather him in suntan lotion, and take him out into the sun. It was hard to believe this kid was the same bad boy rock star he'd seen in the YouTube vids. This guy was tiny and bruised and barely breathing.

Phone light filtered out from under the blanket, so he knew LJ was awake. That was something.

"So how about we go for a swim today? You've got that great pool out there, just... sitting."

"Go ahead. I don't mind."

"No, I've already been." He was up at dawn, working out and doing laps. Keeping fit. "But I'll go with you." He stood and went over, tugging the cover off LJ.

Those huge, near black eyes stared at him, the bruises underneath a deep, dark blue. "Pardon me?"

"Let's go swim. Get some fresh air. Frankly, you need it, buddy." He was allowed to do what he wanted, though. As long as he kept LJ clean.

Clean had to mean healthy, right? Eating, drinking, showering, moving around. Wasn't the guy supposed to want to make music or something?

He held out his hand. If LJ didn't take it, he was putting the kid over his shoulder and carrying him down.

"I don't go outside in the sun."

"Maybe you should start. Ten minutes and a sandwich, and I'll let you come back up here to hide some more."

"You don't get to tell me what to do. I just have to not use. That's it."

"Actually, no. I'm also supposed to keep you alive. And this isn't living. So take my hand and come downstairs with me, or I'll make it happen."

"Shoo." LJ pulled his legs up under his chin, bent back to his phone.

Well, that made it easier to pick LJ up.

Bending, Rye slid his arms beneath LJ's shoulders and knees, then picked him up.

"What? Put me down! I said no!"

Christ, the kid couldn't weigh a buck and a quarter. How much had Ms. Heard said he'd gained in rehab? How much had he lost in the last few days?

Rye should have done this sooner.

He ignored LJ, kept carrying him down the stairs.

As soon as they left his quarters, LJ went stiff, silent. The bigger part of the house had been party central, and Rye had flushed everyone out, had the place cleaned top to bottom, made sure there weren't drugs or booze anywhere.

It was quiet, almost echoing, as he moved into the huge great room, with its floor-to-ceiling windows. He kept going, heading for the pool. He knew there were towels out there and had no qualms over what he was about to do.

The place was a shrine to decadence, to excess, and LJ didn't look at anything, just hid in his hoodie, his baggy clothes.

"Pool," Rye said, as he went out into the huge backyard with its enormous pool set into the place to look like a pond.

"Very nice. I want to go in."

"Exactly, you're going in. We both are."

"No. Inside. I want to go back inside."

"No, the pool, a bit of fresh air. If I put you down, will you strip or run?"

"I don't want to get wet. I want to go inside. I haven't done anything wrong."

"You're not living, LJ. You're just… fading away, and I gave my word I wouldn't let you go." With that, he dumped LJ into the water.

LJ flailed, fighting with the heavy, too-big clothes for a second before just going limp and sinking to the bottom.

Jesus Christ.

Rye took off his shoes and jumped in after LJ.

Stupid little fuck.

He grabbed at the hoodie, but LJ slipped away, leaving him holding the fabric. Growling, he let the hoodie go and grabbed for LJ.

The little bastard was quick, scrambling up the stairs and running for the house.

After jumping out, Rye gave chase, grabbing LJ just before he got to the door. He pulled the kid up against his body. Skin and bones, that's what LJ was.

"Let me go! Let me go! I haven't done anything bad!" LJ struggled against Rye, fists battering at him.

This was more life than Rye'd seen out of the kid since he'd picked him up, and he simply held LJ, let the kid work the anger out.

It didn't last long—it couldn't, LJ wasn't eating—and then the kid just passed out, pale as milk.

Christ.

Fucking Christ.

Rye laid LJ down on a deck chair and grabbed a thick towel from the little cabana. Then he stripped LJ quickly and dried him off.

LJ finally came back to. "I… I want to go back."

"Back where?" Rye looked into that pale, pinched face.

"I want to go back to the hospital."

"You have a life to live." A tour that started in less than two months.

"I want to go back."

"It doesn't work that way, LJ. You know that."

He wrapped the kid in the towel, but didn't bring him back upstairs yet. LJ curled into a tiny ball, almost disappearing under the towel. Acting on instinct, Rye grabbed LJ and tugged him against his body.

"I don't—" The too-skinny body just shuddered.

"Shh. Shh. Just warming you up, okay?" He needed to get heat and food and water into LJ, needed to. He gathered LJ up again. "Kitchen. Food. We'll get something in you."

"N-n-not hungry."

"Too bad. Your body is starving to death, and if I let you die from malnutrition, your manager is going to hunt me down and carve me up."

"Not hungry."

Stubborn boy. "I got that. You're still eating." Maybe a milkshake. There was ice cream in the freezer, milk in the fridge. Fresh berries. Oh, that would make a great smoothie.

Once they were in the kitchen, he sat his towel-wrapped burden down.

LJ looked around the room, wide-eyed. "It's bigger than I remember."

"When was the last time you were in here?" Rye took some bread out to make a couple of sandwiches and buttered them.

"Long time. I don't cook."

Or eat, apparently. "No? I like it." Cooking was easy, and then you knew what you were putting in your mouth. He pulled tomatoes, lettuce, and sliced turkey breast out of the fridge, along with the mayo and mustard.

"I'm going to take a shower. I'm cold."

"We can go back upstairs when I'm done with the sandwiches." Sandwiches were totally portable. And he wanted to keep LJ out of the bedroom he was hiding in as much as possible.

"This is my house. I don't need fucking permission to take a shower."

Rye put the sandwiches together, not pointing out that LJ hadn't made a single move to actually get up off the stool he was sitting on.

Finally, LJ got up and headed for the fridge and got a bottle of water, towel dropping away.

Pale-as-milk skin broken by dark tattoos Rye wanted a closer look at, and so fucking skinny. Definitely a grown man, though. Wait. "Is that metal in your prick?" It was amazing he hadn't noticed earlier, but then he'd been trying not to notice anything.

"Yeah. Double PA, got a dydoe, a frenum, and a hafada. It's a thing."

A fucking sexy thing.

Rye pushed that thought away, along with the sudden thought that all that pale skin would bruise amazingly.

"They let you keep 'em during rehab?"

"They're not made of uppers. They weren't concerned about my prick."

"Yeah, that makes sense. I didn't know if they wanted you to eschew all the trappings of the lifestyle that you were in while hooked or what." He put the sandwiches on a couple of plates. "How about we go sit out in the sun while we eat?"

"I'm a vampire, remember? No sun."

Look at them, having a conversation. "We'll slather you with SPF 1000."

"I tell you what, I'll go shower, dress, and then I'll meet you outside, okay?"

"It's a deal." It was far more than he'd expected, actually.

"Cool." LJ disappeared, sliding out of the room like smoke.

They'd had an actual conversation; LJ had not only been downstairs, but promised to come back; and there was the potential for getting food into that too-skinny body.

And all Rye'd had to do was throw the guy into the pool.

JEFF TOOK a long shower, luxuriating in spray battering at him from all sides, the scent of his soap—roses and sandalwood. He'd showered in rehab, of course, and it had been luxurious, but this was home. This was his shower.

He cleaned himself over and over, touching himself, letting himself feel something good.

Letting himself feel.

Maybe he could just stay in here. Would the giant allow it?

Probably not. He needed to call Donna, have her back the big guy off a few notches. Hell, she gave him a day off, right?

He kept touching himself, tempting fate.

Finally, though, the promise of music and warm clothes drew him out. He dried off, found a pair of huge sweats and an even bigger shirt, his ubiquitous hoodie, socks, stompy boots, and full makeup.

Not January's costume, but some hybrid between Jeff and January.

To his credit, Rye was sitting out on the deck, looking unconcerned about where he was. And the man was in the shade instead of the sun too.

Jeff headed out, hiding in his hoodie, burrowing deep in the shadows.

Rye gave him a smile that made him look really handsome. "Got your armor on, I see."

"There are cameras everywhere."

"You've got a nine-foot privacy fence and nothing behind the house...."

Jeff shrugged. There were pictures online of everything, even a few of rehab. Those people were clever, crafty.

"It's got to be hard, wearing the bad boy facade all the time." Rye handed over a plate with a sandwich on it.

"Yeah, it totally sucks having groupies and money." He winked, putting the sandwich on the table. Honestly, he didn't care about that. He wanted the music, wanted the lights and the pulse of the crowd. He loved that, being everything Jefferson Smart wasn't.

"So why'd you turn to drugs?" Rye handed the plate with the sandwich back.

"I like them." It was as simple as that. They were everywhere, they made life faster, made him better, smarter, happier.

"They've got some pretty severe side effects. Not to mention they're illegal." Rye smiled, taking out the sting of the words.

"Yeah. They stopped my heart. It was great." What did he care about illegal?

Rye snorted but let the subject drop. "Eat. Take the sandwich apart and have the bits you want if the whole sandwich is too intimidating."

He looked at the food. "I need a cigarette."

"No, you need food." Rye had a stubborn set to his jaw.

"I don't want to eat." He'd eaten in rehab, tons of protein shakes at first, then mashed potatoes, scrambled eggs.

"Too bad. Eat. If you give me a list of the foods you like best, I'll have Brigitte start stocking the fridge. But you have to eat."

"Or what?" He took a deep drink of water, letting it fill him.

"I'm not going to leave you be until you do."

"Okay." He was exceptional at being lost in his own brain.

"No, it's not okay. You are going to die, and then your manager is going to kill me. I'm very fond of living."

"Donna is a sweet old lady." Sort of like Elizabeth Bathory had been at the end....

That earned him another snort. "Right. Like the sun is a little hot."

That actually made him chuckle. "When is she coming to see me?"

"Have you invited her?"

15

"No. I haven't called anyone." He grabbed his phone, dialing "Mom."

"Jeff? Is that actually you, honey?" Donna's voice sounded just the same as he remembered.

"Hey. Where are you?" *Why haven't you come?*

"Working. Are you doing okay?"

"Like you aren't getting reports."

"All I know is that you're still alive." Her voice was dry.

"I am. Go me." Suddenly all his adrenaline was gone, and all he wanted in the world was to sleep. "I need to go. I'm tired. Bye."

He stood up and headed inside, his feet feeling heavy, like his boots were filled with sand.

His phone rang, but he ignored it.

All of a sudden he was off his feet, Rye scooping him up and carrying him.

"What are you doing?" He couldn't handle anything else.

"Carrying you up to your room before you fall down the stairs."

He fumbled with his phone, dialing Jim, even as Rye carried him. *Please. Please answer.*

"Jim here."

"I want to come back."

"Oh, honey. You can't live in stasis. You're stronger than you think."

But he wasn't.

"What happened?" Jim asked.

"Nothing. Nothing at all. I'm so tired."

"Have you been eating?"

Rye set him down on the bed.

"I'm not hungry."

"You gotta eat, honey. Taking care of yourself is part of the program."

"I'm not hungry, though. I'm too tired to eat."

"Honey, they'll have to come in and put in an IV. They won't bring you back here. They'll put you in the psych ward."

He started to cry, silently, just lost and lonely and old.

Rye took the phone out of his hand. "Who is this…? Yeah. I'm trying. I don't want to force-feed him. Yeah, okay. I'll tell him you said bye."

Sitting, Rye pulled him into the strong arms. "Shh. Shh."

Jeff sighed softly, tears sliding through his makeup. He cried for a long time before sleep took him again, offering him peace, silence.

All the while, warm arms held him.

R YE HELD the skinny body long after LJ was asleep. Then he called Brigitte and gave her a grocery list.

He was glad he'd pulled the phone from LJ when the kid had started crying; the guy, Jim, had a bunch of solutions for getting nutrition into LJ—Jeff, actually. The sponsor had called LJ that. Interesting that someone called Jeff by his given name, because nobody else ever did.

After hanging up the phone, Rye settled back in his chair and grabbed his tablet.

A few hours later, Brigitte arrived, and he met her in the kitchen, helping her put away the groceries.

Once she'd gone, he prepared a chocolate milkshake, added protein powder, and headed back upstairs.

Jeff was dreaming, writhing on the bed, stretching out, then curling around his belly. He had to be starving to death.

Sitting on the edge of the bed, Rye put his hand on Jeff's shoulder. "Jeff. Time to wake up. I've got a chocolate milkshake for you."

Those dark eyes flashed open. "A milkshake?"

Bingo.

"Yep. A chocolate one."

He tried not to notice how huge Jeff's eyes looked with his makeup smeared around them.

"Smells good." Jeff's hands shook, and Rye held the glass, steadying it so Jeff could take a drink. He wanted to cheer when Jeff took two long swallows. Calories, yay.

He put his arm around Jeff and kept him sitting up, encouraged him to drink some more.

"It's good. Cold." Jeff wiped his cheek, brushing away more makeup. "I.... Everything's a little fuzzy."

He imagined so. "You're a little hungry, Jeff."

It was hard to reconcile the Jeff before him with Lord January's bad boy image.

"Not really. You'd think so, wouldn't you?"

"You are, you just don't realize it." He put the glass back to Jeff's lips. Jeff drank again, deep, swallowing hard. There. There. Good man. Rye nodded, encouraged Jeff to lean against him.

"Sorry. I'm not a snuggler." But Jeff still pushed close, shivering and cuddling.

"Okay." He ran his hand up and down Jeff's arm, trying to warm him up.

Jeff drank half the shake before pushing it away. "No more."

"You can have the rest later." It was probably better if Jeff didn't drink it all at once anyway; that poor stomach would likely just send it all back up. "How are you feeling?"

"I don't know."

The sad part was that he didn't think Jeff was lying.

"You like movies, Jeff?"

There was a huge TV across from the bed—they could watch something.

"I do, actually. I watch them a lot."

"Then how about we sit and eat. I could even make popcorn."

"I.... Okay. Yeah. We could. You know... you know you don't have to hang out. I know I'm shit company. I'm just so fucking tired. I can't wake all the way up."

It was more words and more information than Jeff had volunteered to date. Rye put it down to getting much needed protein into the guy, and just maybe the care he took of Jeff was starting to sink in.

"I bet once we get you fed and out in the air a little, you will. I'm going to help."

"Okay. What movie?"

"I'm a closet Keanu Reeves fan." It wasn't something Rye shared with very many people.

"*Matrix* or *Dracula*?"

"Let's start with the *Matrix*. There's three of them."

Jeff nodded. "I'm going to wash my face first. I itch."

"Sounds good. Are the movies listed alphabetically?"

"Oh, they're all loaded onto hard drives so I can take them on the road." Jeff pulled out a laptop, opened up some software, and showed him a huge long list. "Just click on the one you want."

"That's pretty cool." He cued up the movie, then zipped downstairs to put a bag of popcorn into the microwave.

Five minutes later he was back up with a big bowl of popcorn and a couple of bottles of water.

Jeff was clean-faced, hair loose, wearing soft, loose clothes. The shake was in his hand, another third gone.

He looked... really good, actually.

"I brought popcorn." Rye held out the bowl.

"Cool. Park yourself wherever."

He put the waters on the bedside table and sat on the bed next to Jeff, the bowl of popcorn between them.

The movie started, the huge TV proving to have a stunning sound system that filled the air. Jeff moved about fifteen minutes into the film, curling around a huge body pillow and lying on his belly.

"You okay?" Rye asked softly.

"Hurts to sit for a long time."

It didn't surprise him; there was no padding on the kid. Rye rubbed Jeff's calf companionably.

Jeff made it almost through the movie before dozing again, but he woke after only ten or fifteen minutes, going back for the shake when he woke.

Rye would make another one once the movie was over. God knows, Jeff needed a couple dozen a day.

Jeff shifted constantly, moving across the bed.

"Hey. Come here." He encouraged Jeff to lie against him between his legs, warming Jeff up.

"Are…. Will this get you in trouble?"

Rye didn't bother to answer until he had Jeff propped up, body not making solid contact anywhere. "Making you more comfortable is not going to get me in trouble."

It took a few more minutes before Jeff relaxed, let go, staring at the TV.

There they were.

Between the relaxation and the milkshake, Rye finally felt like he was doing something for Jeff. When Jeff dozed off again, Rye held on, then started the next movie.

CHAPTER TWO

RYE WAS sleeping—sleeping hard—so Jeff headed down to his studio. They'd been in the house for more than a week, and they'd watched a hundred movies together, the music and the visuals easing him almost as much as the way Rye helped make him comfortable.

Now he wanted to play for a few hours, make some music.

The studio was quiet, dusty, and he wandered for a few minutes before he pulled out a guitar and started playing. He ran through standards, a little Spanish flamenco, just playing, exploring his fingers again.

The door suddenly flew open, Rye rushing in. "Oh thank God." Rye leaned against the doorjamb.

Jeff looked up, eyebrow arched. "What's wrong?"

"I woke up, and you were gone. You never leave your room."

"I wanted to work a little." He'd maybe needed to, even. He felt better today, like a real person, and who knew how long that would last?

Rye nodded. "That's great. It is. I just had a moment of panic. You should wake me next time. I won't mind, I swear."

"You looked happy." And Jeff didn't know what to do. Most of his security, he'd basically ignored, and his friends…. Well, he didn't have friends. He could, he supposed, with a phone call. Maybe Jim would come over.

Maybe.

If he could stay awake for more than ten minutes at a time.

Why was it so quiet around here?

"I must have been having a good dream." Rye nodded to his guitar. "Do you mind if I sit and listen?"

"No. Please. I love an audience."

Soon he'd have to call others, start jamming. Not yet. Not yet.

He put his head down and started playing, his fingers moving on their own. Rye was quiet, just letting him play. He played until blood stained the strings, until his body was shuddering with muscle aches and hunger.

"Okay, Jeff. Let's get you some food." Rye took the guitar from his hands.

"You can't...." Could he? No one. "That's my...." Oh. Confused.

"What are you trying to say?" Rye took his arm and helped him up.

"I was working. Playing. That's my guitar."

Rye looked at the guitar he was still holding. "I know?"

"Let me put her away." He reached out, blood dripping on the floor.

"Whoa, you're hurt." Rye set the guitar down against his chair, then took Jeff's hands, tsking. "Your poor hands."

"It doesn't hurt. I was.... Did it sound good? It felt good."

"It did. Not at all what I expected."

Rye led him from the studio up the stairs to the kitchen where he grabbed the first aid kit from the cupboard under the sink.

"What did you expect?" He looked at Rye curiously.

"Well, I've seen your videos...."

"That's my job—the drama and wildness. That's what they pay to see. I'll have to go back to that, and soon. Soon there will be people everywhere again." He knew that the only reason no one was here now was because of Donna.

Rye shook his head. "I get it on the road, but you don't have to do that in your home. This is your private space." Rye bent over Jeff's fingers, putting antibiotic cream and bandages on the worst of them.

"Not here. Up in my rooms."

"I say the whole house. I can't keep you safe if the place is full of groupies and hangers-on. You can have friends over, of course." Rye put away the first aid kit and pulled out the blender, moving around the kitchen with easy familiarity.

"It's the lifestyle. Hookers, groupies, musicians." He watched, fascinated, as Rye moved. "What are your vices?"

"I'm not allowed to have vices." Rye gave him a teasing smile.

"See? You're not allowed to. I'm not allowed not to."

"It's not going to be easy, pretending to be that bad boy while you're on tour but having to do it clean."

Rye put ice cream, frozen strawberries, a bit of ice, and some protein powder into the blender.

Jeff shrugged. He'd fail. There was no other answer, unfortunately. He had a touring contract, but without the speed, he was boring, normal, simple. Just a man. On the road there would be need and opportunity.

Just thinking about it made him tired.

The conversation was cut off by the blender, Rye whirring up his mixture before pouring it into a large glass and setting it down in front of him.

"If I made soup and sandwiches, will you have some?"

"What kind of soup?" He took the shake, drinking deep. *Oh. Oh, so good.*

"Well, tomato soup and grilled cheese sandwiches have always been my favorite. I'm pretty easy, though."

"I like tomato soup." He didn't eat meat, he didn't think. He liked eggs. Potatoes. Soup.

"What else do you like?" Rye pulled out a cookie sheet and grabbed a bunch of tomatoes, a couple of peppers, and some onions and garlic. He cut them all up, sprinkled them with olive oil, salt, and pepper, and then put them in the oven.

"Eggs. Mashed potatoes…. What are you doing?"

"I'm making tomato soup."

"Soup comes from a can." Everyone knew that.

"It doesn't have to." Rye grabbed the blender and put in more berries and ice, whirred it up, and put it in a glass. He came over to sit next to Jeff, drinking the smoothie.

"You can't make soup in an oven."

"Well, no, but I can roast the ingredients that are going into the soup. Then I'll blend them together and voila—soup. I like cooking. With my job there's lots of time to look up recipes, read about techniques, and put them into practice."

Okay.

Okay, Rye was weird. "Are you queer?"

"Because I like to cook?" Rye chuckled and went on without waiting for an answer. "I am. Are you?"

"I'm asexual. I don't go for it." All his love went into the performance; that's what the shrink thought, and the shrink said that was okay.

Rye looked at him like he'd lost his mind. "Seriously? With all those piercings?"

"Yeah. Those are for me, not for other people." He had had sex, but really, other people worried him with their diseases and hang-ups and things. Music was the best lover.

"You've never been in love?"

"No. Well, I am with my job, I guess. That's exciting and worrisome, and it tried to kill me. That's like love." His job was to be a vampire king.

Rye snorted. "I'm not sure that love is trying to kill you."

"Oh, look at the songs. Love is dangerous and deadly." Entire careers proved that.

"It doesn't have to be."

"You can either be normal or be insane." And as peaceful as this normal was, it was fleeting.

"I don't think anything is that black and white, Jeff."

Jeff looked down at his black clothes, his dyed perfectly black hair, his white skin, and he giggled, the sound a touch hysterical.

Rye caught his gaze and chuckled. "Your choice in clothing and lack of sunshine notwithstanding."

"Even my ink is black. I live in a different universe."

"Extremes are part of why you wound up in rehab. You need to find balance."

Jeff thought about that for a second, then rejected the thought. He only knew how to function on the edge. His career depended on it.

The timer on the oven dinged, and Rye went over and pulled out the tray of vegetables. Most everything was turning brown, a lot of it blistered.

After grabbing a big pot, Rye poured the vegetables and the juices on the tray into it and added cream. Then he grabbed a... hell, something, that he put into the pot, and it made noise like the blender.

Craziness.

It was sort of fascinating, honestly.

The pot went back onto the stove, and Rye added more salt and pepper. "Be ready in two minutes."

"Are you sure that's how you do it?"

"You can be the judge of that when it's finished." Rye stirred the "soup."

Jeff drank the rest of his shake, feeling more and more solid. "I like the strawberries."

"Cool. I was told the chocolate shakes were your favorite, but the fruit ones are better for you." Pulling down two bowls, Rye then ladled out the soup and brought it over. "There you go. Tomato soup."

"I like strawberry shakes almost as much as chocolate...." He eyed the bowl. It looked like soup. Sticking his finger in, he swirled it around, then sucked it clean. Spicy, warm, creamy. It was good. He stared up at Rye. "It's soup."

"I told you. You want sandwiches or just toast points with it?" Rye went back and cut a couple of slices of bread from a loaf of something dark.

"What the fuck is a toast point?" Jeff dipped and licked again.

"Toast cut into triangles." Rye gave him a shit-eating grin that lit his whole face up.

"Why do they call them toast points, and no, I don't need them. I had a shake."

Rye shrugged. "I don't know. They just do." Rye put a single slice of the dark bread into the toaster. Then he brought over a spoon, along with the salt and pepper shakers. "In case you need either, though it's pretty well seasoned."

It was all so very fucking normal.

Quiet.

Nice.

Rye's toast popped, and he cut it into triangles, coming back to sit next to him and eat. "So what do you usually do when you aren't touring or playing guitar?"

"Write music. Sleep. Make appearances."

"No hobbies?"

"I write programs." Sometimes. He liked his computer, his phone, liked being anonymous.

"Oh? What kind of programs?"

It was weird; nobody had ever really asked about him, been interested in him outside of Lord January.

"Just stuff. Like with the movies. Apps. Silly things. I like code. That's what my degree is in. Engineering, with a minor in music." Music was just math, after all.

"You've got a degree in engineering? That's pretty cool." Rye grinned. "Nice to know you've got a mind under all that hair."

"Hey. I'm a lord of the undead." His lips twisted.

Rye laughed for him, eyes crinkling.

Jeff ate the soup before standing up, restless. Maybe he should explore the house.

Rye watched him, but it wasn't like how everyone else watched Lord January. It was… more personal. Less groupyish.

"Thank you for the soup. It was nice." Nice. God. He wandered off, heading into the main part of the house.

It was dark and heavy, ponderous, with solid leather furniture and Gothic decorations. There was a huge painting of January in the living area, gaunt and odd.

Rye trailed him through the empty rooms.

There were bedrooms and rooms with video games, a room with a pool table, and one with a huge cross in the middle of the room. Weird.

"You have a St. Andrew's Cross?" Rye went over and checked it out.

"Do I?" Jeff shrugged and headed to look in cabinets and such. There were tons of sexual things in there, bondage and pain. He thought he recognized some of them from the Bonds of Agony tour.

"I'm surprised you've got all this stuff, given you said you're asexual."

"This is from a tour. I'm too tired to have sex." He waved one hand, dismissing the conversation.

"Seems to me like you're too tired to do anything most of the time. You need to be more careful of your health, or you won't even be able to tour anymore."

"That's what the drugs are for." That was what this healing was for, to get healthy enough to tour.

"You can't do the drugs anymore, Jeff. You're going to have to get through the next tour by eating properly and exercising."

Exercising.

Him.

Ha.

"I'm not fat."

"No, in fact, you're far too skinny. The exercise is to help with your stamina."

"I told you, that's what the drugs are for. There's no help for it. We all know it." It was inevitable.

Rye shook his head. "No. It's not happening. You're off the drugs for good."

Rye was adorable. Maybe the fact that the man's head was so far away from his feet made him a little stupid. Blood flow was important.

"Don't look at me like that. You're staying clean. Full stop."

"You're very cute." He headed out into a room with an indoor infinity pool. Oh, that was cool. He wondered when that had been put in. Or had it been there all along? He'd been high so much, he might have just never really registered it as any more than a huge tub, if that.

"Swimming's a really good way to up your endurance. I'd be happy to do laps with you."

"Is that why it's so narrow? You just go and the water goes around you?"

"Yeah. There's a motor moving the water and it pushes against you so it's like you're actually swimming, kind of like a treadmill only for your arms. You have to be a little bit careful because if you don't actually swim, it'll push you into the back wall." Rye pointed to the heavy curtains. "And it's private. No way anyone's going to see you."

"Wow." He leaned down, touched the water. "It's warm."

"All the better to entice you into it." Rye leaned over him, sliding his hand through the water too. "I like swimming. Makes you feel weightless, like gravity doesn't count anymore."

"I don't know how. Just dog paddling."

"It's easy enough. If you can doggy paddle, I can teach you some basic strokes. That's all you need."

"Maybe. Maybe, yeah. I like being wet." He touched the water again. It was like it was alive.

"You want to go now?"

"Can we? Is it safe?"

"Sure it's safe. As long as you don't do it alone or when impaired." Rye started to strip down.

Well, it should be easier without his clothes, he guessed.... He wouldn't have done it if anyone else but Rye was there, but then he wouldn't have been even considering going into the water if anyone else was there.

Jeff stripped down too, then sat at the edge and stared into the water.

Rye had an amazing body, lots of muscles over smooth skin. There were scars too: two on his abdomen and a nasty mess of them on his right thigh. Rye left on his underwear and slipped into the water. It went up to his hips.

"What happened to your leg?"

"I was shot. The bullet shattered my bone."

"Oh. Did it hurt?" It had to hurt. Shattered the bone? "Is your leg metal now?"

"Some metal alloy, some plastic. And yeah, it hurt like a son of a bitch." Rye held out a hand, inviting him into the water.

"Does it hurt now? Was it a bad guy? Can I touch it?" He reached out and let Rye ease him into the water. It felt good around him, making his cock bob gently.

"It hurts sometimes. It's a cliché, but I usually know when it's going to storm. And yeah. I used to be a cop, and it was a drug bust that went bad." Rye brought his hand to the scars.

"Oh." The skin was ridged and hard, odd, but fascinating.

"I know it's ugly."

"No, it's different. Lots of people like scars. I've got some." He showed Rye his back with the patterns sliced into his skin. The scars were tiny, white, barely noticeable. "I let people do it on tour."

"Seriously? That's dangerous." Rye touched each of the little scars, fingers warmer than the water. "I'm not letting anyone near you with a blade, Jeff."

"Are you coming?" Now that was interesting. That was new.

"I am. Eight weeks at home, followed by thirty weeks on tour. We're going to need to really work on your stamina to get you through thirty weeks."

His brain wasn't ready for that.

Thirty weeks.

"What do I do in here?" Jeff asked, looking at the water flowing around him.

"Are you okay with putting your face in the water?"

"Yeah." He guessed. Surely he was.

"Okay. So you float on your stomach and then do this." Rye put his arms over his head and then dropped them down in what would be a dragging motion in the water. "That'll pull you through the water. I can hold your belly for you until you get the hang of it."

Jeff hadn't learned anything new in a long, long time. He hoped he didn't drown.

CHAPTER THREE

RYE WAS going to disconnect the damn house phone.

Between the people calling up from the gate wanting to be let in and the actual phone calls, he was being disturbed at all hours.

He still couldn't quite believe Lord January had allowed everyone and their uncle access to the house, to him.

So far, Rye had managed to keep anyone from disturbing Jeff. The only calls allowed were Donna and Jim, and they both had Jeff's cell number anyway.

It was the sound of glass breaking that woke him at 4:00 a.m., and he grabbed his gun out of the lockbox and went to the bed first to check on Jeff.

Jeff slammed his hand down on a button, and Rye heard locks clicking. "They can't come in. This is my place."

"What rooms did you just lock?" He knew Jeff could not only lock-down his private area of the house, the part Rye thought of as "Jeff's," but also turn the bedroom and bathroom into a panic room that was totally inaccessible once Jeff hit the button.

"Here. The sitting room. Bathroom. The door in the garage."

"Okay, go into the bathroom and lock the door. I'll check the sitting room and the garage first. Then I'll go out and lock the door behind me again. Once it's clear, I'll call you on your cell, okay?"

"Stay here. Don't go. What if it's scary?"

"I need to make sure they didn't get up here before you hit the locks." He reached out and touched Jeff's shoulder. The alarm would have alerted the cops, but Rye knew it would take them at least a few minutes, and anything could happen between now and when they showed up. "I need to check these rooms, and we'll let the police deal with the intruder after that, okay?"

"Okay. Okay, be careful. I like you."

He gave Jeff a grin in the dark. "I like you too. Now into the bathroom and lock the door like we practiced. And don't open it unless it's me and I say Ollie Ollie Oxen Free."

"Okay." Jeff moved silently, locking himself in.

Satisfied after hearing the lock, Rye slipped out of the bedroom, closing the door behind him as silently as Jeff had done.

The sitting room was clear, as were the stairs down to the garage and the garage itself. His app told him the break-in had occurred in the living room, and it looked like they'd gotten Jeff's private area locked down before anyone could make their way in farther.

After hoofing it back up the stairs, Rye called 911 and reported the break-in, just in case the automatic notice hadn't gone through, or hadn't been taken seriously. He let the operator know that he and Jeff were safe in rooms locked away from the rest of the house and they'd stay there until they got an all clear on his cell phone.

By the time he'd confirmed his number with the operator, he was back at the bathroom.

Knocking gently, he called out, "Ollie Ollie Oxen Free."

The door flew open and Jeff came out, eyes wide. "Are you okay?"

"I'm fine. You hit the locks soon enough, and we're safe." He opened his arms, and Jeff came to him, letting Rye hold him close.

Jeff squeezed him, held on tight.

This from the man who didn't shake hands.

Rye leaned against the wall and held on, breathing slowly. He was still on alert, but the initial rush of adrenaline was beginning to fade.

The sirens came, and he sighed and backed off. "They'll want to see you too."

"Okay. I'll get dressed."

"Okay. No makeup, though. They'll respond to you better without it."

Jeff gave him a bittersweet smile. "Just remember, I'm LJ. Only LJ."

"Okay, sir." He would remember that far more than LJ. Jeff wasn't LJ to him anymore.

In fact, Lord January was nothing to him.

Jeff, though…. He was beginning to care an awful lot for Jeff.

Jeff pulled on a sweater, made sure the safety was on his gun, and waited for the cops to call with the all clear.

The knock on the door downstairs was huge. "Sir? Police! Open up."

He checked his phone. No missed call. He'd been pretty clear with the operator.

Jeff looked at him, eyes wide, and then the phone rang.

"Sir? Sir, the intruder has been arrested, and the police are knocking."

"Thank you. We'll let them in."

Rye held his hand out to Jeff. "They've arrested the intruder. It's safe to go down."

Jeff took his hand, and they went together to the stairs, at which point he put Jeff behind him as he unlocked and opened the door. He kept his gun to his side, but he was ready.

There were two uniforms standing there, faces serious. He handed over his driver's license, and one of the cops examined it, checked his phone, then nodded.

The second cop addressed him as he took back his ID. "Sir. We apprehended the guy, but there's some damage, and the press is already gathering."

Jeff's heat disappeared from behind him.

Jesus Christ.

"We can deal with the damage, and I know there isn't anything you can do about the press." He assumed they knew better than to try to climb over the gate, which was no doubt what the perp had done.

"Can you tell me about the perp? Was he armed?" How dangerous had been his intent?

"Looks like a fan. Broke in, cut his arms up and bled everywhere."

That was fucking gross. Rye was going to have to call someone in to disinfect the whole place. How could Jeff live like this? Oh, right. The drugs.

Clearly the perimeter alarm had been useless. He was going to have to look into that. Then he was going to have a serious talk with Jeff about beefing up their security measures, making the place less accessible through the barring of the windows and doors.

"Thanks, I appreciate the heads-up. Will you have a patrol car go by every half hour or so?" It would keep the press from getting overly enthusiastic about trying anything.

"Absolutely. Can someone come down and see if anything is missing?"

"I'll do it. Give me a minute, please."

The officer nodded, and Rye closed the door, locked it again, then went up to find Jeff.

Jeff met him halfway, totally in Lord January mode, white makeup, black eyes and lips, hair slicked down, and wearing skin-tight jeans and a silk blouse.

Rye shook his head. "I don't want you going down there." Jeff didn't need to see what that freak had done.

Flashes happened in the bushes near the garage. Fuck. Fucking leeches.

"Lock yourself in the bathroom, and I'll tell them to get off the property or I'll have them arrested. I have to let the cops know if anything was stolen too. Then I'll be back up. Same code words as before, okay?"

Jeff didn't answer, just lifted his head and nodded.

"I'll wait here until I hear the lock on the bathroom door." He took Jeff's hand and squeezed it. "You're safe."

"Thank you." Jeff's eyes were… wrong.

Really wrong.

"Hold up. What the fuck?" Frowning, he took Jeff's chin and tilted it up so he could get a better look. The man looked like a demon.

"Contacts, Rye. Black contacts."

Oh, man. Fucking scary. "Christ, that's spooky. For real."

"Yeah. January is a spooky fucker."

"Yeah, you can say that again." He was about to ask how Jeff had gotten all… January, but there was a knock on the door at the bottom of the stairs.

"Sir?"

"Coming. Go on, Jeff. I won't go until I hear the bathroom door lock."

"Okay." Jeff sashayed into the bathroom and closed the door.

Rye shook his head and waited for that click. Then he went out to deal with… well, everything.

JEFF STARED at himself in the long mirror, at his pale face, the way his hips pointed, his black eyes.

"I hate you."

For a second, in the dark, he thought January smiled.

Jeff chewed on his bottom lip, then grabbed his phone and texted Donna. *Someone broke into the house. Press here.*

Call 911.

We did. Rye downstairs.

You're safe?

Yes. Worried. Tired.

Sad. He was sad. January was going to come back.

Do you need to call me?

Yeah.

His phone rang immediately, and he answered it. "Donna."

"Hey, honey."

"I'm so… I've been spoiled. It's been a good week."

"He's taking good care of you, huh?"

"I'm trying to swim." He liked swimming, even.

"Right now?" He could hear the note in her voice that said she was teasing.

"Yep. Glub, glub. There will have to be meetings soon, huh? Rehearsals?"

"I've been dealing with the meetings for you. And you've got a few more weeks before the rehearsals start, time to get strong. I'm sending Rye with you, okay? He's there to help you, honey."

"I'm so scared, Donna."

"What are you scared of, honey?"

"I can't be January without the drugs." And that was that.

"Of course you can."

He sat on the lid of the toilet, rocking himself, biting his bottom lip until he tasted blood. "Will you come see me now?"

"I'm in London, honey, but I'll be in the city next week."

A knock on the door had him jumping. "Ollie Ollie Oxen Free."

"Rye is back." He lifted his head. "Coming." He opened the door, offering Rye a smile. "You'll come next week? Promise?"

"I swear," Donna promised.

"Who was on the phone?" Rye asked after he hung up. "Wait, is that blood?" Rye took his chin and tilted his head, frowning.

"Donna. Blood?"

"On your lips. Were you hurt?" Rye's thumb landed on his lower lip, tugging on it.

"I was biting."

Rye tsked him and wiped the blood off, gaze on his mouth.

"Is the house broken?" Jeff asked.

"A window's shattered, and there's some vandalism. I'm leaving a message with the regular service for a cleaning crew to com first thing in the morning." Rye was on the phone for only a moment, then his arm came around Jeff's shoulders. "Let's get you back to bed."

"I... I need to shower. I'm dirty." And he was going to lose it. He blinked at Rye, who winced.

"Can you take out the contacts?"

"What? Oh yeah. Sure." He eased them out and put them in their containers.

Nodding, Rye pulled him close and held him. "You're safe now. And now you know I'm not going to let anything happen to you."

"I knew that." He sucked in a deep breath. "I'm going to cry. I need a shower."

"I hate leaving you alone like this."

"I'm okay. I just—" He pulled away, tugging at the tight, restrictive clothes.

"You need to get out of his skin." Rye helped, getting buttons and zippers for him that his fingers just couldn't seem to make work.

"Yes. Yes." God, Rye understood.

The only part of him that was warm was where Rye's fingers brushed against his skin.

They moved into the shower together, Rye still touching him, holding him. "Let me get the makeup off."

"Please."

Rye tilted Jeff's head back into the spray, hands following the flow of the water.

The pomade was washed from his hair, the makeup from his face. Rye's hands were gentle, careful.

"Are you my friend?"

"Not like all those people who call themselves your friend. I care about you."

"Those people just want something from me."

"I want something *for* you."

Jeff nodded, and they headed out of the shower. Rye wrapped him in a towel. Then he was picked up, and Rye carried him to his bed, laid him down, and tucked the covers around him.

"I.... Can you...." He lifted the edge of the covers. "Just tonight?"

Rye nodded and pulled off his sopping-wet clothes before slipping on a dry pair of jeans. Then he slipped in with Jeff, putting an arm around his shoulders and bringing him in against the solid body.

"Thank you." He settled, the steady rhythm of Rye's heart easing him into sleep.

RYE WOKE with an armful of naked, warm boy, and a raging hard-on pushing painfully against the zipper of his jeans.

Man, he should have taken the damn jeans off and just slept in his underwear. It wouldn't have been very professional, though. Of course, neither was having a raging hard-on for his client. Still, Jeff wasn't like most clients and required a different level of security, of intimacy.

Jeff was sleeping hard, face relaxed, body snuggled against him. It had been fucking terrifying last night, seeing Jeff turned into LJ. Hell, it hadn't even been LJ. That had been Lord January.

He'd already figured the tour was going to be a nightmare of trying to keep Jeff safe and clean; now he knew for sure it would be.

He stroked a lock of ebony hair from Jeff's face, the touch earning him a smile. The man trusted him, and beyond Ms. Heard and Jeff's sponsor, Rye knew that was rare.

That trust would make things easier.

Rye figured he was going to have to play the part of the evil bodyguard who didn't let Lord January do anything, who kept the man's fans away from him, while January sneered and complained about him. He could live with that, as long as he knew that the real man behind that persona trusted and liked him.

Jeff's eyes opened, slowly. They were dark, but a dark green rather than black. "Morning."

He smiled, ignoring how his cock tried to throb, at those big eyes so close. "Hey. How did you sleep?"

"Good, barring the whole weird breaking-glass thing. That sucked."

"Yeah, that really did. I'm going to implement a number of options to make the place even less accessible. Cameras on the fencing, and barbed wire at the top to discourage people climbing it to break in." Maybe some loud-assed alarms that went off if anyone breached the house itself, given that the damn perimeter alarm was either a piece of crap or badly installed. He'd have someone check it out as well.

"Now that they know I'm here for sure, the groupies will come."

That was already happening. "Yeah, I'll say. The press has shown up now too. I'm not sure how statements and stuff work. Are they likely to back off if Lord January goes out there and flips the bird at them and tells them to fuck off?"

He'd bet Lord January got away with a lot of bad behavior with the press and such because of his persona.

"I'm never seen during the day, so I have a little leeway."

"So we have time to decide how to handle it, I guess."

"I'll go out in the yard after dark, make an appearance, then schedule some sort of public outing in a week or two."

"Have you ever wanted to just chuck it all away?"

"Lots of times, but the guys in the band depend on me, Donna, my tour manager, my driver. There's dozens of them, from the social media girl to the publicist. It's a machine." So straightforward, so sure. There was no hope in Jeff's voice.

"Ever thought of changing your image?"

Surely not all the fans were there just for the... stuff. Some had to be in it for the singing.

"Not really. Eventually the age will catch up with me and plastic surgery won't do it. This isn't forever. My star will fall."

"You're a good singer, though. And you write songs and stuff. There's got to be more to your career than just the vampire stuff."

Jeff chuckled and sat up, grabbed the remote, and turned the television on, along with the laptop. In a few seconds, there was Lord January, big as life, writhing and snarling on stage. The words were husky, pure sex, but somehow cold, inhuman.

It was fascinating and repulsive all at once.

"Do you think I'm a good singer, Rye?"

"I have to admit that's not my kind of music. Why don't you sing me something less... uh, goth?"

"Life is what it is, my friend. There's no altering that." Jeff slipped from the bed, wrapping himself in layer after layer of too-large clothes. "I assume I should stay up here until a cleaning crew comes?"

Rye was a little disappointed Jeff wouldn't sing him something—the guy played all sorts of nongoth music on the guitar. He put that aside, though. He wasn't here to get sung to.

"Indeed. I'll go make you a milkshake." It was nasty downstairs, and he didn't want Jeff seeing it. People were seriously fucked up. This had been a random fan—he had the man's photo and name on his phone now, sent by the cops, and it wasn't any of the names from his credible threats list. Even so, he would be careful.

"Can you bring me my acoustic guitar, please?"

"You got it."

He headed downstairs to the kitchen. The cleaners showed up while he was making a couple of milkshakes, and he let them in. Then he headed back upstairs, detouring into the studio to grab Jeff's guitar.

Jeff was waiting, sitting cross-legged in the center of the bed, typing on his laptop.

Rye handed over the guitar and set their milkshakes down on the bedside table. "Have a few sips of the shake before you start."

"What kind is it?"

"Cherry." He was going to have to put more frozen fruit on the shopping list for Brigitte.

Grabbing his, he ignored the sudden desire to sit on the bed with Jeff and went to the chair he'd begun to think of as his. He silently told himself off—just because Jeff had needed him close in the aftermath of the break-in didn't make it more than just that.

Hell, Jeff wasn't even his type. Jeff was skinny and pale and emotional. Still, there was something about the kid and those big, green eyes....

He cleared his throat and downed some of his milkshake.

Jeff sipped a little, just a bit, then put it aside and started playing his guitar.

He didn't like the crap that Lord January did, but just Jeff and his guitar? He could listen to this all day.

Softly, Jeff began to sing to him, voice gentle, low, unique, and wonderful.

Oh damn. He put his milkshake and his tablet down and just listened. He didn't know anything about markets or music, but he knew when something was honest and real.

One song slid into another, then another and another.

He hardly even noticed the passage of time, simply entranced by Jeff's voice. How come he was playing Lord January when he could do this?

Finally, though, Jeff's voice cracked, and he knew it was time. Rest. Food. Now.

Standing, Rye clapped. "Yes, I think you're a good singer, Jeff."

Jeff pinked and rolled his eyes, but there was a smile there, a real, warm smile.

"How about you finish up that milkshake, and I'll go see if the cleaning crew is done yet."

"I'll have some."

"You know I'm just going to nag you until you finish it." He played it off lightly. It was true, though; he would.

"You'll be downstairs." Jeff took a deep drink, though, humming over it.

"I'll bring up another one." Actually, he was going to bring up a sandwich. He'd learned that if he cut the bread really thin and kept the ingredients vegetarian, he could get Jeff to eat solid food.

"Thank you for sleeping with me. It helped."

"You're welcome." He touched Jeff's shoulder. "I'll be back in a few, okay?"

"I'll be here." Jeff took another sip of his shake and grabbed his laptop.

"Cool." Rye headed downstairs, finding that the cleaning service had let in the carpenter, and the window was almost done. So, apparently, were the cleaners.

Good.

By the time he had their sandwiches made, a plate of cut-up vegetables beside them on the tray, the cleaners and carpenter were ready to go.

After seeing them out, he locked the door behind them.

He balanced the plates and headed up into the quiet, private quarters. *The Avengers* was playing on the TV, and Jeff was watching it, head hanging off the edge of the bed.

Rye sat their plates on the bed and climbed on. Jeff would eventually come sit or lie on him, letting him cushion Jeff's limbs.

"Does the house look okay?" Jeff slowly rolled over, stretched.

"Yep. You'd never know anything happened. We can go swim."

"Yeah?" Jeff was becoming quite the swimmer, enjoying the water, the exercise. His stamina was really getting up there too. It was good to see.

"Yeah. After you eat the sandwich."

Jeff looked over, grabbed a carrot. "Hummus?"

Was that hunger? He pushed the hummus over, not saying a word.

"Thank you." Jeff dipped a piece of red pepper, noshed on it. And Rye ate his own sandwich, feeling chipper.

"Do you play games?" Jeff asked.

"You mean like checkers?"

"Checkers. Chess. Backgammon. Halo. World of Warcraft. Spades. Scrabble."

"Hey, I've heard of all of those," Rye teased.

"Do you play any of them?"

"Sure. All except Scrabble. I'm a shit speller."

"I have a backgammon board. It was my dad's."

Oh. So Lord January had a family. "Yeah? You used to play with him? Are you a backgammon shark?"

"I'm not bad, but yeah. I used to play a lot." Jeff got out of the bed, headed for the closet, and pulled out what looked like a tiny little suitcase.

"Cool." Rye shifted so he was sitting cross-legged on the bed.

Jeff grinned, settled across from him, and set up the board. In seconds, they were playing.

All through the game, Jeff kept picking up a new vegetable and dipping it into the hummus. It made Rye happy to see Jeff eating, relaxing. Interacting with him.

He'd thought the man was totally empty, but he'd been wrong. Jeff had been tired. Tired and hungry.

Jeff won the first game, and Rye won the second one. By then they'd both eaten their sandwiches, and Jeff had demolished a good part of his vegetables.

"Tiebreaker?" Jeff asked.

Rye loved the life in Jeff's green eyes. "Of course." He rubbed his hands together. "Prepare to go down."

"Not a chance, man."

"We'll see. Time will bear me out."

"Oh...." Jeff grabbed his laptop and typed furiously for a second.

"Hey now, you're not trying to cheat, are you?"

"Huh? Cheat at what?" Jeff looked up at him. "I was writing that down. Time will bear me out. It's a killer lyric."

"Oh yeah?" Rye grinned. "Does that mean I get cowriting credit?"

"I'll thank you in the liner notes. Inspired by someone I beat at backgammon."

"Hey, we're tied at a game apiece. Come on, it's time for the rubber match." He liked this: the teasing, the happiness, the hints of brilliance.

This whole month had been a study in watching someone come alive. Even last night's events didn't seem to have fazed Jeff too badly.

They started another game, and it quickly became apparent that Jeff was likely to win again. At the end it was close, though, and Jeff barely squeaked by.

"You've got a lucky touch with the dice." Rye believed some people had it and some didn't when it came to games of chance. It looked like the dice liked Jeff well enough.

"Sometimes. Sometimes no matter what you do, it sucks."

"That's a pretty good metaphor for life, isn't it?" Rye closed the board up. "We should go swim. And I found your mini gym. We could start with some weights—get some muscles built up."

"I can't have muscles. I have to be spare." Jeff stood up and looked at himself in the mirror. "I've gained weight already."

"You're still too skinny. And I'm not talking muscles-muscles." He put up his arms and flexed. "I'm talking wiry muscles. You can be both skinny and strong."

"You're not skinny. You're a giant. It's amazing."

"A giant...." Rye chuckled. He supposed he might seem like one next to Jeff. Jeff wasn't short by any means, but Rye was over half a foot taller and maybe had at least a hundred pounds of muscle on Jeff.

"Yeah. My own personal giant." Jeff put the board away, carefully tucking it in the huge closet. "Do I need to buy you clothes for the tour?"

"I guess that depends. I have plenty of jeans and T-shirts and a couple of suits. But if you want me... in costume, then, yes, you do." He wasn't going to like it, but he'd wear whatever Jeff wanted him to, as long as it didn't obstruct his sight lines or movement.

"Suits are fine. No colors, but black and white and you'll be fine."

"I've got two that fit that bill." They'd be at hotels, and he could have the one suit cleaned while he wore the other; it would work.

"You know if you need things, Donna will do it. She's like a superorganized machine." Jeff headed for the door. "Swimming?"

"Yes, swimming." He followed Jeff. The swimsuits and towels were kept in the small cupboard in the pool room.

Jeff made it to the door of the main house and took a deep breath. "No one's in there, right?"

"Nope. The cleaning crew left. But I can go ahead of you. It'll be good practice for when you're on tour." He put Jeff behind him. "Put your hand on my back, so I know you're right there."

Jeff's hand rested on the small of his back, right above his belt.

"Perfect. Then you just keep up with me. Tap on my back if I'm moving too fast or people are touching you, and I'll drop back to you. But most of the time, I'll be able to forge a path through people if I'm ahead of you." He opened the door into the living room.

"What happens if I disappear?"

43

"From behind me?" Rye shook his head. He wasn't letting that happen. "The second your hand disappears from my back, I'll turn and grab you."

"The crowds can be scary. I try to out intimidate them."

"You want to go ahead of me, then? I can loom over you and help with the intimidation." Like an extension of Jeff.

"I don't know. We'll have to experiment."

"Yeah, see what works best, huh?"

"Will you use the same team as before?"

They headed into the swimming area, the water clean and clear, the room warm and comfortable. This was quickly becoming Rye's favorite room.

"Team?"

"There were... three? Four men? I don't know. Enough to protect the stage with the band."

"Ah. Ms. Heard said she'd take care of that. It'll be new people, though." He'd insisted on that. Guys who knew Lord January was clean now and could be trusted to honor that, to make sure any groupies who hung out weren't carrying. Anyone with drugs would be turned away.

Jeff started stripping down. "New security? Are you sure? You know people?"

"Ms. Heard is taking care of it. I gave her a list." Ex-cops, every one of them.

"Oh." Jeff slipped into the water without another word.

Rye stopped Jeff with a hand on one shoulder. "You'll be safe. On my life."

"No. No, you're not allowed to get hurt. The road is ugly. It always will be."

"Then we'll get through it together."

Jeff looked away, then patted his belly. "It's time to swim."

"It is." Rye stripped down, getting into the water as Jeff started to swim. He was going to miss swimming naked when they started using the hotel pools.

Every so often, he would adjust Jeff's stroke so that he wasn't causing wear and tear on his shoulders. It felt good, working his muscles, the water on his skin. Knowing he was helping Jeff out.

He was used to watching the black ink move, muscles making the dark shapes shift. It was kind of mesmerizing, like Jeff himself. Different from what he was used to, but compelling. Fascinating.

Rye swam until he was tired, and then he patted Jeff's shoulder. "Time to stop." He'd make them some roasted red pepper soup. Jeff was even eating the toast points now too.

"Already?" Jeff was relentless.

"Yeah. Your body needs a break now and then."

Jeff sighed, eyes rolling dramatically.

Chuckling, Rye climbed out of the pool and offered Jeff his hand. Jeff's hands were shaking, and Rye made sure everything was steady before he let go. Grabbing a towel, he ran it over Jeff's limbs, then handed him a robe before drying himself off.

The gate bell was ringing when they headed to the kitchen, a couple of news vans waiting.

Jeff winced. "I should call Martin. He deals with the press."

"Okay. Meanwhile, I'm going to tell them to go away."

"Please." Jeff sighed and headed back up to his rooms.

Growling, Rye grabbed the phone. "Who is this?"

"Lisa Jonston from KFAA, News 12. We were wondering if Mr. January had a statement on the arrest of one of his fans last night."

"No comment. Talk to his publicist." He hung up.

The bell rang again immediately. No wonder Jeff stayed upstairs. He took a breath. If he answered he was going to be rude. If he went down there, he was quite possibly going to be violent.

He turned the ringer down low and put the peppers on the burners to roast the skins.

At some point he was going to have to break down and eat a steak the size of his head.

Maybe they could go to a restaurant. Him and Jeff, not Lord January.

He would like that, to see Jeff actually go outside.

Like a real person.

He'd have to broach the subject. He doubted Jeff would go out today, but Rye would wear him down, and maybe in a couple days they could do it. Somewhere quiet where they served vegetarian and meatatarian meals.

Somewhere no one would recognize Jeff.

Somewhere trustworthy.

Continuing to ignore the phone, which was still fucking ringing, Rye made the soup and grabbed a package of crackers instead of making toast. He made another milkshake with protein powder for Jeff too. It all fit on a tray, and he headed back upstairs, making sure to close and lock the door on his way.

He totally got the temptation to lock the rest of the world away and stay safe in hiding, but Rye wasn't going to let Jeff be a prisoner of Lord January's fame.

CHAPTER FOUR

"THE BAND is coming in tonight, LJ, and you have an appearance Thursday night at midnight at Clockworks. Do you need me to order in food and supplies?" Donna asked, her voice warm even over the telephone.

"Yeah. Yeah, that's fine. Call Rye and tell him when to open the doors." Jeff stared out the window of his bedroom. It had been good, vacation, but it was over.

All of it.

"Okay, LJ. You feeling ready? The tour starts in two weeks."

"One week of music rehearsals, one week of dress rehearsal, and then we're off. Got it." He was going to die.

Rye came in with a tray of food, moving easily.

"Is there anything you need?" Donna asked again.

"Bri will want M&M'S, Roach likes beer. Scooter and Brandy bring their own shit."

One of Rye's eyebrows went up and he mouthed, "Who?"

Jeff held up one finger. "E-mail me all the details for Thursday and make sure Rye gets all the information."

"You've got it. I'll keep you updated if there's any change. Take care of yourself, honey."

"I will."

He hung up, tried to smile. "Vacation is over. Time to earn my pennies. The band is here starting tonight. The appearances start Thursday."

"Okay. You don't need to do the whole January schtick with the band, do you?"

"No. No, there will be some strangers, so I'll be LJ."

Rye made a face. "All right. But remember he's just a shell."

"He is." Jeff sighed and stretched. "There will be deliveries today—food and booze, all that. They all have rooms here."

"Do they know I'm going to search them and their stuff for drugs?"

"Oh, that's going to go over well." Roach was going to scream.

Rye shrugged, not looking terribly concerned. "They should be happy I'm letting them bring in booze."

"I only drink booze when I want to blow fire."

That eyebrow of Rye's went up. "And do you do that often?"

"Couple times a week on tour." Whenever he had to.

Rye made a face but didn't actually say anything. He set the tray down. "Come and eat."

"What is it? It smells good."

"Figs and cheese on crackers, vegetables, and baba ghanoush."

"Do I like figs?" Jeff came closer, eyes curious.

"You tell me." Rye picked one up, offering it to him.

Jeff took the bite and nibbled, then nodded. "I like figs."

"I'm glad."

"Yeah? The cook will be back tomorrow, and you won't have to do it anymore." He was sad. He liked Rye's food.

"Yeah? Does the cook know what you like?"

"No." How could she? Jeff hadn't known.

"Then we'll have to tell her."

"Yeah." Really, he'd just have toast in the morning. It would be enough.

"Hey. I'm still here, and I know you're not LJ. You need to remember who you are, you look to me, okay?"

"Just remember, if you hate January, that I'm still your friend."

"I know. Me and Jeff, we're like this." Rye crossed his fingers together.

"Yeah. Yeah, good friends."

Rye smiled that smile where it made his face the handsomest thing around.

He ate another fig cracker, sighing as his phone rang. Roach. He grabbed it, answered. "Roach."

"Boss. Tonight, huh? You really clean?"

"Yeah."

"You get religion?"

"No."

"Great."

He rolled his eyes, and Rye dipped a carrot in hummus and handed it over to him.

"Thank you," Jeff mouthed. "You have a song list in mind?" he said out loud.

"Of course I do." Roach cackled. "I know exactly what all those little bloodsuckers want."

"That's my Roach." He chuckled. "I can't wait to see you play." That was the truth. Roach was solid as a rock, unflappable, and cynical as fuck.

"Ditto, LJ. Been too fucking long."

Ten months. He hadn't gone that long between tours ever. "I'll be ready. We'll rock the house."

"You know it, LJ. The place full of groupies yet?"

"No. No, not yet."

"It will be. Live like rock stars, huh?"

He supposed so.

"Okay, LJ, I'll see you tonight." Roach cackled some more and hung up.

Jeff put his phone away and headed into the closet. He needed his costume, to become LJ.

He sighed, and he thought he could hear January in the back of his head, laughing.

RYE FOLLOWED Lord January downstairs to meet up with the band, with some misgivings. That the band themselves already hated him—he'd done his drug check when they'd arrived and flushed several joints down the toilet—didn't bother him.

49

But Jeff's alter ego made him itch. He couldn't help but think that January was toxic for Jeff. It was his job to make sure Jeff didn't get totally lost.

LJ was in a silk shirt open to the waist, skintight leather pants, and dark, thick eye makeup and heavy silver jewelry.

It was ugly, stark, and weirdly distasteful. Rye wasn't sure what that said about him as a person.

Was it fucked up to think that Jeff was the attractive one? That the loose, gauzy pants or jeans and sweat shirts, hair clean and loose, was Jeff at his most beautiful?

This LJ character was supposed to be more powerful than his Jeff, but....

God, man, Rye growled to himself, *fucking focus.*

The four guys who made up January's band let up a cheer as Jeff came down, and Rye scanned the room, making sure it was just them, that there were no threats.

They swarmed January, hugging and shaking, looking him over.

They all had the same basic look: lean, skinny, underfed. The bassist was bald and fierce, her sharp teeth flashing. The percussionist was the only one with any meat on his bones, and he picked LJ up and spun him about.

Rye tried not to growl, made himself stay where he was. These were Jeff's band members, not vultures.

"Oh, man. You look great."

An older guy with a terribly scarred face—Roach—looked LJ over. "You know, Scooter, he does. You look healthy. Weird."

Rye ground his teeth and stayed right where he was, not saying a word.

"Yeah, yeah, yeah." LJ flipped Roach off. "And you look like a starvation victim."

"Sort of been. It's a thing. You want to work or talk, asshole?"

"Work!" The entire band spoke together.

They settled quickly into the music, and Rye sat back. He couldn't help but compare this session to the music Jeff made when it was just the two of them.

This was raucous and furious, Jeff screaming and jumping up and down, head whipping around feverishly.

Rye kind of hated it.

It was going to be a long fucking tour.

They played five songs, and then they broke, LJ and Roach's heads together making plans. The beers came up, and then a couple of people he didn't know wandered in.

Whoa.

Hold up.

Rye got up and got into their faces. "Excuse me. Who are you?" And how the fuck had they gotten in?

"We won the *101.2 contest*. Lord January! Oh my God!"

Another man walked in, smarmy written all over him. "Marvin Reynolds. LJ's publicist. They're with me. Hey, LJ. Looking good!"

"You can all stop right there." Rye started with Mr. Fucking Publicist, patting the man down. He was going to have words with the man later. He hadn't been informed of this contest. Not to mention this was Jeff's house—having fans wandering in and out was crazy.

"What the fuck! LJ, tell this guy who I am!"

Jeff looked over. "You just did, Marv."

"No one gets in and out without a search, Mr. Reynolds. I'm going to have to ask for your key too." Luckily the guy was clean, and he held out his hand for the key.

"Dude! LJ!"

"He doesn't work for me. Works for Donna. Call her. I'm working." Jeff looked positively tickled for a second.

Rye puffed up, making himself look even bigger, and kept his hand right there, waiting on that key. No one was getting past him until he had it.

The key was handed over. "Your ass is fired, man."

"Do your worst. And when these ladies' visit is over, we need to have a word about these *contests*." Turning to the girls, he managed a small smile for them. "Are either of you carrying drugs or knives?"

"I… I have a pen knife. I was hoping… I mean, everyone knows…."

He held out his hand. "Sorry, no knives." People were fucking insane.

"You'll give it back later?" The tiny goth handed over a little knife with vampire teeth sketched on.

"I will." He turned to the other girl, eyebrow raised.

This little girl looked terrified. "I just… I'm Amy's friend."

"Barb! My goth name is Dru!"

"Sorry. Sorry." This kid was going to lose it.

Rye crouched down in front of her. "Is that a no, honey?" He really didn't want to have to frisk these girls if he didn't have to.

She nodded. "I have my phone and money for a cab home."

"Okay." He stood and moved to stand behind Jeff.

"Okay, Roach. Let's do 'Fucking and Narcoleptic' for the girls." Jeff's voice was husky, rough. "Give them a show."

Rye kept half his attention on the girls, the other half on Reynolds. Frankly, he was more worried about the publicist than the fans.

The band got to their microphones, and the screaming guitars started.

Rye pretended he couldn't hear it.

They ran through the songs, LJ writhing, humping the air, the act obscene, ugly. No wonder Jeff didn't have sex, if that's what he thought it was. Even kinky sex wasn't meant to be… vicious.

The girls were clearly pleased, though, screaming and clapping.

Rye couldn't wait for it to be over.

Finally, the music stopped, LJ breathing hard. "Take five, guys. Need a breather."

"Lord January! Can you come sign things for the girls?"

Rye sort of hated that Marv guy already.

"Sure. Somebody get me a Sharpie."

Rye found it and handed it over. "You need some food."

"After." Jeff met his eyes.

52

"Soon," he countered.

Jeff nodded once and headed over to the girls, muttering low, growling, and making the girls scream.

Christ on a crutch. He reminded himself he needed to get used to this.

The band played another five songs, and it wasn't until nearly the end of the last one that Rye realized LJ didn't get the break he asked for.

He stepped forward. "Okay, guys. Break time. And Reynolds? It's time for the contest winners to be escorted out."

"Yeah. I'm done," Jeff said. "You guys staying here?"

Roach nodded. "I'm yours 'til the tour's over." The others piped up in the affirmative too.

"Okay, cool." Rye put a hand on Jeff's shoulder and guided him toward the kitchen.

"I need to go upstairs now."

"Okay. I'll bring your food up, okay?"

"Hot tea?"

For that poor voice. "You got it." He made sure Jeff got to the stairs and that the door was locked. Then he headed for the kitchen to make a meal. He'd make sure that Reynolds and the girls were gone before he brought it all upstairs too. This whole thing was earmarked for disaster.

He put together tomato soup and cheese sandwiches, along with a strawberry milkshake. He put a teapot with teabags in it on the tray and started the kettle. Then he did a sweep of the house.

Roach was still in the studio, playing with the guitar, making notes.

"Reynolds and the girls get out okay?" Rye asked.

"I think so, yeah. Bri wanted to fuck them both, but the little one started crying, and he scrambled. Unwilling isn't his thing."

"Not here at the house, okay? It isn't safe." He knew that kind of thing used to happen here all the time, but things were changing now that he was on duty.

"Yeah. Who are you, man? Security?" Roach asked.

"Personal bodyguard. I'm the guy who makes sure he gets out of this tour clean and alive."

"Cool. I'm not into the speed and shit. Not my deal. I just lead the band." It was fascinating to watch his mouth move with the scars.

"Good to know. Sorry for the pat down earlier, but I'm not taking any chances."

"Whatever, man. I don't give a shit. This is my job. You don't screw with that, I'm easy. We're just making music and money."

"I won't screw with your job." Even if he did think Jeff could be so much more real on that front. "Don't let anyone in."

"I won't. There anything to eat in the fridge? Sandwiches?"

"Yep. There's a list on the fridge. Add anything you want. The housekeeper will pick it up. Night."

Rye double-checked the doors, reminding himself he had a bone to pick with Reynolds, but they could do it tomorrow.

He headed back to the kitchen to grab their food.

Brandy was in there, making a peanut butter sandwich. "Yo."

"Hey." He was going to have to get used to there being other people in the house. Pouring the hot water into the teapot, he then grabbed the tray for upstairs. It was uncomfortable, stressful. He didn't like his Jeff in so much danger.

"Don't let anyone in without my approval, okay?" He'd repeat it until he was sure everyone had been told and understood he was serious.

"You know it. Night." She had a voice like a crow.

It was all that screaming. It couldn't be good for any of them. He headed for Jeff's rooms, double-checking the lock before going up.

The shower was running, *Star Wars* blaring on the TV.

Rye set the food on the bedside table and went into the bathroom, knocking on the door and calling out. "Hey, Jeff. It's just me."

"Hey." Jeff's voice was barely there.

Jesus. How was he supposed to survive the tour? "Food and beverages are in the bedroom. How are you doing?"

54

"Okay." The water went off, and Jeff came out of the shower, pale as milk. "Tired."

"You look exhausted." He wrapped a towel around Jeff and began drying him.

"I am. You're okay?"

"Yeah. Just adjusting to having other people in the house." He finished drying Jeff off and grabbed the robe on the back of the door, put Jeff in it. "It's been just us. I liked it."

"Yes. It will be sort of like this on the bus."

"Oh, it'll be easier to police on the bus." Far less places for people to hide.

Jeff nodded, then shocked him by pushing into his arms, hugging him tight for a breathless second before pulling away.

"Let's eat." Rye ignored the fact that his throat was tight, his voice thick. He turned the movie down a little and passed Jeff his bowl of soup.

Jeff sat, wrapped in his robe, sipping the soup. "Tomato. My favorite."

"I know. I found a recipe for carrot and ginger—asked Brigitte to pick the ingredients up for it."

"Carrot soup? I would like that."

"Yeah, I think you would."

When Jeff had finished his soup, Rye passed over the cheese sandwich. "There's a strawberry milkshake for dessert." It felt good, getting back to what was normal for them.

"Can I just have the shake?"

"How about eating the cheese without the bread?"

Jeff shook his head, but picked the sandwich apart, eating the crispy outside, some of the cheese.

Pleased, Rye handed over the milkshake.

Jeff took a deep drink, moaning low. "Oh, my throat hurts."

"I'll put lozenges on the grocery list."

Finishing his own food, Rye set everything back on the tray before settling against the headboard. He held his arms out for Jeff.

Although there was a little more meat on those bones now, it was still more comfortable for Jeff to use him as a cushion.

Jeff crawled over to him and snuggled into his chest. "Did you like it? The rehearsal?"

"Honestly?" Jeff nodded, and he continued. "No. I didn't. You're an amazing singer, but you couldn't tell with the songs you guys were doing."

"It's the act."

"I know, and it's clearly popular with the fans. How did you get into the goth thing to start with?"

"Roach and I met in college. I minored in music. He had a band that had gotten signed to a label, and the lead singer cut his own throat on stage, bled out. I looked like him."

"Oh my God." What a horrific legacy.

"Yeah. I became Lord January, and no one even knew."

"Seriously? That's fucked up."

"I know, right?"

"Yeah, right." He shivered, held Jeff a little closer.

Jeff sighed and leaned, resting hard, eyes on the TV. "I love Chewie."

"Great big teddy bear?"

"Violent chess player."

Rye put his head back and laughed. God, Jeff was… good. A fun, interesting, good man. He ran his hand across Jeff's shoulders, hoping to ease Jeff's tension. It only took a few minutes before Jeff was sound asleep, curled against his chest.

Rye held him, pushing away the thought that he would protect this man with his life for more than just the job.

CHAPTER FIVE

JEFF WOKE up when the sun went down, heading to the bathroom to gargle salt water and bathe. He had been dreaming about wandering through a house filled with blood spatter, with razors and knives.

Rye popped his head in while he was in the tub, debating whether to top up the hot or get out. "Morning! I've got breakfast, when you're done."

He snorted. "Morning? I like that."

"Well, you just woke up."

"I did. How are you?" Jeff floated, feet bobbing in the water.

"Eh. I have to get used to the new schedule."

"It's hard. On the road it's easier. You sleep when we travel."

"Well, it's good to hear there will be some advantages to traveling." Rye stepped out, then came back and gave him a milkshake, complete with a straw.

"Thanks." He was going to have to watch his weight.

"How are you feeling about last night? About having the fans here and shit."

How was he feeling? He wasn't. He didn't want to feel anything.

"I'm having words with Reynolds today. This is supposed to be a safe place. No more fans."

"He won't let you do it." Not even Donna would agree to that.

Rye snorted. "Too bad. Unless they want me strip-searching your fans, they'll agree to keep meet and greets off the property."

That would cause a stir now, wouldn't it? Naked, panicked fans running amok.

"You need anything else?" Rye asked, nodding at his milkshake.

"No. No, I'll get dressed and ready for rehearsals."

"Sounds good. We're breaking for food, though. And you need to get some swimming in today."

Jeff nodded, but he knew better. There'd be singing, planning, then more singing, then bed.

"Don't turn into a prune," teased Rye as he headed for the bathroom door.

"I won't." He was going to turn into a vampire.

By the time he was made up and dressed, he'd dumped the shake and decided on the playlist for tonight.

"You haven't had any veggies and hummus." Rye looked at the tray, frowning. "You need to eat, to keep your strength up for rehearsals. Even more so once you start touring."

"I'm not hungry." He wanted to just crawl back into bed, hide from the world.

Rye's mouth twisted. "You need to eat, Jeff."

"I will. Later."

"Have a carrot, Jeff." Rye was looking particularly, immovably giant-like.

"Later." It was sort of cute, really.

"One carrot, dipped in hummus. Then I'm out of your hair."

"My hair's greasy. You wouldn't want to be in it."

Rye went to the tray, grabbed a baby carrot, dipped it into the hummus, and handed it over to him.

"I read the little carrots are poisonous." Still, Jeff ate it, because it was good.

"You want me to be your food taster too?" Rye's eyes twinkled for him.

"You could just eat for me."

"I would if that's how it worked." Rye touched his shoulder.

Jeff reached up and held Rye's fingers for a second.

Rye squeezed his hand. "You're going to make it through this."

He didn't think so. "I will."

"You will. Even if I have to drag you through it kicking and screaming."

"I only do that for work, you know."

Rye stared at him for a moment, then chuckled for him.

Jeff leaned up and kissed Rye's cheek. "Time for work now. Time to be someone else."

"I know. I've got your back."

"Good." He wrapped Lord January around him and headed downstairs, chin held high.

RYE WAS about done with this whole Lord January rehearsing thing.

Jeff wasn't eating, he wasn't swimming—he wasn't doing anything but drawing back into himself.

Rye wanted to shout and hit things. It had been three days since there'd been any sort of break during rehearsal, and he wasn't letting it happen again tonight.

When he was ignored, he went over to the power outlet and unplugged three or four things.

The entire band turned to look at him.

"It's time for a break. LJ needs to eat. I imagine the rest of you do too."

"Are we still making that appearance at midnight, man? We need to go full-on psycho if we do." Roach looked perfectly gleeful.

"Full-on psycho?" Rye did not like the sound of that.

"Lord January at his foul, gruesome best." Brandy clapped. "We haven't seen you dripping with blood in eons."

Rye fucking hated this. Hated it.

"Yeah. Let's take an hour, meet downstairs. The limo will pick us up. They paid for two hours of mayhem." Jeff didn't even seem like the same person.

"An hour." Rye nodded and grabbed Jeff's arm, tugging him toward the kitchen.

Jeff followed along. "Where are we going?"

"You need to eat."

When they got to the kitchen, he put Jeff on a stool.

"I don't want much. Just a little."

"A shake and some veggies. I won't take no for an answer."

"Just a little."

"Just a few, yes." Rye pulled the cut-up vegetables and hummus from the fridge and set the prepared plate in front of Jeff. "Go ahead. I'll make your milkshake."

"Are you coming tonight?"

"I'm your shadow, Jeff. No matter where you go."

"It's going to be ugly."

"Yeah, I got that." He wasn't going to enjoy it. At all.

"Just remember the money. They pay for it. It's just a show. A sick, dirty show."

"Is it worth the money?" Rye was thinking more and more that it wasn't.

"It's part of the deal. Appearances. I'll be all over the Net in the morning."

"We live in a crazy world." He put extra protein powder in the shake, whirred it up, and handed it over. "I expect you to drink it all."

"I don't want to throw up. The fake blood packs are nasty."

"Are you expected to drink them?" Please say no. Please say no.

"No. You bite them and let them drip out of your mouth."

Thank God it wasn't worse than that. "I'll look into things, see if I can find something less nasty for you to deal with."

"At least it doesn't stain."

"I still can't believe people want crap like that." He sat next to Jeff and had one of the carrots. "You've got an amazing voice when you're allowed to use it."

"It's the shock value, the gore, the death." Jeff stirred the shake, stopping when some of the band came in.

Rye leaned in and spoke so only Jeff could hear him. "Drink it up. We're not going anywhere until you do."

"Are you wearing the black robes today, man? The heavy ones?" Brandy asked Jeff.

"I don't know. Maybe the leather."

"Leather is better armor," Rye pointed out.

"They'll hold your gut in too." Brandy smiled at him as Roach snorted.

"Yeah. He's huge. Bah."

"He's too fucking skinny," growled Rye. The last thing Jeff needed was to be told he was overweight, joking or not.

"Oh, I think he looks good." That was Scooter. "Just remember to ham it up, lots of writhing and gyrating on the dance floor. It won't take long."

"Oh, LJ doesn't eat meat." Rye managed not to smile even when he said it.

It took a second, and then the band started cackling, pushing and shoving each other.

Smiling, Rye poked Jeff. "Drink up."

"I think I'll take it upstairs."

"Good choice." Rye gave the guys in the band a nod and followed Jeff upstairs.

Jeff's steps slowed, each one heavier than the next. Rye put his arm around Jeff's waist once they hit the stairs and were alone. "Almost there."

"I'm okay. I just... I miss the uppers. I miss the rush."

"So you need something else to give you a rush." Rye had a few ideas on that front, from roller coasters to scary movies to kinky sex.

Jeff chuckled softly. "What I need is a few minutes of quiet, probably. Janie will be up here soon to get me in costume."

"More costumey than what you usually wear?"

"God, yeah. This requires contacts, teeth, paint, hair."

What a zoo. Rye kept his mouth shut, though. He figured Jeff knew well and good how Rye felt about Lord January and all the crap that went along with it.

Jeff sat in one of the wingback chairs, legs crossed, eyes closed.

Rye regarded him for a moment, then went to stand behind him, hands dropping to Jeff's shoulders, and he began to massage. Jeff's muscles were hard, stiff as rocks. Rye didn't say anything; he just kept working the tight muscles, fingers digging in. Finally they let go, easing under his touch.

He kept massaging, keeping them loose, wanting to give Jeff something good to hold on to.

"Can I have a little of my shake?"

Rye handed it over, relieved Jeff was having something to eat. Stretching, he moved to sit next to Jeff.

Jeff sipped, quiet, still. It was a bit like the man was being drained, day-by-day. He'd tried not to interfere too much; he'd tried to let things roll the way they always had. But it wasn't working. Rye was going to have to start putting his foot down and insisting on stuff like food, like swimming.

Like sunshine and happiness and backgammon. There was no reason on earth Jeff had to inhabit Lord January twenty-four/seven.

None.

Lord January was a... a role. Just a role. One not worth dying over.

He smiled encouragingly as Jeff drank most of his shake.

"Do you like your job?" Jeff asked.

"Most of the time, I do."

"What will you do when you're done? Find another person?"

Rye found himself not really wanting to think about moving on from Jeff. He simply shrugged.

Jeff's phone rang, and Jeff didn't answer, just buzzed someone in. "She's here to get me ready."

"Okay." Rye headed down the stairs to meet Janie at the door. "I'll check her out," he called back to Jeff.

"Check me out? I'm not a hooker, sweetie. I'm a makeup artist."

Oh dear God.

This amazing woman with a huge pink beehive and orange cat's eye glasses stood there, at least as wide as she was tall, cracking her gum and staring at him.

"Janie!" Jeff called from the top of the stairs. He actually sounded tickled. "Oh, I've missed you!"

She pushed past Rye and grabbed Jeff in a hug. "Oh, you look great! I've missed you. My Allie had her baby, did you hear? I have pictures!"

Rye blinked. "Okay. Just a second. From now on, no one comes in here without a pat down."

"A pat down? Now that's more action than I've gotten in twenty years."

"I'm sorry, ma'am, but it's security measures. I'll need to look in your cases." No drugs, no weapons were getting in on his watch.

"Sure. Go for it. I'll show LJ my grandgirl." She was totally unconcerned. "Oh. Oh! I smuggled you in something!"

"Oh God. Honest?"

"You know it!" A paper bag was held up. "Rugalach from that bakery on Third. There's a couple of bagels too."

Food? Jeff was excited about food? Rye started going through Janie's stuff. There was nothing—makeup and brushes and shit. Curling irons and such.

Jeff pulled out the sweets, taking the tiniest bite. "Oh, that's just like my mom's. You brought a ton."

"Put it in the fridge. Make it last."

"Or you could do something radical like actually eating it all quickly." Rye was sure they could get more rug… ruglatch.

"No way I'm eating this fast. You want a bite?" A tiny square of pastry was held up, the scent of cinnamon and butter on the air.

"Sure. I want to try any food you're excited about." Rye came over and took the bite. Flaky and delicious, the pastry melted on his tongue. "Oh wow. Yeah, those are amazing."

"There's a tiny kosher bakery near my house. I try to grab them when I can." Janie grinned, gold tooth shining. "LJ, I'll get set up. What are you wearing? Do you know?"

Rye stole another bite of the treat and stepped back out of the way.

Soon Jeff and Janie were in the bathroom, creating Lord January. First Jeff got stripped down and Janie painted him, making him even paler, highlighting him with gray.

Making him look even worse than when he'd first gotten out of rehab.

Pure black contacts went in, and she dressed him in a tight, tight leather corset, lace-up pants, high-heeled boots. Then the sharp fake fangs went in, dangling rings in his ears and fake piercings in his nipples, thick dark makeup, and then a wild, black wig.

Christ.

He looked like the antichrist.

Rye's fingers curled into fists.

"Am I sex on a stick?"

He answered without even thinking. "You were before you put on the Lord of the Vampires."

"The corset fits beautifully, honey. Let's do your lips. Red or black?"

"Black." Those empty, black shark-eyes stared at him.

Rye looked away, not sure why he'd said what he'd said. Oh fuck it. He knew why he'd said it. Because he was attracted to Jeff, for all he wasn't his type.

And Lord January simply looked like death.

Lord January—because that wasn't Jeff, it didn't even sound like Jeff with the teeth in.

Sighing, he glanced at his watch. "We about ready to head out?"

"You don't have to come, if you don't want to. There'll be security at the club."

"You going to make me say it again? Wither thou goest…." He winked, hoping Jeff was still in there under January.

"I will go." Jeff reached out for him, fingers brushing his wrist.

Rye let his own fingers touch Jeff's briefly. His Jeff was in there, and he'd make sure Jeff could shake January the minute they got home again.

"Time to go to work. Are you ready to go on the road, Janie?"

She nodded. "Just a little bit longer."

"Make sure you bring more of the ruglatches, please." They were good, plus it made him happy to watch Jeff eat.

"If she makes them, I'll bring them."

"Thank you, Janie."

Rye went to the door and checked the stairs. "Let's head out."

"Time to work."

LJ LET more blood drip from him, writhing with a bunch of young girls, bumping and rolling with the music. God, he was bored and nauseated. Tired. And his feet hurt. This was so much easier when he was high, when he didn't care. Rye had been there stage-side the entire time, though, and was right next to him now, watching. It wasn't like he had anything on him anyway. Of course, someone would have something if he wanted it. It was a good thing Rye was there to help him stay accountable.

Rye's big hand suddenly landed on his shoulder, tugged him back against a solid wall of warmth. "Time to go."

"Promise?"

He looked up, hating the way Rye flinched away.

"I swear. Stick with me." Backing up, Rye moved them toward the venue's exit.

LJ leaned back, leaning on Rye's strength, trusting in it, wholeheartedly.

When the fans realized he was leaving, everything reached a fever pitch, and they began pushing. Rye sort of wrapped around him, his own personal giant simply pushing his way through the crowd.

The head of security at the club came up to Rye. "You want us to get the band somewhere, Hoss?"

"The limo's in the alley behind the club."

"Good deal. You have transportation of your own?"

"Yep." His SUV was on the side road, close but far enough from the limo that they could slip away. "Thanks for your help."

This club had good people.

"Anytime. I'll have someone keep an eye on you 'til you leave."

"Good deal." Rye squeezed Jeff's arm, and they started moving again, hitting the door and pushing out into the street.

They had enough lead time on the fans that they got to the SUV without too much trouble.

Rye bundled him into the front passenger seat and closed the door. Jeff heard the lock shoot home and watched as Rye hurried around the front of the vehicle. Locks clicking again, Rye climbed into the driver's side and started the engine up. They moved off quickly, Rye visibly on high alert, checking the mirrors and the street.

"Home?" Jeff asked, feeling everything inside him clenching.

"Just as quickly as we can."

"Good." He slumped back, burning eyes closed. Hurt. Hurt. Hurt. "Oh God. Rye. Gonna hurl."

Rye pulled over, and Jeff rolled the window down, the big hands helping turn him so he could lean out the window. He spit his teeth out into his hand before he lost it, heaving over and over.

Rye's hand stayed on his back, rubbing and soothing, easing his muscles as they clenched with the effort of throwing up.

Finally, he was empty, slumping to the seat. "Home. Please."

Rye got them going again. "Window up or down?"

"Down. The wind feels good."

"It'll be twelve minutes. You want some music?"

"Nothing loud." Nothing ugly. Nothing angry.

"No, I have just the thing."

Soft music began to play, a lone male singer accompanied only by an acoustic guitar.

"Mmm." His eyes closed, his muscles relaxing.

They drove in silence aside from the music, but it wasn't awkward or heavy or anything like that.

Just quiet.

The corset pressed against him, the edges slick with sweat and uncomfortable, and he smelled of smoke and other people.

"Almost there," murmured Rye. "I'm going to do up the window, keep you safe from the photographers at the gate."

"I got you." He was holding his teeth in his hands.

The window went up, and they rounded a corner, Rye opening the gate remotely as they drove up.

There weren't many photogs—maybe three—but Jeff wasn't in the mood to deal with them. He'd already done his duty for today, mixing it up with the fans, giving them exactly what they wanted.

Rye drove into the garage, the door closing behind them, then came around to help him out. "Straight to the bathroom to get rid of January."

He nodded. "I need to brush my teeth."

"And shower. I don't suppose we can burn those clothes?" Despite the words, Rye was smiling, making the words seem less harsh.

"No, they cost a fortune."

And the corsets looked good.

"I bet. Custom leather is expensive, no matter what it's customed into." Rye took his hand, and they went up the stairs to his rooms.

"You don't like guys in corsets?"

"Oh, I like the corset. It's the rest of it." Rye gave him a sideways look. "You'd rock a colored corset. A dark red or emerald green would look amazing on you."

"I never wear colors, but thank you." He shrugged the heavy coat off and turned his back to Rye. "Loosen me?"

"Sure." Rye's fingers began working on the lacing, fingers warm where they moved against his back.

The pressure eased, and he could breathe, could unfasten the placket in the front and free himself. The silk shirt went next, then the skintight pants.

As soon as he was naked, Rye put him in the shower, turning it on nice and hot.

"My contact case, please?"

Rye passed it over and began to strip.

Jeff popped his contacts out, put them away, and turned his face to the water, letting it beat him down.

Rye stepped into the shower with him, big hand soaping him up, helping him wash the last of Lord January away.

Suddenly he could breathe, could focus. He leaned back into Rye, the solid body supporting him. He loved that Rye was comfortable enough to be naked with him, that they could touch skin on skin. It was comforting.

"Close your eyes," murmured Rye, and when he did, the big fingers slid soap over his face. "Just getting rid of the last of the makeup."

"I did it." God, he was exhausted.

"You did. Just one more of those before the tour starts, though."

"Yeah. Just one, two nights before, and it's faster."

That one he'd show up, let them take pictures, and go. It would take longer to get dressed than he'd actually be there.

"Good. I've told Reynolds any interviews during the tour will have to be onsite at the hotels or right after sound check at the venues. That you won't be making appearances after the shows at clubs and stuff."

"No. No, I can't. Not and do the shows. I'm tired already." And on the road, it would be impossible.

"I know. He was pissed, but I told him he went by my rules or you wouldn't even be doing the interviews." Rye chuckled. "He called Ms. Heard, and she told him exactly how the wind blew. If I say this is how it goes, then this is how it goes."

"How cool is that?" Leaning out of the shower, Jeff grabbed his toothbrush and the Crest, making short work of doing his teeth. Then he grabbed the shampoo and washed his hair, fingers tangling in the long mess.

Rye grabbed a hairbrush and started working through the wet tangles. "It's pretty cool. It means I get to do more than just keep you safe and clean. I get to keep January from killing you."

"He's our bread and butter." He stretched out for Rye, the gentle brushing a comfort. "You know I'll have to take the uppers, don't you? It's inevitable. I won't be able to help myself."

"Nope. It's not happening." Rye's brushing stayed in rhythm. "We'll figure something out. Just keep me in the loop of how you're feeling."

"I promise. Will… will you promise to stay my friend, even when I suck and I'm January?"

"I will always be your friend. I hate what January does to you, but I don't hate you."

"Okay. That's good enough for me." And it was. He needed someone that saw him, a little bit. All the time.

"Can you do me another favor?" At his nod, Rye went on. "Only put the contacts in when you absolutely have to? The all black is… unnerving."

"Oh God yes. They hurt, itch like fire. You should see the bleeding ones. So. Gross."

"Sounds awful." Rye finished doing his hair and pushed him back under the spray. "There. Are you ready to come out?"

"I am." Jeff stepped out of the shower, and somehow a towel was wrapped around him, cradling him.

Rye dried him off thoroughly, then wrapped him in a robe and guided him to the bedroom.

Jeff crawled into the bed, leaving a side for Rye. He slept better with the big man close, with the sound of that steady heartbeat.

"You hungry?" Rye asked, drying himself off.

"I don't think so."

"I could grab a milkshake, just in case…." Rye stood by the bed, waiting for his answer.

The man was rather stunning naked. Well, he was stunning not naked too. "Did you know you were hot? I mean, do you have a girlfriend? A wife?"

Rye looked startled for a moment, then chuckled. "I'm queer, remember? So I don't swing that way. And with the scars…." Rye shrugged.

"Huh. Really?" Jeff didn't remember, but he supposed it didn't matter. "I think the scar thing is probably in your head. Come to bed. I'll eat tomorrow." The scars were just scars. Jeff was covered in them.

Rye climbed in and tugged him close. "That's a nice thought, but I've been told the scars on my thigh are... less than attractive."

"I think they're fine." He touched them, exploring the skin. "They don't bother me."

"Thank you." Rye's voice was slightly thick, like when he'd just woken up.

Jeff curled in close, head on Rye's chest, hand on his hard belly. Rye's arm slid around his shoulders, and he felt completely safe.

He kissed the broad chest. "Good night. Thank you."

Thank God he was home.

RYE WAS getting used to pushing his weight around.

Lucky for him, he had a lot of weight to push with. And that Donna Heard appreciated the fact that he'd kept her client clean, that what he was doing was working, and she'd laid down the law.

He was going to have to have a talk with her about Jeff's chances as a songwriter and singer away from the Lord January persona. Because Jeff was fucking talented. And he had a lot of money in the bank because he didn't spend anything on himself now that he wasn't buying drugs.

Because January was fucking killing Jeff, sure as he was breathing.

He could totally understand the lure of the drugs, how they had helped Jeff deal with being January, but that wasn't going to work anymore. He had an idea now of how badly Jeff probably wanted a hit when he was on stage, and Rye was impressed that Jeff hadn't said anything about wishing he had some, hadn't whined about it, but had just dealt. Rye didn't see it getting any easier, though.

They were holed up in Jeff's room after the last fucking public appearance before the tour. Jeff had been right; it had been a quick "show his face, spew blood, and leave" event.

There were apparently lots of rumors going around that January was dying and the tour would be cancelled, because he hadn't been available to the public the way he used to be, but time would bear that out as wrong, and frankly, Rye didn't give a shit. Jeff came first.

He'd brought a tray of food and the ubiquitous milkshake up and was trying to coax food into Jeff.

"I'm not hungry, Rye. Thank you." Jeff was sitting in the center of the bed, staring at the chaos. Everything was being packed to go: makeup, costumes, guitars.

"We could make it a game," Rye suggested. He was getting desperate. Jeff had to eat. Had to.

"A game?"

Oh.

Eye contact.

Bingo.

"Uh-huh. Like Truth or Dare, only with hummus and milkshakes." Okay, so that wasn't the greatest comparison, though he'd answer questions or do dumb stuff if it got Jeff to eat.

"Truth or Dare with hummus...." Jeff grinned at him, then started chuckling. "You are desperate to get that into me, aren't you?"

"Yeah, I totally am." Man, could someone misinterpret that sentence.

"I'll have a sip of the shake, just to ease the worry."

"Then we'll play something for more." A sip was only a step in the right direction.

"Okay. I like games." Jeff took a tiny sip, then another.

"I know. You want to do a board game, a card game, or some variation of Truth or Dare?"

"Let's play cards. Something simple." Jeff pulled out a deck.

"Stuffed poker!"

"Stuffed poker? Is that strip poker backward?"

"It's strip poker with eating food instead of taking off clothes. I can see you naked anytime." He waggled his eyebrows at Jeff.

"Oh, the romance is gone!"

The little joke, the tease, made Rye want to applaud. He simply chuckled instead, grabbing his cards up when Jeff dealt them. He looked at his cards. Two pair, not bad.

Rye pursed his lips. "I bet a carrot dipped in hummus and two sips of milkshake."

"What.... Do I bid the same stuff and you eat if I win?"

"If you want. Or we can come up with something else."

"Well, you don't need my clothes."

"They would be a bit on the small side."

Jeff giggled, the sound charming as fuck. "You think so?"

He held his hand out, two fingers almost touching. "Just a little."

"I'm so glad you're here." The words were careful, gentle. "Okay, one carrot and two sips."

He was more pleased than he could say. "Me too. You gonna fold?"

"No. No, I need a card."

He handed the card over, watching closely.

"Okay. I'm going to stay. You?"

"I'm good." He had two pair. He'd bet Jeff would have to eat.

Jeff had a pair of aces, so he dipped the carrot and held it to Jeff's lips. They brushed against his fingertips, leaving tingles behind. Rye was beginning to worry that his soul was lost to this gentle, amazing, lost man.

Licking his lips, he grabbed the glass and waited until Jeff had finished chewing, then held it up to Jeff's lips as well.

"Strawberry?"

"Of course." Tempting worked better if it was one of Jeff's favorite flavors.

"Thank you." One good sip and one tiny one was taken.

"Okay, next hand."

"Okay."

They played four hands, and he won three. He usually wasn't quite this lucky playing games against Jeff. Looked like fate wanted Jeff taken care of too.

"I'm done playing, Rye."

"Finish the shake? For me?"

"I'll try."

"Thank you." He touched Jeff's cheek and smiled.

Jeff leaned into his touch, swallowing hard like he was fighting tears.

"What's wrong?"

"I'm scared."

"I'm not going to let anything happen to you." He'd die first.

"But we both know I'll fail. The drugs will be there, everywhere, and I'll be so tired, I'll need it so much. All I'll have to do is let Roach know I need."

"Then I won't let you be alone with Roach. I won't let you be alone, period." Rye was clear on his mission. No drugs for Jeff. None.

"If it's not Roach, it'll be someone else. The fans have stuff. Some of them are pushers. I'll wind up getting my hands on them somehow."

Rye shook his head. "I'm not going to let you have them. I'll call the tour off first."

"You can't. That's bigger than us."

"Hopefully it won't come to that. This should be the last one, though, Jeff. You can't keep doing this."

"What else would I do? What else am I? I'm nothing. LJ is the money, the power, the talent."

"No. I've heard you sing, I've heard the songs you've written. LJ is just a part you play. You're the real talent."

"One more drink, right?"

"No, you're supposed to drink the whole thing."

"Damn." Jeff quirked a half smile, obviously trying to play.

Rye grinned and reached out, squeezing Jeff's hand.

Jeff managed the shake and then handed him the glass. "Stay with me tonight?" Every night Jeff asked.

And every night Rye said yes.

Stripping down to his skivvies, he climbed into bed and held his arm out for Jeff.

Jeff curled right in, hand on his belly. "I don't know what I'd do without you, Rye."

"Let's make sure you never find out, okay?" He rubbed Jeff's shoulders. Jeff needed some coping mechanisms on his own. Maybe not during the tour—that was probably too much to ask of anyone— but after, when he gave it up, there would still be stressors.

"Okay." He thought Jeff cried a little again, but then Jeff was asleep. The man was depressed, worried, stressed out. Wasn't this touring and performing shit supposed to be good? Exciting?

Instead of doing it for himself, Jeff was doing it for everyone else now. People who would find other jobs if this one disappeared. Jeff had to stop taking the weight of the whole thing on his shoulders. No, he needed to stop, period.

What would Donna do if he called her and asked her about relaunching Jeff as an indie artist?

Rye's big worry was that she'd fire him if he rocked the boat too much, and he couldn't lose access to Jeff. The man needed him.

More than that, he was beginning to believe, more each day, that he needed Jeff.

JEFF WANDERED in his tour bus, going from space to space, exploring. This ride was new, shiny, and sort of unbelievably gorgeous.

Donna grinned at him. "Suitable?"

"It's amazing. Did you see the bed?"

It was good-sized, taking up a large portion of the space. She'd stocked the place with guitars, movies, and games. He was actually tickled.

She smiled fondly at him. "It's all state of the art, and I've been told the hydraulics are amazing—you won't even be able to tell you're on the road."

"Cool. I like all the creams and golds. There's a blender?"

"There is. Rye was pretty clear about what needed to be stocked in the kitchenette and fridge."

"He does clear really well."

Donna snickered and patted his cheek. "You're happy with him, yeah?"

"Yeah. Yeah, he's good. He doesn't hate me, talks to me, plays backgammon."

"Oh, plays backgammon, that's a keeper." She gave him a hug. "I worry about you, honey."

"I worry about me too."

She chuckled softly. "I guess that's a good sign."

"I worry about Jeff too." Rye came up behind Donna, gave them both a smile. "So he's going to be just fine on this tour...." Rye looked like he was going to continue, but he closed his mouth instead.

"Of course he is. It's only, what? Thirty weeks?"

Thirty weeks.

Fifty shows.

God.

"What do you think about—" Rye shook his head, clearly holding himself back. He cleared his throat. "I'm going to check the bus out again."

She arched an eyebrow. "What's he got to check?"

"Zombie garden gnomes? Stray tour bus gremlins? I don't know. I think life on the road unnerves him a little."

"His job is to keep you clean, so yeah, I bet it does." Donna took his hands. "You scared me to death, honey. You *died*. I can't do that again."

"Well, it's a little inevitable that I will, at some point, die again."

"Hush. Not for a long, long time, and not until I'm long gone myself."

"That's the plan." Jeff hugged her tight. "I love you." He needed to sit with Harry, the tour manager, make sure everything was working, was right.

"I love you too, honey. Call me if you need anything, okay?"

75

"I will. Have… have you heard from Jim? From rehab? I tried calling, and his phone isn't working." Jeff had been calling once a week, mostly, just to say hi.

"No, honey. I haven't."

"Huh. I guess I could call the hospital, huh? He worked for them."

"Are you sure you should be worrying about this, honey?"

"He was good to me." He looked at Donna. "He went back, didn't he? He slid."

"I honestly don't know, Jeff."

Rye joined them again. "We'll find out."

"Okay. Okay. I just… I don't have too many friends." If Rye said he'd find out, Rye would find out.

"You have me and Rye, honey." Donna hugged him again. "Okay, I have to go. You guys need to get on the road. Can't be late for your first gig."

"Woohoo." He nodded and waved. "I'll call."

"Good luck, honey."

Rye came and stood with him as they waved Donna off.

Barney, his driver since forever, got on and closed the door. "We ready to go, Mr. January?"

"If the other buses are ready, I am."

"Okay, let's get on the road." Barney talked into his Bluetooth, and a few moments later, they were off, the ride as smooth as Donna had promised.

"So we've got, what, a couple days before we're at the first venue?" Rye asked.

"It's Tuesday. The first show is Friday. We'll get there late-late Wednesday, and Thursday we'll check out the stage and stuff." Jeff was pretty sure Rye knew this already; still, it was nice to feel like the one who knew what was going on.

"So we have two days on this beast, huh?"

"Yeah. Basically. Barney will stop as he needs to."

"So, you want a game of backgammon and a milkshake?" Rye asked.

Jeff sat on the couch and shook his head. "No. You want to talk? Do you like the bus?"

Rye sat with him and looked around, nodding. "I do. It's homier than I thought it would be."

"It's nice. Luxe. Roach and Scooter share a bus, and then Brandy and Bri. Everyone else has another."

"I'm glad. Feels kind of like we're back at the house."

"Yeah. More mobile, but home sweet bus."

Chuckling, Rye tugged him to lean back against the strong chest.

"We have access to all our movies and stuff, just not our pool." Jeff was going to miss the pool.

"We'll have to swim at the hotel stops."

"If they have a quiet one, maybe." He sighed softly, shook his head. "Just think, we're on the road again." It was a weird thought, a bit of a mind fuck.

"I want this to be your last tour, Jeff. I want you to retire Lord January."

"You know I can't. I have responsibilities."

"You have a responsibility to yourself as well, you know."

"I'm replaceable." Hell, he'd been a replacement. And why were they having this conversation?

"Then let yourself be replaced. Let someone else play Lord January, so you can have a real life again."

"I…." Jeff stood up, started pacing. "Stop it. A real life? I don't have one of those! You forget who makes all the money! No one wants me!"

"I want you, Jeff. Just as you are. And if someone else plays Lord January, then you don't have to worry about anyone else. I bet you have money saved up until you're on your feet, and if you don't, you can sell that big house. You can stay with me." Rye sat forward. "You have a beautiful voice and could use it, be your own person. I just wanted to float the idea."

"Don't. Don't make me have ideas. It'll just lead to disappointment."

"I want you to have ideas. I want you to think about it, because we can make it happen."

"I...." He paced, back and forth, feeling the bus move beneath him.

"Seriously, Jeff. You could let someone else wear January. That way everyone keeps working, keeps making the money, and you get your life back, your hopes and dreams."

"Hush. Hush. I can't... I can't think right now." He wrapped his arms around himself, anxiety flooding him.

"Hey." Rye stood and stopped his pacing, wrapping those strong arms around him. "You don't have to make any kind of decision right now. I just wanted to float it."

"I.... I need a Xanax. Those are approved, right? One Xanax, from the doctor?"

"You don't need a Xanax." Rye sat and tugged him down to sit between Rye's legs. The big hands dropped onto his shoulders. "Just close your eyes and relax."

"I need one. It's not an up—" Oh. Oh God. Good.

Those huge hands surrounded his shoulders, squeezing. "Close your eyes," murmured Rye.

Jeff let his eyes drift shut, let himself lean. Humming, Rye kept working his shoulders, the warmth and relaxation sinking into him. He found himself melting and floating, breathing with Rye. Rye always made him so warm, and he could feel each breath against his neck. The touches were perfect.

Delicious.

"I want you to have something good to hold on to on this tour."

"That's you."

"Okay." Rye squeezed him tight. The hug felt good, and Jeff leaned into it, enjoying it. Rye leaned his cheek on top of Jeff's head.

"Tell me a story? About you?" Jeff asked.

"Well, when I was little, my family was the crazy one in the neighborhood."

"Yeah?" He loved stories, and he wanted to know Rye.

"Yeah. We had goats and chickens in the backyard, and my mom was rabid about pesticides and healthy eating." Rye chuckled. "We were vegan until I was fifteen, and she just couldn't keep me fed."

"I haven't eaten meat in a long time." Little vegan Rye baby. God, the cuteness of that image.

"No? I have a lot of mass to feed. And I'll admit that I like my red meat a lot."

"Sometimes I wish I could just not eat, ever again."

"When you're tired, I bet."

"Yeah. Yeah." Rye knew him.

"Ironically, that's when you need it the most."

"Do you…. Do you get tired of me? I do, sometimes. I was more fun, on the uppers."

"You were out of your mind on the uppers. I don't need you to entertain me, Jeff. And I like you just how you are."

God, he was a loser, but Jeff held on to the words like a drowning man.

A soft kiss was pressed to the side of his head. "This is the best job I ever took."

"I kind of love you, man. Really." Stupid, but true.

"Me too."

"We're a little stupid, you and me."

"I don't know. Maybe it's the smartest thing either of us has ever done."

"Maybe. We'll see." He didn't think it would really matter.

"So we'll hold on to each other, and you'll make it through this tour."

"I hope so." Jeff hoped a lot of things.

"You will." Rye sounded so sure. He hoped Rye was right.

Chapter Six

Rye grabbed hold of Jeff as he came off the stage after the second encore. Looming over Jeff, he then pushed through the people assembled there, going straight to the dressing room.

The place was lousy with groupies, and he put his mouth next to Jeff's ear. "You need the toilet or anything before we go to the car?"

"Go." Jeff was pouring with sweat, dripping with fake blood, and smelled like rot.

Grabbing hold of one shoulder, he loomed over Jeff again, getting them back out into the hallway and making the trip down the corridor to the back doors.

"Package on its way," Rye told Big T, who was driving.

"Mailbox ready for package, boss."

The crowd was still roaring in the stadium above, stomping and screaming. It was insane.

They hit the back door, and Big T opened it for them. He hustled Jeff in, the door slamming behind them. Seconds later they were on their way, Big T getting them out onto the road with a minimum of fuss.

"Here." Rye put his hand in front of Jeff's chin. "Spit out your teeth."

Jeff nodded, pushing them out. Next were the fucking contacts. Rye had the containers for both with him. He slid the containers in his pockets and grabbed a couple of baby wipes, trying to deal with some of the blood smeared on Jeff's face.

"How was the show? Did you enjoy it?" Jeff asked.

It had been… insane.

Blood and screaming guitars and smoke and props and Jeff flying on wires. "You know how I feel about Lord January, babe." He wasn't going to lie to Jeff.

"I know, but... at least say I was impressive."

"Oh, you were very impressive. It was rather... amazing in a terrifying way."

"That's my job. Big, spooky vampire lord."

"I think Jeff is far more compelling."

"You're biased." Jeff leaned back, eyes closed, as he started to shiver, sweat drying.

"I am. Doesn't mean it's not true." Rye hit the controls, heat blasting from the vents.

"I can still hear the music inside me."

"Do you like it?"

"Like what?"

"The music. Do you like it at all?"

"I love music. I minored in music in college."

"Yeah, you'd said. The vampire stuff, though. Does that really count as music?" He hoped he wasn't being insulting.

"Sure it does. The lyrics are good, for the most part, and the music is solid—just ramped up, distorted."

"Huh."

They pulled up in the back of the hotel, and Big T went out to make sure the way was clear. A moment later he knocked on the door.

"Okay, let's get you upstairs and into the shower," Rye suggested.

"God, yes. Please. A long hot shower. I...." Jeff swayed, suddenly pale. "Rye. Sick."

"Okay." He pulled Jeff out of the SUV and supported him as he threw up on the ground. Rubbing gently, he soothed Jeff as best he could, Big T blocking them in case anyone was looking down the alley.

As soon as Jeff was done, he hurried the man upstairs.

"Sorry. So sorry."

"Shh. It's okay." Rye went straight to the bathroom and began stripping Jeff's clothes off.

The clothes were foul, heavy with sweat and makeup and stinking of smoke. Rye dumped them in the corner and got the shower going as Jeff brushed his teeth. After stripping himself down, he pulled Jeff into the shower with him.

This was going to be their routine for forty-nine more shows. Shit, they were all going to need to eat their Wheaties. He swore that Jeff had lost ten pounds just from one show.

He tilted Jeff's face into the spray, supporting the slender body. The concert makeup didn't come off as easily; it was so greasy. He kept at it, soaping and resoaping, rubbing.

Finally, Jeff's face was clean, and Rye stared down at it, fingers tracing Jeff's features.

"Hey." Jeff smiled at him.

Smiling back, he slowly lowered his head and touched his lips gently to Jeff's. It was the most gentle touch, just a chaste, easy kiss.

Then he grabbed the soap back up and washed the rest of Jeff.

JEFF STARED at his cock, totally stunned that he was erect. He didn't get hard-ons. He didn't have the energy for it. He hadn't gotten hard in months. Maybe longer.

He didn't.

Huh.

He pulled his pants up and on, then headed out to play his guitar.

Rye was sitting on the big, ornate couch, frowning at his plate.

"What's the matter?"

"They gave me sunny-side up eggs. I can't eat sunny-side up eggs—they're *looking* at me."

"Oh." Jeff went to the phone, hit the concierge number, and started screaming, going full-on asshole Lord January "get me more motherfucking eggs right now." "There you go."

Rye blinked at him. "You didn't have to do that. I could have just eaten the bacon and toast—"

"I pay a fucking fortune for this room." He grabbed his guitar and started playing, but his mind was going a million miles a minute.

"Hey." Rye came and sat next to him. "What's wrong?"

"Nothing." He couldn't meet Rye's eyes.

Rye grabbed his chin, tilting his head up. "Tell me."

"I got hard." The demand surprised him so much, he answered.

"Oh." Rye gave him a small smile. "That's a good thing, isn't it?"

"I don't get erections anymore. It's… unnerving."

Rye stroked his cheek. "I think it means your body is healing from the drugs, from the starving."

He opened his mouth to answer when a knock came to the door. "Your eggs are here."

Rye kissed him again, quick and short. "Thank you." Then he got up and went to the door.

A squeal came from behind the room service guy, and Jeff ran, hiding in the bathroom. He could hear Rye shouting—not the words, but Rye was angry.

A few minutes later, there was a knock on the door. "Jeff, it's me. Ollie Ollie Oxen Free, the room is safe."

"Sorry. Sorry. Your eggs?" He opened the bathroom door.

"My eggs came with a half-dozen groupies. I told room service off, then I called the front desk and told them off."

"Mean giant security guy." He was actually a little tickled.

"That's me." Rye flexed. "Grrrr."

"Go eat your eggs." Jeff snickered, following Rye out into the main room.

"I'll eat my eggs if you eat something too. I ordered you a bowl of tomato soup and a grilled cheese sandwich."

"I'll try." The last hotel had been nasty, and he'd refused any of the food. Maybe this one was better.

"If you don't like the soup, I'll get one of the guys to go pick up some tomatoes at the market, and I'll make you some." Rye took his hand and led him to the couch, sat with him.

"We're back on the bus tomorrow, right?"

"Yeah. Although I'm tempted to put you on it tonight, right after the show." Rye shoveled in a mouthful of eggs. "It feels more like home than these big hotels."

"Yeah. I'd like that. The bus is home."

"All right. I'll call Barney and make sure he knows to have all his pretravel shit done before the show's over. That way when everyone comes down to the busses, we're already there. We'll miss having to move you through the groupies and fans waiting to steal a touch." Rye looked gleeful at that.

"Perfect. Then we can have our own bed." He looked at the cheese in the sandwich. He wasn't eating that. No. Way.

Rye caught his look and went over to his bag, pulled something out of it, and tossed it over. It turned out to be a bag of mixed nuts. "Have some of those—they're good for you." Then Rye grabbed his phone and began texting.

"Okay…." Jeff picked out the pecans and the cashews and, oh, pistachios.

"There." Rye set his phone down. "Shopping list sent. The fridge in the bus will be restocked by this afternoon."

"Good. I only want your soup." He only wanted the not-from-a-can stuff.

"You're going to give me a swelled head."

"You're already really big, Rye. Like really."

Leaning against the couch, Rye chuckled. "All the better to keep you safe, my pretty."

Jeff chuckled and ate another pecan before settling back again.

"I asked them to close the pool this morning. Roach and the boys are going to spend a bit of time in the lobby, centralize the fans so we can slip upstairs and use it unnoticed." Rye looked pleased.

"You did that? Really?" Rye was good to him, truly. "That sounds fun."

"It does, doesn't it? Although if you tie your hair back and wear something with color, I bet no one would even realize who you play onstage."

"I don't have... do I have swim trunks?"

Rye gave him a grin. "Of course you do."

"Oh. Cool."

"Thank Janie. I told her you needed a pair, and she made it happen."

"You must think I'm useless."

"Nope. I think you're stressed, and you have the weight of this entire tour on your shoulders."

Jeff searched Rye's eyes, looking for the truth in the words. The blue eyes met his head-on. He pushed into Rye's arms, hugging tight. Rye held him close, warm and solid and good. His body started to tighten, his cock beginning to fill, so he pulled away, the sensation unsure.

"What's the matter?" Rye pushed his hair out of his face.

"Nothing. I'm okay."

Rye looked into his face a moment longer. "Okay. Wanna go swim?"

"Uh-huh." God, he was nervous.

Unnerved.

"Okay, I've got both our suits in my bag—figured it was better, just in case someone got snoopy in your stuff."

"Cool." He got up and paced to the window, to the door of the suite.

"You're like a cat in a room full of rocking chairs today."

Jeff nodded. "I am. I'm nervous. I'm—" He waved toward his groin. "Weird."

"I'm still thinking a hard-on is a good thing. Your body is recovering from being a drug addict. It's coming back."

"It's worrisome."

"Why?"

"I don't like having sex."

"Then you've never done it right."

85

"That's what everybody says, Rye." He chuckled, went over for another hug.

Rye held him close and whispered in his ear. "It's true. Sex is fantastic."

"It isn't all that."

"Maybe one day I'll be able to change your mind about that."

If anyone could, it would be Rye. "You convinced me to eat your soup."

Rye's laughter rubbed them together. "I did, indeed."

He lifted his face, begging for a kiss. Rye gave it to him, gaze holding his as their mouths met softly. Jeff sighed. This connection made his belly ache, deep. Rye's tongue flicked out and touched his lips. His tongue touched Rye's, barely stroking it. Groaning, Rye touched his back. He liked how Rye tasted, the caress.

One big hand slid along his back, slowly up and down, leaving warmth and tingles in its wake. Jeff's eyelids got heavy, too heavy to hold open, and the kiss went on and on.

Rye's other hand cupped the back of his head, tilting him slightly as Rye's tongue slipped between his lips. Jeff's hands slid up Rye's arms and wrapped around the huge, broad shoulders.

A low sound filled his mouth, and he could feel Rye's breath brushing on his face. He arched, body pressing into Rye for a moment. That earned him another groan.

What a fascinating sound.

The hand on his back kept moving, warming up the bones of his spine. He leaned into it, almost like he was dancing to Rye's music. In fact, Rye hummed for him, and the sounds and the touches and the kisses joined together like a beautiful harmony. His cock filled, going heavy and solid.

Oh God.

Rye just kept kissing him, filling him with a surprising amount of pleasure. Rye's strength supported him, held him firm even when his knees buckled. Shifting him closer, Rye brought their bodies together, and Jeff could feel that Rye was hard too. Hot through their clothes. Hot and hard and big.

Like really big. Just like the rest of Rye.

Their lips parted, Rye resting their foreheads together and panting.

"It's good?" He loved Rye's eyes.

"I think so. I hope you do too."

He nodded, grinned. "No one would believe it, that I liked necking."

"I'm not planning on telling anyone. This is ours."

"Our secret." Jeff loved that.

"Yes." Rye rubbed their noses together and took another kiss. This one was light, playful, making him giggle. Rye picked him up, squeezed him.

"One day, can we go to the mountains? Like a cabin? Just us?"

"Baby, we can do anything you want."

"Okay. I want to go to the mountains together one day."

"Sounds good." Every day he spent with Rye felt good, strong. "So… swimming or more kissing?"

He sighed happily and leaned into Rye again. He could swim at home.

KISSING JEFF was as easy as breathing.

Wrapping his arms around Jeff, Rye picked him up, carried him to the bedroom, and looked into the pretty green-flecked eyes.

He wanted…. God, he wanted so much, so many things, but right now he wanted Jeff's joy. He sat them on the bed and took another kiss, pressing their lips together.

Jeff stayed in his lap, close, responding to every single kiss. It was as wonderful as it was unexpected. Jeff—with his piercings and his ink—kissed like a tentative virgin.

Rye knew he was the only one who got to see this side of Jeff. He was going to protect this gentle soul with everything he was. He took one kiss after another, fingers moving over Jeff's face, tracing the lovely lines. He didn't push, didn't attempt to touch anything below the shoulder.

He knew how big just this was. Hell, Jeff had been... almost outraged by his own body when he'd become hard. Rye licked across Jeff's lips before dipping his tongue back into Jeff's mouth. Jeff's fingers moved against him lazily, exploring his skin.

Time disappeared, the warmth of the kisses blocking everything else out. He couldn't quite believe it, that Jeff was hard against him, erect. Jeff wanted him. It was a luscious feeling, almost decadent.

His tongue teased Jeff's, encouraged it back into his mouth. Jeff actually wiggled a bit, rubbed against him. He finally slid his hand down along Jeff's spine, stopping just above Jeff's ass.

Jeff took a long, shaky breath. "Oh. I need to get up, walk around."

"Why?" Rye thought Jeff was doing great, right where he was.

"I'm... tight inside."

"You need an orgasm." The words shot out before he had a chance to even think about them.

"I.... I don't.... What if I can't, and then we're both mad?"

"Jeff." He took Jeff's hand. "I'm not going to be mad at you either way. I promise."

"I just...." Jeff pressed against him, rubbed a little more.

Rye tugged Jeff's legs, encouraged him to wrap them around his waist so Jeff could rub against his belly. "It's okay. You're doing what feels good."

"Uh-huh. Doing what feels hot."

"Good." He cupped Jeff's head and tilted it, taking another kiss. So nervous, so worried. What baggage was Jeff carrying about sex?

As they kissed, he slid a hand down to cup Jeff's ass, encouraging the rubbing. They slipped together, slow and easy, keeping it light. Jeff's ass rubbed against the top of his own cock, and he wanted so badly to be naked with Jeff. He could be patient, though.

That fine ass was taut, perfect in his hands. Their kisses deepened, Jeff moving faster against him. *Please, babe. Please, let me feel you.* His hand tightened on Jeff's ass. Jeff moaned for him, the sound low, sweet.

"Skin would feel so good." If Jeff allowed it, he'd open Jeff's pants and let him rub against his belly.

"Please. Please, Rye."

Oh God. Yes. His fingers were almost trembling as he undid the button and zipper of Jeff's jeans. "Do you want to feel me too?"

"I'd like that."

He tugged Jeff's jeans open and pushed his underwear down, freeing the hard cock. The jewelry glinted, caught in the light.

"I liked getting them done."

"Yeah? Tell me about it?" Rye touched the Prince Albert, the silky flesh around it.

"Oh." Jeff shook his head, then nodded. "You'll think badly of me."

"Have I yet?"

"I liked the sting and the weight of it. I was still... functional then, and I liked the ache."

"You're functional now," Rye pointed out.

"I know. Weird."

"I like it." Rye touched it again, then reached for the frenum. "What about this one?"

"It bled a lot, but after, I would twist it."

"Like this?" Rye twisted it.

Jeff jerked, precome dripping, hot.

"And the hafada?" Rye reached down to stroke it and Jeff's balls.

"It didn't hurt. It felt so good."

"You're a bit of a pain slut, aren't you?"

"What?" Jeff's eyes went wide, and he backed off Rye's lap. "No. No, I.... Can we go swimming?"

"Shh. Shh. It's okay. Let's just get you off first, okay? No more questions." He lifted his shirt and pulled Jeff closer, letting that sweet cock rub on his belly.

"I'm not like January."

"You are nothing like January." The words were fiercer than he'd intended, but he didn't like January one bit. Jeff, though.... He loved this man.

"That's right. Nothing." Jeff was working himself into a lather.

He cupped Jeff's face and took a kiss, not making it hard, just easy and gentle. Jeff slowly relaxed and eased into him. That was better.

Rye moved one hand down to cup Jeff's ass, once again encouraging the easy rubbing. Jeff's eyes were closed, the look on the lean face blissful, happy. Better. His own cock was still trapped, but it rubbed against Jeff's ass as he moved the slender body, making him moan. So good.

As was the sensation of Jeff's velvety flesh on his abdomen. The piercings were hot from Jeff's body, but felt different than the hard cock they were attached to, bumping along against him. The dragging kisses became slick, Jeff's cock leaking for him. Fuck. Fuck. It was good, so very good.

Rye licked into Jeff's mouth, touching Jeff's tongue with his own. Jeff groaned softly, hips moving faster, dragging that cock harder. He dug his fingers into Jeff's ass, helping him rub harder.

"Rye." The little sound was a hiccup, a whimper.

"Right here, baby. I've got you."

"I need."

"Then take."

Jeff arched, body shaking, shuddering against him.

"That's it, baby, take it."

"Rye. Rye. Rye—" Jeff bucked, heat spreading between them.

He shuddered at the scent. Fuck. He'd just made Jeff come. Rye held on, cradling Jeff in his arms. Rocking them gently, he ignored his own erection in favor of making sure Jeff came down slowly, making sure Jeff was okay.

"Oh, Rye. That was so big."

"Yeah. Kind of huge."

Jeff nodded, cuddled into his chest.

He kissed the top of Jeff's head and held him close for as long as Jeff needed him to.

THOUGHTS FLASHED through Jeff's brain—too fast to understand, just snatches of ideas, whispers.

He'd orgasmed, for Rye. On Rye. Rye'd touched his rings. He didn't know what to do, what to think. Rye wasn't upset with him; in fact, his own personal giant was cuddling him close against all those muscles.

He squeezed his eyes closed, hoping the thoughts would go away, the sensations fade. Rye rubbed their cheeks together, humming softly.

"I came." Jeff couldn't believe it.

"You did. My belly is magical."

The words shattered the thoughts rushing through his mind, and he looked up. "Yes!"

Chuckling softly, Rye brought their mouths back together. His lips felt swollen, full, tender from all the kisses.

"Are you happy?" Rye asked him when the kiss was over.

"I am. I'm nervous. Excited. Worried."

"About me?"

"About everything. Nothing." He didn't know.

"You don't need to worry—that's my job."

"Does it work that way for people?" Jeff pondered that. He let Rye worry about lots of things, without even considering it.

"It can, if you set your mind to it."

"Next week is a break. Are we going to go home?"

"We can go home. We can go somewhere nobody knows who we are. The world is your oyster. Or at least it should be."

"Where would you go?" He wanted to give something to Rye, something special.

"If I could go anywhere?" Rye pondered that. "I think Iceland would be fascinating."

"Let's go. I'll call Donna."

Rye chuckled. "Just like that?"

"Uh-huh. Just like that."

"Are you sure that's where you want to go?" Rye looked into his eyes.

"I want to give you a trip, a gift. I'm sure."

"Thank you, baby." Rye kissed him again, quick and hard.

Jeff didn't want to be selfish, to be empty, not like January. Rye looked really pleased about it too.

"A whole week without all—" Rye waved his hand in the air. "—this."

"A week just being... us."

"It sounds glorious." Rye's fingers moved on his skin beneath his shirt, swirling.

He hoped so. For Rye's sake.

"You still want that swim?" Rye asked, fingers still moving, making his skin tingle.

"Do you want.... Do you need to come? I'm not a bastard. I'm fair."

"I didn't want to push, but yeah. I need to at least undo my jeans."

"I've seen you naked, Rye. I've slept with you. I'm not scared." Not scared at all. Rye loved him. Him. Jeff.

"Then, please...."

Jeff reached down and opened Rye's jeans, shoving them down and loving the way Rye felt against his palm.

Groaning, Rye pushed against his hand.

Jeff dragged his fingers down Rye's thighs, pulling the jeans all the way. He ended up kneeling in front of Rye, mouth near the heavy cock, so he leaned in to inhale.

"Oh damn. Baby...." Rye's voice was thick, sounding strained.

His tongue flicked out, dragged on Rye's skin. This time Rye didn't say anything; he just made this garbled, moaning sound. Oh, neat. He lapped his way up, intent on the fat, mushroom head.

The muscles in Rye's thighs went tight, another moan filling the air. Jeff made himself wait to actually taste the slit, but as soon as he did, it made him tingle.

"Jeff. God. Please."

"I won't make you hurt. I promise."

Rye snickered. "Oh, baby, you're not hurting, trust me."

"Taste good." He licked over and over, tasting.

Groans and moans and whimpers came from Rye, those strong thighs trembling now, Rye's hips beginning to rock gently. Jeff wrapped his lips around the tip, sucking nice and slow.

"Jesus, that's good." Rye's hands slid into his hair, tugging just a little bit.

"Mmmhmm." It was good, the pressure on his lips.

Rye moved his hips, the thick cock sliding in Jeff's mouth, leaving drops of liquid on his tongue. His eyes closed, and he pulled, keeping it gentle, soft, quiet. Rye's fingers stroked through his hair, rubbed on his head. It was the easiest thing ever, to hum, to let the sound vibrate through Rye.

"Jeff." His name was choked out, Rye moving faster now, jerky, like he couldn't help it.

Jeff braced himself on Rye's huge thighs, the heavy cock spreading his lips wide.

"Don't let me hurt you."

Rye wouldn't. Jeff knew that.

He sucked harder, slapping the fat shaft with his tongue. Rye jerked, pushing in deeper. He took Rye halfway, and he brought his hands in to play for the rest. Rye seemed to let go after that, sliding faster along his tongue, pushing harder into his mouth. Jeff's jaw was beginning to ache, but he wouldn't stop. He wouldn't.

"Jeff." His name was a whisper, and Rye's cock throbbed just before it released his come.

He swallowed some, and then the rest splashed on his face.

Rye's prick slid from his mouth, Rye dropping to his knees. "Thank you, baby." Then Rye licked at his face, cleaning him. That was erotic as hell and made his spent cock bob.

When he was done, Rye rested their foreheads together and smiled at him.

"Better?"

"Yeah. Things were getting a little tight in my jeans."

"You taste right. Clean."

"I am clean. I get tested every six months."

"That's not what I meant."

"No?"

"No. I meant you taste… pure. Like something good."

"Oh." Rye's cheeks heated a touch, but he looked pleased. "Thanks." Then Rye hugged him, hands sure and warm. "You still want to go swimming, or do you want to nap together?"

"Nap?"

"Sure, I'm easy." Rye stripped the rest of their clothes off efficiently and tucked them both in bed under the covers.

It felt different this time, cuddling against Rye's body. It felt like this was his. Purely his. Rye held him close and kissed the top of his head.

"Love, huh?"

"Yeah, Jeff." He got another kiss on his head. "I love you too."

"Oh, good."

"It is. And I'm not letting go."

The words were a comfort, following Jeff down into his dreams.

CHAPTER SEVEN

THE TAXI let them out at the chalet that was theirs for a week. A whole week in this amazing country. Rye had been reading up on it ever since Jeff had said they were going. There was lots to see: hot springs and mountains, snow, auroras.

He paid the driver and brought their bags in. The Hotel Borg overlooked a square, the art deco building lovely, charming, but swank.

They checked in, and it amused Rye that Jeff could wander around unrecognized as long as he didn't wear anything that was Januaryish.

Jeff was in T-shirt and jeans, hair pulled back, no makeup, so he looked fresh, young.

He looked sexy too.

Of course, part of that might have been because they hadn't done anything but literally sleep together since that one time. They'd been busy and tired, and it just hadn't happened again.

Rye hoped it did this week.

They headed up into a decadent room: hard wood floors, a large bed, huge windows.

"Wow. This is gorgeous." Rye had been to all kinds of fancy hotels, and this was one of the nicer, if not the nicest.

The hotels on the tour had all been okay, a couple even ritzy. Maybe it was because here they were on holiday, but this place was stunning.

"Lots of windows." Jeff closed one, staying to the shadows.

"You should come into the light, baby. It loves your skin."

"If I get color, though…."

He held his arms open, and Jeff came right to him. He wrapped Jeff in a hug. "I bet Janie has a makeup for that." Janie was easily one of Rye's favorite people. She was always cheery, always ready to cheer Jeff up. And she brought him food that he ate.

Speaking of which.... "You hungry?"

"No, love."

Rye's lips tightened. He wasn't sure, with the time changes and the flights, how long it had been, but it had been too fucking long.

"I am, though. I'm going to order some stuff, okay?"

"Sure." Jeff nodded and settled on the bed, searching through a guide book.

Rye perused the room service menu and called down, getting the veggie platter and a plate of fries. He'd never offered Jeff fries before. Fried potatoes—what was not to like?

"We can look at whales." Jeff sounded excited about the prospect.

"Oh yeah? Like out on the ocean?"

"That's what it says here. There's all sorts of things to see."

"I want to swim in one of the hot springs too. I think that would be really neat."

Jeff nodded and curled up around the pillows. "Are you glad we came?"

"I am. It's going to be fun, don't you think?" Hell, simply being here with Jeff—only the two of them, no entourage, no groupies, no business, absolutely no January—just that was wonderful.

The rest was icing on the cake.

"It's weird, to travel like this, without the drama."

"Good weird, though, yeah?" Rye climbed onto the bed, spooning up behind Jeff.

"Yeah, it's like... I went to rehab and everything shifted. Everything is different now."

"What was important changed," he suggested. Before it had been all about the money, all about playing January for everyone—everyone but Jeff himself.

96

"Something did. I was supposed to want to die, you know? That's like, the end game, to kill yourself, but when my heart stopped, I wanted to live."

Rye hugged Jeff tight. "I'm glad. And I really think you need to pass the baton. January isn't good for you."

"That's all I am, though. That's the money."

"First of all, I don't believe that. Second of all, I bet you have a ton saved up."

"Probably. Donna handles that."

"And there's your house, and I haven't spent a dime of my salary. So you've got a lot of time to figure out what would work for you."

"Maybe. I'll have to worry about it after the tour."

"I think you should tell Donna that it's the last tour you're doing. So it doesn't come as a surprise to anyone."

"But what if.... What if I can't? What if I.... Just shh."

Rye chuckled and leaned in to whisper in Jeff's ear. "You can. You are amazing just as you are. And I'll hush now, but you need to think about that."

"I'm just a shell. Something to be on stage."

"I've heard you, baby. It's like magic when it's just you, your guitar, and your own songs."

Jeff was really good, and Rye had to believe that with Donna's contacts, he could get heard by someone who put out that kind of music.

"Shh. No talking." Jeff's fingers were trembling against his lips.

Rye licked at them, then pulled them into his mouth, sucking gently.

Jeff's eyes went wide, then slowly closed.

Ah, distraction. Rye ran his tongue across the tips, then bit gently.

"Toothy man." Jeff chuckled for him.

"Do you like it?" he asked around Jeff's fingers before nibbling them some more.

"Uh-huh."

"Good." He turned Jeff in his arms, still sucking on the slender fingers, and pulled the lovely body up against his.

"Hungry man." Jeff fit against him, curled in with a happy moan.

"Hungry for you," Rye agreed, dropping his hand down to cup Jeff's ass. He didn't know how long he had until room service came, but Jeff seemed to be happy to pet and play.

Foreplay, food, more foreplay, and possibly more. It sounded like a great way to stave off jetlag. Then tomorrow they would play tourists together.

He rubbed against Jeff, pleased to feel Jeff was responding. Sometimes his touches got nothing but happy sighs, but more and more, Jeff's body was healing, learning to be eager for pleasure.

And Rye could be patient. He hadn't pushed for them to do more like this since that first time. Now, though, this week was for them.

There was a discreet knock at the door, and he bit back his groan.

"Your food, my giant."

"Yep." He gave Jeff one last kiss, then called out, "Coming," and headed to the door for their food. At least he hoped he was going to get some of the veggies and fries into his far-too-skinny lover.

His lover.

Yeah, that's what Jeff was. Even if they'd had one orgasm each together—what they had was way deeper than just sex. There wasn't any other man he could say that about.

Rye answered the door and signed for the food, pulling the table into the room himself. Jeff was on the bed, watching him. He loved how Jeff looked at him, stared at him.

Smiling, he wheeled the table right over to the bed. "I bought fries for us to share. They've got a couple neat dipping sauces with them." Lifting the lids off the two plates—one veggies, one steaming french-fried potatoes—he made a "tada!" motion.

"You didn't get you a steak?"

He was pleased to see Jeff reach out and steal a fry. "Nope. I figure I'm going to wait until we stop at a restaurant where they'll do it right." He hadn't found hotel steak to be terribly exciting.

"I bet you'll find lots of fish here. Do you like fish?"

"I do. What about you? I know you don't eat meat—are you a vegetarian, a full-out vegan?" Rye had always been happy to get anything into Jeff. He supposed he'd been feeding Jeff stuff that vegans wouldn't eat.

"I like cheese. I just... after all the blood from work... there's no way I can eat meat."

"Ah." He nodded and dipped a fry in something mayonnaisey, handing it over. "I get that."

Jeff touched his tongue to the sauce, then nodded. "That's okay."

"Then eat. I love french fries, though a nice baked potato is even better." Rye dipped a fry into something ketchupy and popped it in his mouth. Oh, salty and hot and yum.

"I like those okay, sometimes."

"So it's a sometime, have a few."

Jeff chuckled but took another fry, then a bite of cauliflower.

They ate, and Rye was pleased, because Jeff did a lot better than he could have hoped, having a bunch of fries and even more vegetables.

He finished up when Jeff begged off, his lover curled around a huge pillow. "You never did say if you ate fish or not." Rye took the table back to the door and set it out in the hall.

"I haven't in a long time."

Well, that wasn't a no.

"Shrimp? Lobster? Crabs? You like the crawly-in-the-water things?"

"No. No. Those are bugs."

"Delicious bugs."

"Uh-uh." Okay, the nose-wrinkling was adorable.

He kissed Jeff's nose. "We'll agree to disagree." He liked seafood a lot.

"I would pay for you to eat anything."

"But will you watch me eat bugs?"

"I would. I wouldn't eat them, but I would sit with you. Roach ate a testicle once."

Rye nearly spat out the carrot he'd been munching on. "What?"

"Raw. It was gross, and he chewed a lot."

"Raw? Did he, like, rip it off someone and eat it in front of them?" He knew logically that wasn't what had happened, but it was what popped into his head.

"Not when I was watching. I think it belonged to a cow."

"That's gross. I mean, even cooked it would have been gross."

"It was gross. Really gross."

"Yeah, can we talk about something else?"

Jeff cracked up, curled into himself, and cackled like a big bird.

"Nut job." Rye rolled his eyes.

"We're evil, remember? Vampire lords."

"January might be evil, but Jeff isn't."

"You don't think so? We're the same person."

"Bullshit." He knew very well that January and Jeff were polar opposites.

"No? You're not scared of me even a little? My mom was, a little."

"I'm not scared of you or January." He didn't like January, but that didn't mean he was scared of the persona. "Is your mom still around?" Jeff never talked about family.

Jeff nodded. "She hates me a little bit. I send money."

"Hates you?" Frowning, Rye moved to sit up against the headboard and tugged Jeff up into his arms.

"Yeah. She's religious. A lot. She says I'm going to hell."

"Ah. Is that because of January or because of being gay?"

"I left home as soon as I graduated high school. I had long hair, I listened to loud music, I got tattoos."

"Yeah, I like all those things about you."

"Thank you. There aren't many people that like me for just me. Some."

Rye imagined that was true of everyone. He hugged Jeff tight. "Do you have any other family?"

"No. No, my father ran off when Mother was pregnant, and I was her only little bastard." Jeff smiled at him. "How about you?"

"I have a mother and a sister. They're both a little out there, but I guess you could say we're close. I only see them a couple times a year, usually."

"Do…. Do you want to…. I mean, you know you can go see them anytime. That would be good."

"They know I'm working."

"Still, if they love you—"

"If you want to meet them, I'd be happy to take you to visit them." His mother would love to mother Jeff, he'd bet.

"They won't like me. They won't."

"Of course they will. *I* like you."

Jeff nodded but didn't say anything else.

"You're a great guy, Jeff."

"I'm okay. I try."

"You just don't have a lot of people in your life who are there for you as your own person." *Just him and Jim*, Rye thought. They hadn't been able to get in touch with Jim yet, though. Rye could think of a bunch of reasons why, and most of them were not good. Jeff had stopped asking, even.

Rye hugged Jeff hard. He would protect this man from everything, anything. And not because he was paid to anymore. He needed Jeff—he needed the smile, the secret looks, the gentle touches. "So whales or hot springs tomorrow?"

"Hot springs, I think. Something easy. We'll be tired."

"Sounds good." He reached over for the hotel's brochure, figuring they'd have information in there. "Private ones if I can find them, yeah?"

"Please. Not too many people."

"I'll see if there isn't someplace meant for couples on their own."

Jeff nodded, kissed his chest. "Sounds good."

"Cool. You nap, I'll get us booked."

101

"You sure?" Jeff's eyelids were so heavy.

"Yep. I'm sure."

His lover didn't answer, just trusted him enough to doze right off. Rye went through the brochure, anticipating a great vacation.

WHALES.

They'd seen whales.

They bathed in springs and walked for hours, stopping on the wash street to see the little shops. Jeff felt young; he felt like he couldn't stop smiling. Rye made him happy, and no one saw him. No one. He was a guy.

Rye had ordered them some room service supper and then run a shower, those big hands washing Jeff thoroughly. Rye had been washing January off him for ages, but this was different. This wasn't getting rid of January, this was... cleaning him, learning him. Jeff felt relaxed and happy, comfortable in his skin.

Something soft landed on his lips, warmer than the water that fell around them.

Rye kissed him again. It was the most natural thing ever, to reach up, wrap his arms around the broad shoulders, and kiss Rye back. Rye's kiss deepened, tongue pressing into his mouth. Jeff moaned, his cock filling, the pressure where they rubbed together delightful.

"I've wanted to do this again since the first time."

"Me too. I'm sorry. My body is slow."

"No, we were busy." Rye pressed him up against the shower wall, rubbing against him.

It should be worrisome, all that weight on him, but it wasn't. It was arousing, comforting, right. Rye dragged a hand along his side, wrapped it around his hip. Jeff nodded, fingers sliding down to tangle in the hair on Rye's chest, tug it gently.

Groaning, Rye pushed their cocks together, the bump and slide delicious. The water made everything slick, made everything better.

Rye's kisses were like a drug that swam through him and made his insides ache in the best way. "Want you. You make me ache."

"I like that. Works both ways, you know."

"I do." Rye never let him think he was unwanted.

"Good." Rye kissed him again, hand wrapping around their cocks together. The big fingers dragged over his piercings.

Jeff's eyes crossed, his entire body tensing.

"Love the way your piercings feel. So sexy."

Jeff smiled at the words. He loved the tugs and pulls, the pressure perfect.

Rye bit at his lower lip, nipping lightly. Jeff gasped and stepped forward with a cry. "I've got you," Rye promised.

"Rye." He pushed into the kisses again.

Rye's arms wrapped around him, picking him up and holding him against all those muscles, the big body. It was the easiest thing ever, to roll, to rock against his lover. "Want you so much."

Jeff nodded. He knew. He got it.

Rye lifted him again, and he slipped his legs around Rye's waist. He held on tight, his cock squeezed tight against Rye's belly. Rye's prick rubbed against his ass cheeks. He burned, his body aching in an entirely new way.

After turning them, Rye leaned against the tile, letting the water warm him as they rubbed together.

"I need…." Jeff shook his head. He didn't know what he needed.

"I have lube in my bag." Rye looked him in the eye. "And condoms."

"Do you think you'll fit, giant man?" He was 99.9 percent teasing.

Rye snickered for him, but quickly grew serious. "I would never hurt you."

"I know." That was the easy part.

Kissing him again, Rye slowly put him back down onto his feet.

When their lips parted, Rye rubbed their noses together, eyes on his. Then he bent over and turned off the shower. "The first time should be in bed."

Rye had so many very definite ideas. They made him smile.

Grabbing a towel, Rye dried him, just like the man had a hundred times before. Only this time… the touches felt more personal, more intimate.

Jeff helped, taking up a huge bath sheet to dry Rye's body. They got a little tangled together, Rye chuckling softly as he caught hold of Jeff and kept him from tripping over one end of the towel.

"Good catch."

"I'll always catch you." Rye picked him up, carried him back to the bed, and put him in the middle of it. "Let me just get the stuff we'll need."

Jeff wrapped his hair in a towel, squeezing out the last bits of water.

Rye leaned over his bag, ass displayed for him. A tiny, needy sound escaped him. He couldn't help it. Not at all. Rye stood, turning toward him, hard cock pointing right at him. "You okay?"

"Uh-huh." He reached down, stroked his cock a bit.

"Just look at you. So sexy, Jeff."

It was funny, because sex was what he sold—sex and violence—but he felt like the most desired man on earth, right here, like this.

Setting the stuff on the bedside table, Rye climbed onto the bed, pushing into a kiss right away. Jeff met Rye halfway, the rush of active desire surprising him, this delicious rush.

Rye's tongue pushed into his mouth, Rye lying prone and pulling him down onto the big body. Jeff spread over the finest mattress ever and kissed Rye back, hands sliding over Rye's chest. Rye touched him too, big hands warming him and leaving tingles on his skin. Rye's touch was another addiction. Nothing made things so right, so simple. One of Rye's legs bent, cradling him in between Rye's hips.

"Oh." Jeff found a perfect spot, cuddling right in.

"You fit like we were made to be together." Which was surprising because Rye was so big and he wasn't at all, but it was true.

"Maybe we were. Like destiny." Except Jeff didn't believe in that.

Rye chuckled. "I don't know if I believe in destiny, but I believe in you."

"Me either. Too. Whatever."

Rye grabbed his ass, rocking them together. "Yeah. Whatever."

Jeff leaned down, kissing Rye's chin, collarbone, all along Rye's throat.

"Have you ever done this?" Rye's voice was thick with desire.

"I did it to people, but I never let anyone in."

"I'm glad you're letting me in." Rye's hand dropped along his spine.

"I am. Only you." He wasn't sharing this with anyone else.

Rye lifted his head and pushed their lips together, a heat to this kiss. Jeff cradled Rye's head with his hands, helping to support. He could feel Rye's cock pressing hard against his belly. He leaned down toward it, sliding their cocks together.

Groaning, Rye slid his fingers along Jeff's crack toward his hole. It was easy not to tense, not to worry. Rye loved him. Those fingers disappeared, coming back a moment later, slick and wet.

"Do you want me to sit up?"

"Not yet. I can start you like this." The tip of one finger pushed into his hole, proving Rye's words.

Jeff's focus shifted to Rye's chest, the tiny nipples. He licked and nuzzled, sucked gently. They hardened beneath his tongue, two little points that begged wordlessly for more. Jeff closed his eyes, focused on the steady suction, the way Rye moaned and twisted.

The finger inside him pressed deeper, then came almost all the way out again, Rye's movements matching the rhythm of his suction. It was as if they were wrapped in a magic blanket, where their touches bled into each other. Which was poetic as hell, but that didn't make it true.

Moaning, Rye rolled them, then put two fingers into Jeff, pressing them deeper now that they'd changed position. Jeff felt that stretch in the pit of his belly, vibrating like a ringing bell.

"God, you're tight."

"You have giant fingers."

Rye laughed, sounded pleasantly startled. Jeff grinned, bit Rye's chin, then hooked one leg over Rye's hip, spreading himself a little more.

Happy sounds turned into moans, and Rye pushed his fingers even deeper, finding a spot inside Jeff that made everything light up. He grunted, his fingers scrabbling on Rye's chest.

"Good?" asked Rye, touching that spot again.

"Uh. Uh-huh. Good."

Rye's eyes smiled down at him, fingers still playing inside him. That touch came again.

And again.

And then again.

Whoa.

Pleasure rushed through him at each touch to that spot, making him shake. "Mmm. So good. Love how you look."

"How do I look?" Rye asked, fingers gently brushing over the same spot.

"H-happy."

"Oh... I am."

"Me too." And that was that, wasn't it? He was too.

Rye beamed at him, and the two big fingers inside him became three, stretching him very wide. Jeff sucked in a deep breath and let it out, trying to make space inside him.

"Nice and slow," murmured Rye, fingers opening and closing inside him but not pushing in and out.

"Big. You're big inside me."

"Gotta make room for my cock."

"Yes. Then we'll make love." He didn't think Rye fucked.

"Yeah, we will." Rye kissed him softly, tongue slipping into his mouth.

Jeff wrapped around Rye and held on tight. The fingers inside him stretched and contracted, pushed deep, then pulled shallow. He started moving, matching the rhythm.

Rye watched his face, looked down at his body, letting loose with small sounds of approval. He moaned, totally caught in the pleasure inside him. It was almost a shock when Rye's fingers slid out of him.

"Rye—" He twisted, searching for that sensation.

"I don't want to wait too long, or it'll be all over before it even begins."

"I want you." His heart was pounding, thrumming in his chest.

"Me too." Rye shifted, moving to kneel between his legs. "I want to watch your face while we do this, okay?"

"Uh-huh. I want. Now."

Rye breathed out softly. "I didn't expect you to be so demanding. I like it."

Jeff chuckled and grabbed Rye's prick, rubbed it.

Rye's eyes closed, a deep moan coming from him. "The, uh, condom is next to you somewhere."

Jeff reached out, searching for it. Rye's hand took his, guided it to the condom. Oh. There. Excellent. His fingers trembled, but they worked the damned thing open. Rye nuzzled his neck as he dealt with the wrapper, not making it any easier at all.

"Be good. I can't do this."

"I could help?" Rye didn't stop sliding warm lips along his throat.

"Uh...." What?

"Tear open the package? Get it on? What do you need?"

"Yes. Please. You make me stupid, Rye!"

"You're not stupid, baby." Rye took the condom and used his teeth to open the side of it. Jeff leaned up and kissed the center of Rye's chest.

Humming, Rye pulled the condom out of its package and worked it onto his cock. Obviously Rye was better at this than he

107

was. Obviously. Of course Rye had probably done it more than he had. Or at least not been high.

"Ready?" Rye asked, putting Jeff's legs over his broad shoulders.

He nodded, shook his head, nodded again.

Leaning in, bending Jeff's legs so his knees were up at his ears, Rye kissed him. All Jeff's thoughts shattered, dissolved in his head.

As they kissed, Rye began to push into him, cock huge but moving slowly. Jeff's body stretched, spread, opened wide.

"Oh fuck. Jeff. So tight." Moaning, Rye leaned their foreheads together, pushing in and in.

Tight? He was so full, he couldn't breathe.

When Rye had pushed all the way in, he rested there, taking deep breaths. Jeff could feel his body clenching and relaxing, over and over.

"Fuck. Jeff." Rye groaned, gaze meeting his. "Ready?"

"Ready. Ready. I want to feel."

"Okay." Rye kissed him, then began to withdraw, pushing back in right away.

Oh.

Oh, that burned, deep inside. Holding his gaze, Rye continued moving. Jeff's hole clung to Rye's shaft, squeezing it. Moaning, Rye kept moving, cock sliding nearly all the way out despite his best efforts. It always returned, pushing into him again.

Jeff moaned, stretching, spreading. His movements made Rye gasp and thrust faster. He stretched, arching his back, rolling his hips.

"Oh God." Rye followed his lead, moving faster, pushing in harder.

They got it going, the rhythm hard and driving, musical. It felt good, just the fact that it was Rye making it special. Jeff hummed as they slapped together, his head spinning. Rye's hand wrapped around his cock, fingers dragging over it, catching slightly on his piercings.

Oh.

Oh fuck. Jeff's eyes crossed, and he arched into the touch. Flicking his frenum piercing with his thumb, Rye sent him soaring. His toes curled hard, spine bowing.

"Come on," murmured Rye. "Want to feel you."

"Do it again."

Rye did, then yet again, the little bit of metal shifting in his flesh. The burn made Jeff clench his teeth, hips rocking. Rye's mouth covered his again, and it was less a kiss and more Rye breathing into him. He gulped in air, his entire body clenching. Moaning, Rye pushed in harder.

"Rye...." Please.

"Gonna come soon, baby."

Rye shifted, and the big cock hit that spot inside him. Hard.

"Soon.... Fuck—"

Rye nodded, kept moving on his gland. His body was singing. Singing. And it was all for Rye.

"I need you to come," Rye told him.

"Me too. Me too, Rye."

That made Rye grin and tighten his hand around Jeff's cock. One thumb flicked the ring in the tip of his cock, and Jeff moaned as he shot. Yes.

"Oh fuck." Rye kissed him again, body jerking into him a few times before freezing.

Jeff was shuddering, shivering, flying. Rye's kisses made him dizzy. His body felt too sensitive, too raw.

Pulling out, Rye got rid of the condom and settled next to him, tugging the covers over them. Jeff cuddled in, then moved to rest atop Rye's broad chest. It made Rye smile, big hands sliding along his back.

Jeff cuddled closer. "Good, huh?"

"Understatement of the year."

Jeff started giggling madly.

Chuckling, Rye held him tight. "I love that sound."

And Jeff loved Rye.

"Are you having a good vacation, baby?"

"I am. It's been magical."

"Yeah. That's a good word for it. Of course, you've been kind of magic from the start."

Jeff knew better. He was a stoner with a psycho alter ego.

Rye nuzzled his neck, cuddling and snuggling with him. Soon they would be heading back, and there would be no breaks, no real rest. Not for weeks. Still, he'd had this.

This was going to be enough.

CHAPTER EIGHT

RYE PULLED Jeff through the backstage area toward the back door, walking fast, refusing to stop for anyone.

A fucking razor. Someone had made it onstage with a fucking razor. He was going to kill someone.

He got Jeff into the SUV waiting for them. "Drive," he snarled at the driver.

"I didn't do my encore." Jeff was trembling, dripping with sweat.

"I don't fucking care." Rye put his arm around Jeff, pulling him close. "I'm not giving anyone else a chance at you. And we're cancelling tomorrow night's show."

"What? We can't do that! Everyone will be pissed. Everyone. We can't."

"If the venue can't keep the psychos out, they don't get you."

Jeff was panting, breathing hard, focused somewhere else.

"Are you okay? Did they cut you?"

"I don't think so. There's so much blood anyway."

"We'll take a shower as soon as we get to the bus." They'd stopped staying at the hotels, choosing to be a little out of the way and private.

Rye was so fucking pissed off he couldn't breathe. He wanted to take Jeff home and tell the whole fucking world to get fucked. He was mad at the venue for fucking letting people with razors fucking inside. He was pissed at the security staff—men he'd hand-fucking-picked himself—for letting the psycho onstage. He was pissed at himself for letting Jeff continue on with the fucking tour when he knew it was eating Jeff up.

He wanted to scream, rage against the world. He wanted to hit something. Hard. If there was one single scratch on Jeff. One.

A bruise.

A nick.

Anything.

They got to the bus, and Rye scanned the area, then went in with Jeff, locking the door behind them. "Shower."

"Let me get my costume off."

Rye helped, tugging at the blood-soaked mess, tossing it toward the front of the bus to get the smell away from them. It was insane, the layers of flimsy clothes, the leather corsets, the boots.

He finally had Jeff naked, then stripped down himself and pushed them both into the little bus shower. The water beat down against them, pounding hard, washing the fake blood away.

Grabbing the shampoo, he worked it through Jeff's hair. His fingers tangled in Jeff's hair, tugging some.

"Careful!"

He closed his eyes and took some deep breaths. "Sorry."

"I'm okay. You did your job."

"You'll have to forgive me if I need to check that for myself."

"Uh-huh. I do. Forgive you. I mean, whatever." Jeff rolled his eyes, the black makeup making him look like a raccoon. "I mean, please. Yes."

"Shit, your contacts." Luckily they had more than one pair. He held his hand out for them.

"Man, you must be wigged out. You never forget them."

"More furious than wigged out." He tossed them out into the toilet once Jeff had taken them out. Then he carefully soaped up Jeff's face, working on getting rid of the makeup.

Jeff seemed calmer—in fact, the more ramped up he got, the calmer Jeff seemed.

Rye got the makeup off Jeff, then turned off the shower. "I need to actually be able to see you to make sure you're not hurt."

Stepping out, he grabbed a towel and began carefully drying Jeff off. Jeff was still, watching him with red-rimmed eyes. Picking

Jeff up, he carried him to the bed. Goddamned people trying to hurt his lover.

He started at Jeff's face, checking the pale cheeks, behind Jeff's ears. There was nothing, barring a few bruises from the harness Jeff "flew" with. He checked every inch too. Very thoroughly.

Finally, he was satisfied. "You're okay."

"I am. Tired, but okay. No cuts."

"No. No cuts. Thank God." He would have had to kill someone.

"Uh-huh." Jeff leaned in.

Rye rested his forehead against Jeff's, just breathing, the fear and anger finally backing off.

"You're okay. I promise. I used to let them cut me on purpose, and I survived it."

"Not anymore. And not by some nut who rushes the stage and gets to you, waving a fucking razor in your face."

"Good. I don't need it anymore."

That actually made him feel better, hearing that from Jeff. Pressing their lips together, Rye took a long, hard kiss. Jeff stroked his side, his back, obviously trying to soothe him.

"It's okay. You're okay." He nodded, kissed Jeff again, working to make it less manic. He was supposed to be soothing Jeff, not the other way around.

"I am. I promise. I'm tough."

"You shouldn't have to be." Jeff should have been safe.

"God, you're a good man." Jeff kissed him hard, framing his face, holding him.

"I'm your man."

"They're just fans. Nothing terrible is going to happen."

Uh-huh. He saw the dark circles under Jeff's eyes, the way his lover lost weight until he was bird-like. "Things happen, baby."

"Shh. I'm a vampire lord, remember?"

"No, you just play one on TV."

"And on stage. That reminds me, I have an interview in the morning with that reporter from the *Times*."

"I know. I've got the alarm set for six." He kissed Jeff's cheek. "You think you can go to sleep now?" Rye was all keyed up, but he'd hold Jeff.

"No. No, let's just stay up all night watching movies."

"A Keanu Reeves marathon?"

"That works." Jeff pushed him into place, cuddled into his arms. "Sit and stay."

He chuckled, easily holding Jeff close. "Yes, boss."

"Good boy." Jeff patted his belly.

That had Rye laughing harder, and he kissed the top of Jeff's head, feeling so much better than he had. "Thank you," he whispered, hugging Jeff tight.

"I can't always be the psycho. Sometimes it's your turn."

"I like that."

It made what they had together more real somehow.

The movie came on, and before he knew it, he was dozing, Jeff on his laptop, watching the movie.

They were together and safe.

SOMETHING WAS wrong with Roach.

Jeff wasn't sure what, but something was weird. The man was just off, and it unnerved him. They were stopped for a few hours, and they were pretending to rehearse, but mostly they were goofing off and playing horrible parodies of their own songs.

Except for a handful of roadies and a couple of groupies, it was just them.

Rye brought him over a smoothie. "You okay, baby?"

"Baby? Since when do you call him baby?" Brandy looked over, eyebrows waggling.

Rye simply stared her down for about a minute, then turned his back on her. "Well? Are you okay?"

"Yeah. I'm cool." He looked at the smoothie, smelled the strawberry, and smiled. He loved the strawberry ones.

"Yeah? You just seemed…." Rye shrugged. "I don't know."

"Me either." He stood, grabbed his guitar. "I'm going to bed. I'm tired."

Roach looked at him, face serious. "You feeling okay?"

"Just tired." And weird. He felt weird.

Rye collected his jacket and his smoothie, his giant following dutifully.

There were a bunch of teenagers standing back away from the bus, and he could hear them whispering. "Is that him? It can't be him. He's too little. Don't be stupid. Of course it's him." On and on.

Rye just put an arm around him and led him to the door, pushing him in ahead and slamming the door closed behind them.

"Are you sure you're okay?"

"I'm fine." Something was weird. Something was wrong with Roach. His friend Jim never called back.

"I'm not so sure that you are." Rye passed his shake back to him. "Drink this, okay? You're too skinny again."

"I was getting fat." Jeff put it down, started pacing.

"No. You were getting healthy." Rye frowned and stepped in front of him, grabbing hold of his hands. "Something is wrong. Tell me."

"I…. Everything. Nothing. I just…. Something's wrong with Roach. I know it. And Jim still hasn't called, and I'm not freaking out and I should be!"

"You're kind of freaking out," Rye told him.

"Well, *now* I am!" He wanted to scream.

"Well, there's one problem solved, then."

"I—" He wanted to do something. Run away. Swim. He wanted to swim.

Rye dropped his hands to cup his cheeks. "What do you want, baby?"

"I need to expend some fucking energy. I want out of this goddamn bus! I want some trouble."

"Yeah?" Rye looked around. "We could go run away for the night."

"Anywhere." But even as he said it, Jeff knew that wasn't true. He wasn't going to go.

"Get changed—jeans and a T-shirt, with a hoodie."

"I can't. What if something happens?"

"I'm going to be there with you, Jeff, and I'm not going to let anything happen to you. We'll put your hair in a ponytail. Hell, your eyes aren't even the same color."

Rye got him in jeans and T-shirt, a colorful hoodie. "I didn't know I owned anything bright."

"God forbid, eh? Nobody is going to guess it's you."

Rye made a couple of calls, and there was a car outside, waiting for them. They slipped out, and Rye told the driver where to go. Jeff thought maybe it was their usual driver, but he couldn't be sure.

"Where are we going, Rye?"

"Neighborhood bar where they've got a couple pool tables. We can have potato skins and play a couple rounds. Be normal guys for a while."

"Oh. I…. Really? We'll just do it?"

"Yep. Like a Nike ad." Rye gave him a grin.

They pulled up and the driver parked. "I'll wait here, boss."

"Good deal. Keep your phone on." Rye patted the guy's back, and they got out, Rye putting an arm around his shoulder. "This place is gay friendly."

"Oh." Should he have worried about that too? "Is it vampire friendly?"

"You're not a vampire today, baby. You're just Jeff. A hot guy with a big, possessive boyfriend."

They went in, the place fairly quiet, classic rock playing loud enough that silences wouldn't be uncomfortable, but quiet enough that you wouldn't have to shout.

They found a table and sat together, and Jeff blinked. A date.

They were having a date.

Rye checked out the menu. "Oh, they have french onion soup. I bet you'd like that. If you don't mind, I'm having the bacon cheddar burger."

"Go ahead. I want the cheese nachos." He could pretend to eat those, and then Rye could finish them.

"Oh, yum. We'll order the large, and I'll steal a few." Rye closed his menu, looking pleased. "What do you want to drink?"

"I want a ginger ale. Do they have those?"

"We'll find out."

Rye smiled at the waitress who came over with perfect timing.

"Large nachos, all-dressed bacon cheeseburger with the fries, and two ginger ales, please."

"You got it. No appetizers?"

"No, thanks."

"Okay, I'll be right back with your drinks."

Rye grinned at him when she'd gone. "I guess they have ginger ale."

"I guess." Jeff looked around, watching the people talking and joking, playing pool. It was mostly, but not all, guys. He wasn't sure he would have known it was a gay place if Rye hadn't said.

"You want to play some pool when we've finished eating?"

"I haven't in a long time, but sure. I remember how." He'd been okay as a teenager.

"We don't have to. This is supposed to be something fun—a way to get away from everything." Rye nodded toward the jukebox in the corner. "I read online that after ten there's dancing."

"Dancing? Really? Like slow dancing?"

"I'm pretty sure there's regular dancing as well, but hopefully some slow songs."

"Would you like me if I wasn't LJ, do you think?"

"Baby, I like you despite the fact you're LJ."

"I mean…. The money, the—" Fact that he was basically worthless.

"I don't care about your money, Jeff. I'm interested in *you*. I love *you*. Not your persona, not your fame, not your money." Rye met his gaze head on.

"But I'm a loser."

"What? No, you're not!"

Jeff didn't argue, but he knew better. He was at his creative best when he was fucked up. His fans were starting to say he was aging, slipping.

"You're not. Have you thought any more about giving up the LJ gig?"

"I spoke to Donna, but…. People depend on me. It's not like when I was new. People know me."

"And they can all get other jobs. If you die from this, they'll be out of a job anyway."

"I'm not ready to die…." The waitress brought their drinks, and his words trailed off until she left. "I mean, when my heart stopped, I didn't want to die."

"Then take your life back and live."

Jeff felt his cheeks heat, the words stinging. No matter what he chose, it was wrong. It sucked.

"You said yourself someone else could play LJ and nobody would know. So let's let it happen."

Then what would he be? A loser with no reason. Crazy rock stars were celebrities. Crazy normal people were committed.

"What's going on in that head of yours, baby? You need to talk to me."

"I don't have anything to say, really. The food's coming."

Rye stayed quiet until they'd been served. Once the waitress had gone again, he spoke. "I'm not going to let anything bad happen to you, and that includes dumping the LJ gig."

"Eat your hamburger before it gets cold, huh?"

"Trying to shut me up?"

"Uh-huh."

Chuckling, Rye grabbed his burger. "I'll eat, but I'm not forgetting."

Jeff picked up a chip, playing with it, his mind going a million miles a minute.

"You need to eat that," murmured Rye.

"Huh?" He looked up and met Rye's eyes.

"You've hardly eaten for weeks. So eat the chips."

"You know me. I don't eat much." He did try a bite, though.

"And you know me. I'm the crazy guy who insists you do eat." Rye took a few bites of his burger, waited until he'd had another cheese-covered chip, then asked, "Did anyone tell you, you were fat or something?"

Jeff shrugged. It happened. He was supposed to be gaunt.

"Jesus Christ, Jeff. You're skinny as a rail."

"How's your burger?" He wasn't getting into this.

"It's good. How are your nachos?"

"Fine. Spicy."

"Good. Have another."

"Uh-huh." Maybe. Maybe later.

Rye watched him for a moment, then one eyebrow went up.

"What?" Jeff held Rye's gaze.

"Eat, baby."

He took a bite, feeling himself vibrate.

"That's a good start."

He wasn't going to eat any more. He wasn't.

"Don't make me do the airplane thing."

"The.... Oh. Don't be a turd." He giggled, tickled at the idea of his giant lover waving the spoon about and making airplane noises.

Giving him a shit-eating grin, Rye took another bite of his burger.

Jeff did eat another chip, before pushing it to Rye.

Rye grabbed a chip and started waving it around in the air.

"Have you lost your mind?"

"Nope. Eat some more, and I won't have to keep faking it."

"I had some. I did." He drank his ginger ale.

"I don't think three chips constitutes 'some.'"

"Stop counting. Eat your burger." Damn it.

"I am eating. I've had half of it." Rye looked at his plate.

"So, I ate too." Sort of.

"Are we going to have this argument for the rest of our lives? Or just the rest of the tour?"

"The rest of our lives. You're a giant—you have an unreasonable idea of how much normal people eat."

"I know normal people eat more than three chips and call it a day. And I am not a giant. I'm big-boned." Rye's eyes twinkled for him.

"Huge. Vast."

"You're just Lilliputian."

"Moi?" He fluttered dramatically, and suddenly they were snickering together, the weird tension dialing back.

Rye finished his burger, and Jeff actually had a few more chips.

"Can I talk you into dessert?"

"Can I have a french fry?"

"No. You can have two, though." Rye picked them up and raised them to Jeff's lips.

Jeff opened, blinked, and ate, the grease and salt so good. Rye's fingers slid on his lower lip, heat in Rye's eyes.

"We should be careful." He licked his lips.

"Gay bar, remember?"

"Uh-huh." What? He was fascinated by Rye's smile.

"Besides, I don't want to be careful. I want to feed you dessert and dance with you."

"Can we have something with ice cream?"

"We most definitely can have something with ice cream. A hot fudge brownie? A chocolate chip cookie?"

Oh. A cookie.

A cookie with ice cream.

"You want the cookie." Rye grinned and got their waitress' attention.

"I just…. Yeah. Yeah, that sounds good."

"Your face lit up when I said it."

Rye was still smiling as he asked their waitress for the dessert with two spoons.

"Why did you become a police officer?" Jeff asked, the question coming from nowhere.

"I know I'm supposed to say something like I wanted to help people, but the truth was, I wanted to go fast, run the light, and carry a gun."

"That's okay. I wanted to be Bill Gates."

"Bill Gates? Why?"

"He's brilliant, rich. I was a geek back then, until I discovered music." Hell, he was sort of a geek now.

"And now you're a music geek."

"Yeah." He supposed so. He definitely wasn't a rock star in the traditional sense of the word.

"If only LJ's fans knew." Rye nudged his foot under the table.

"Yeah, yeah. They're all probably IT guys during the day."

"Oh, here's our dessert." Rye licked his lips as the waitress set a plate with a huge cookie on it, two scoops of ice cream slowly melting over it.

Christ, it was huge. Jeff took a bite and let the ice cream melt on his tongue. The cookie was warm, soft, gooey.

Rye made a great face as he ate his first bite. "God. Good."

"Uh-huh." He ate another bite.

Rye took a spoonful of cookie and ice cream and offered it to him. "Dessert tastes better if you feed each other."

"That's a big bite." Even so, he opened and ate it.

"You've had a big bite from me before," murmured Rye, a naughty look on his face.

"Rye!" That made him laugh, right out loud.

Rye looked so pleased at his reaction, and he waggled his brows.

"Butthead." Jeff scooped up a bite, fed it to Rye. It was surprisingly intimate. Weirdly exposed. Rye slowly took the dessert off his spoon, lips closing over it, sliding off it. Someone liked sweets. Oh hell. Rye liked food. Lots.

"Give me another bite, baby." Oh, that was a switch, Rye not trying to feed him, but getting him to feed Rye.

"A big one?" Jeff didn't wait for the nod, just scooped up a bite with cookie and ice cream. Rye opened his mouth and took the bite, but Rye's gaze held his, made the feeding even more intimate. He could feel his cheeks heating, and he wiggled on his seat.

Rye licked his lips. "You want another bite, baby?"

"A little one."

Rye didn't try and feed him a huge bite, instead offering the small bite he'd asked for. The ice cream was his favorite part, slick and cold and creamy. It felt good against his throat.

Rye ate most of the rest of the dessert, teasing another biteful into him now and then.

The music started—goofy and rhythmic, light, with the barest beat behind it. Still, people started dancing, gyrating on the floor.

"You want to?" Rye asked, nodding toward the little dance floor in the corner.

"Okay. Okay, sure." He danced for a living, didn't he? Dancing with Rye shouldn't be weird.

Standing, Rye took his hand and helped him up, then drew him over to the dance floor. Rye wasn't the best dancer in the world, but he was good—he could move. Jeff let himself lean in, not working too hard, just enjoying himself.

The music slowed after a couple of songs, and Rye pulled him into the strong arms, swaying with him. Oh, that was lovely.

Jeff leaned and let his eyes drop closed. One hand settled in the small of his back, the other on the curve of his ass, and they just swayed easily. It was like a high school fantasy, wasn't it? Slow dancing with the perfect guy.

They danced until the music changed again, and then Rye took his hand and led him back to their table. "You want to play some pool? Have another ginger ale? Call it a night?"

"I think I'm ready to go home, snuggle for a while." He was full, tired, warm, and things felt okay.

"Cool. I can get behind that." Rye pulled out some bills, sticking them under his glass, then took Jeff's hand again, leading him out.

The driver was sitting in the car, snoring away.

Snorting, Rye banged on the window, making the guy jump. Then the back door was held open for him.

"Good nap?"

"Yes, sir. Fab." The guy backed out. "Good evening?"

"Yeah. Yeah, it was, thank you."

Rye smiled. "It was great." Rye put an arm around Jeff and tugged him in.

Jeff leaned over, sighed happily. It had been. Normal and wonderful and different. It was just too bad they were going back to the bus and the tour.

CHAPTER NINE

JEFF WAS napping, and the hum of the bus's engine threatened to send Rye to sleep as well.

Rye shook his head and grabbed his phone. It was as good a time as any to talk to Jeff's manager. Just feel the woman out about getting Jeff out of the January business.

Donna answered quickly. "Rye, is everything okay?"

"Everything is just fine."

He heard the relieved sigh from her end.

"I just wanted to talk about possibilities."

"Possibilities?"

"About what possibilities there are for Jeff post-Lord January. Have you heard him do his own stuff? He's amazing."

"No. No, I haven't, at least not lately. Why? Is he looking to transition away in the next few years?"

Next few years? Was this lady really this oblivious?

"Let me lay it on the line for you, Donna. This needs to be his last tour."

"I'll call and speak to LJ."

"Don't you dare guilt him into staying in a job that will kill him."

"Pardon me?" Her voice went icy. "What did you say?" She was a stone cold bitch, he knew that, but Jeff was too important to back down on.

"He thinks he has to keep doing this thing he hates because there's all these people who depend on him, that if he doesn't keep playing January until it kills him, he's letting you and the whole machine down."

"LJ and I have been working together for years. Years. You've known him three months. I'll let him make his own career choices."

"I have no problem with that. I just want to make sure you let him know that he does have choices."

"Good day."

Click.

Now, that hadn't gone like he'd hoped.

Rubbing his face, he got up and paced in the little space he had to do it. God damn it. Why was he the only person in Jeff's life who gave a damn about Jeff himself?

Well, him and Jeff's sponsor. Donna had never found him. Had she tried? It didn't matter if she had or not; he had a guy, a private detective.

Rye went through his contacts on his phone, found Brandon's number, and texted him the details.

He got a text back with a "got it."

Leaning back, he closed his eyes a second and let himself relax. It wasn't hellish. Jeff was doing okay—he was clean, safe, working hard. Rye could see it, though, see the way playing January was killing something inside of Jeff.

It didn't surprise him that Jeff had turned to the drugs. How else was he supposed to cope? It was a totally unhealthy way of living.

He didn't think Donna realized quite how hard it all was on Jeff, that the drugs had been his only way of coping, an escape. Rye sighed and rubbed the bridge of his nose. Damn it. He headed for the bed at the back of the bus and sat on the edge of it, smiling down at Jeff.

Jeff cracked an eye open. "Everything okay?"

"Yeah, yeah. It's fine. I talked to Donna."

He didn't want Jeff to find out from Donna that he'd called her. And Jeff needed to know someone was going to fight for him.

"Why? Are you quitting?"

"God, no. I wanted to ask her about her thoughts on this being your last tour, what she thought about finding you a new gig."

"And she said she couldn't discuss business with you, and she'd call me."

"Basically. I think she was pissed that I suggested you might need a change."

Jeff shrugged. "I trust her. She's my manager."

"I just want her to give you options. That's all, baby."

Jeff nodded again, still settled in the covers.

Rye lay down next to Jeff, pulling Jeff against him. "I want you to be happy."

"I am happy."

"Yeah?"

"I think so. I have you. I have money. I have a job."

"You don't like your job, though. You'd be happier with a different one, wouldn't you?"

"I've never had a different one." Jeff looked at him, face still, quiet. "And I might not be a better person as just Jeff, and then what would you do?"

"I'm not asking you to be a better person. I'm just asking you to have a different job."

"Why?"

"Because this one is killing you, and you don't like it."

Jeff stood up, slipped from the bed. "I think I need a shower, Rye."

"Are you going to run away every time we talk about this?"

"Probably, yeah."

Jeff headed for the bathroom, seeming quiet, small.

"Baby…." God.

He was worried he was screwing this up. He couldn't give up, though. This was too hard on Jeff.

He truly believed Jeff needed to give up January to live.

Getting up, he followed Jeff to the little bathroom. "Want me to wash you, baby?"

"I want a hug."

"I always have those for you." He opened his arms.

Jeff squeezed him tight, just for a few seconds. "I don't want to talk about quitting or LJ or anything right now. I'm tired."

"Okay, baby. We can just stand in the shower and be." At least Jeff was talking to him.

For now that was going to be enough.

"DO YOU want me to fire him? He's taken this whole thing about taking care of you too seriously, LJ. You're not a child. You have to look at your responsibilities and decide what's best for you."

Jeff nodded. "Okay."

"I'm serious. One phone call, and he's gone."

"No. No, it's good."

Jeff was tired, and his throat hurt, and he felt... like he was fading.

"Are you sure?"

"I am. I need to start getting ready for the show."

Janie was coming, and it was a big one tonight because they were closing out a festival. The crowd had been there three days, drinking and dancing, and the sound already rocked the bus.

"Okay. Have fun, sweetie," Donna said before hanging up.

"Uh-huh." He hung up and went to the bathroom, grateful that Rye was out having a security meeting. He grabbed a razor blade and cut a tiny line on his arm, following an old scar so Rye wouldn't notice.

It wasn't a good high, but it was something. He did it three more times, leaning against the bathroom door as he bled, breathing nice and slow.

"LJ? Honey? You ready?"

"Two minutes. Turn some music on? Loud?"

"Sure thing, honey."

The music came on, loud just like he'd asked.

He washed up, then opened the bathroom door, just a little buzzed. "Okay, lady. I think the bat wing leathers today. It's muddy out there."

"All right. Is that big burly man of yours going to be around to help lift them on?" Janie asked.

As if on cue, Rye came in, closing the door firmly behind him.

"He is." Jeff pulled on the tight black shirt that went underneath. "Still crazy out there?"

"Bug fuck nuts." Rye shook his head. "I'm going to be right offstage, okay? I can reach you in two and a half seconds."

"I'm not worried." He'd worked worse shows.

"You don't have to be—that's my job." Rye seemed to be trying to keep things light, but his giant was in full-blown protector mode.

They got Jeff dressed in the heavy leathers; they'd protect him from any thrown beer bottles.

"I'm pulling you if it gets too bad."

"I'll be fine. We've done worse." He was used to the drama. Hell, he was used to it and buzzing a little.

Grunting, Rye grabbed his chin and looked into his eyes. "Are you okay?"

"Excited, I guess. Something in the air."

Rye held his gaze for a long time.

"You want to test me, Rye?" Rye thought he was using. Cutting wasn't using, though. Was it? Rye would be upset to know he'd done it. Would probably freak right out. Would he leave because of it? Jeff tried not to think about how that thought made everything in him tighten.

Rye answered him, distracting him from his thoughts. "No. I'm just trying to figure out why you're more animated tonight."

"I just want to put on a good show."

"You always do, baby." Rye glanced back, but Janie was at the front of the bus, talking to Barney. Leaning in, Rye gave him a quick, hard kiss. "You always do."

Jeff smiled and reached up, held on for as good of a hug as he could get.

"Love you," whispered Rye.

"Ditto. It's okay. I swear, it'll be okay."

"Stop stealing my lines, baby." Rye hugged him again, then turned and led him from the bus.

The band was ready, and they went across the back, moving fast. The wind was beginning to blow, storm clouds building.

Rye was a solid giant immediately in front of him, Jeff's hand on Rye's back the whole way.

Arriving at the curtain, Rye stepped aside, squeezed his hand, and let him go on.

They hooked him into the harness, ratcheted him up behind the curtain, and Jeff held on to the scaffolding, watching the band set up.

The roadies were starting to hurry, rushing through everything.

He thought he saw a flash of lightning in the distance.

"Come on. Come on," Jeff muttered. They needed to get a few songs out before the lightning shut them down. Rye had wanted to cancel the show, but he'd flat-out refused, noting that the storm wasn't supposed to hit until after the scheduled encore.

Things got moving, and they were announced, the crowd surging forward, pushing at the stage. Jeff felt the scaffolding shift—weird.

Then he was flying, and he started screaming out lyrics, the wind pushing him in the air.

Something jerked him, and he dropped suddenly, the ropes coming to a stop about eight feet from the stage. He was still swinging madly, the wind whipping into a frenzy.

He looked back for Rye, but everyone, from roadies to fans, was all scrambling, the stage really moving. Oh fuck.

Oh fuck.

The stage was going down. *"Roach! Rye! The stage!"*

The crowd surged forward again, and sparks flew, the risers letting go.

His ropes held, but he was flung around by the wind, and it felt like he was in the middle of a tornado.

He watched as the back of the stage went, the crowd pouring over the side, wild. Police and security were everywhere. The scaffolding bent, fire catching along the equipment in the wings. Oh fuck.

All Jeff could see as he went down was a writhing mass of people, screaming and reaching for him.

CHAPTER TEN

RYE WATCHED it all happening like it was in slow motion, and his only focus was Jeff.

He was running right for the spot where Jeff went down, but he knew he wasn't going to be there to catch him.

The fucking crowd was too thick.

Of course, that crowd was going to keep Jeff from slamming into the ground, which probably would have killed him.

Rye waded in, shoving people aside with sheer size and strength. He shouted into his Bluetooth, but he'd be damned if he could hear a damn thing. The roar of people and wind, thunder, lightning, and the stage falling to bits filled his ears, turned almost into white noise.

He pushed two more kids out of the way and grabbed hold of Jeff's leg, climbing Jeff's body hand over hand until he had one arm around the slender waist. He wasn't fucking letting go.

Jeff was still in the harness, knocked out cold. People were pulling at him—tugging and tearing at his clothes, his jewelry, his hair.

Fucking animals.

There was a sound louder than the rest from the back of the stage, sparks flying. Jesus, the whole fucking stage was exploding. Didn't these kids have any sense of self-preservation? Tapping his ear piece, he tried in vain to communicate with his team.

Rye tugged and pushed, finally getting Jeff out of the harness and into his arms. He shouldered a couple people out of the way, looking around wildly for the best egress. The stage area was in flames, which meant backstage was out.

He turned again, suddenly coming face-to-face with Jude, one of the guys who usually stood in front of the stage and kept the kids off it. Jude pointed to the left, mimed pushing through, and Rye nodded, ready to follow in Jude's wake.

"My band," Jeff moaned, then screamed as someone tore at his hair.

Rye kicked out with his foot, hard, and the offender shouted and let go of Jeff's hair. Rye shifted Jeff, using his shoulder to protect Jeff's head.

Jude kept moving, slowly but surely, and Rye had to believe the man was leading them to a clear exit where he could get Jeff to safety.

Then he'd go back, get the others.

Lightning flashed, hitting the stage, and everything stopped for a second—his senses frozen, trapped in light and the scent of ozone.

Fuck.

Fuck. Fuck. Fuck.

The screaming increased, the fans finally hitting self-preservation and pushing this way and that, scrambling to find a way out of the open-air arena.

Thank fucking God he was as big as he was or he would have fallen, and they both would have been trampled. He still had Jude, though, and he could see now where they were headed; the crowd was starting to thin out as everyone scrambled for safety. He pushed through, his muscles screaming even as the first responders pushed toward the stage.

All of a sudden, the crowd opened up like the venue had spewed them all out into the parking lot.

Jude turned back around. "Bus?"

Rye nodded. If they could get there, get Jeff into the SUV, they could get him to the hospital while he figured out where the rest of the band was. He tapped his Bluetooth a couple of times, amazed it was still attached to his ear. "Sit rep!" He repeated his demand for a situation report a few times, trusting that Jude was taking them to the SUV as quickly as possible. He could see the flashing lights coming from the east, so at least fucking emergency services was here.

"Boss, we got injured, man. Hardcore. Someone stabbed Roach, Brandy's burned. We need help!" The words were shouted through his earpiece.

"God damn it. Where are you?"

"Back of the stage. The fucking civilians are everywhere. I got a young teenager, girl. Broken leg. I got a couple guys down. Lots of blood."

"I'm on my way." He turned to Jude. "Get LJ to the hospital. I'll be there as soon as I can. And keep me up-to-date on his condition." Rye settled Jeff in the back of the SUV. "Baby? Jude's taking you to the hospital. I'll be there as soon as I can, okay?"

"Get the others. Help them."

"I will. And I'll be there soon. Jude will be with you." He gave Jeff a kiss, not caring who saw, then closed the door and turned back to Jude again. "Do not leave his side until I get there. No press, no fans, nobody but the doctors and nurses. Okay. Go. Go."

"You got it, boss. Be careful."

He nodded and took one last look at Jeff, who was a hell of a lot better than stabbed or burned. Then he turned back into the fray. God fucking damn it. This was insane. Nobody should have to live through this just to make a few bucks.

He found an EMT and made sure the guy followed him out back; he had at least three people in need of the man's services. And he imagined that was just for starters.

"I WANT to know what the fuck is going on!"

Jeff was two seconds from total meltdown. His leg was in a cast, his head was stitched up in four different places, and he had three broken bones in his hand where he'd been stepped on. They had him in a room, drugged up and fucking restrained to the bed, just because he'd hit a doctor. The man had hurt him.

He knew everyone was busy, he knew this was crazy, but it was nearly five in the morning and no one knew anything about

Rye, about the band, hell, about the other acts that had gone before or the roadies.

"I know it's not fucking visiting hours! I've just spent eight hours pulling people out of a fucking disaster! So don't tell me to calm down!"

"*Rye! Rye!*" Jeff bellowed, fighting the restraints.

"Jeff!"

Seconds later, Rye came bursting through the door. "Oh thank God."

Rye came right up, relieved face turning furious, and Rye turned on the nurse who'd followed him in. "Why the fuck is he restrained?"

"He attacked a physician."

"Let me go. I was freaked out. I'm okay. Please."

"Can we undo these, please? Wait a minute." Rye looked in his eyes. "Jesus Christ, did you people drug him?" Rye leaned their foreheads together. "It's going to be okay, Jeff, I promise. We'll get this sorted. I'm going to get you out of here." Then Rye turned back to the nurse. "Well?"

"I…. Just keep him in the bed, okay?"

Rye nodded. "He'll be fine. And no more drugs. He's been clean over a year." Rye started undoing his bindings. "Jesus. I should have come with you. I should have." Rye looked tired and dirty, and he had cuts on his face, his hands. And there was an alarming amount of blood on his shirt.

"You… you hurt?" Jeff relaxed as the restraints were removed, even though his broken hand started throbbing.

"No. The blood isn't mine." Rye tugged a chair over and sat, holding on to Jeff's good hand. "You weren't so lucky."

"They shaved big parts of my head."

"Yeah." Rye touched his scalp carefully, hands warm, even through the bandages. "The rest of the tour is going to be cancelled."

Rye met his eyes.

"Brandy got burned. She's going to be okay, but she's going to be out of commission a couple months. But Roach… he got stabbed.

When they got him on the gurney and cut off his shirt, they found a stent in his chest. Baby, he's got cancer."

"What? He has…. Where is he? I need to talk to him."

"Not at five in the morning, baby. I'll find out how he's doing after the shift change and take you to him at the start of visiting hours if he's up to it, okay?"

Cancer?

Roach?

Rye stroked Jeff's cheek. "So you've got a broken leg and a broken hand? And what did they do to your head?"

"Tore my scalp. They ripped my hair out."

Roach had cancer.

"I'm sorry, baby. I should have gotten to you sooner."

"You came. The… the stage fell. I…." He looked at Rye. "The stage fell."

"I know. It was the scariest thing I've ever seen."

"How could Roach have cancer? Roach is my friend."

"I know, baby. And I'm so sorry."

"I…." The morphine made his eyes cross.

"Baby? Damn it, that's the drugs, isn't it?" Rye stroked his cheek. "Fuck."

"Morphine. I was freaked out and hurting."

"Shit, I'm sorry. I hope the withdrawal isn't going to be a bitch. I'll help you through it, though, you know that."

"I just… I want to see Roach, Brandy. How about the others?"

"They're okay. Nobody died, but there were a lot of injuries. The organizers got lucky." Rye squeezed his hand. "You can't see anyone until at least ten—visiting hours. Why don't you try to get some sleep?"

"Stay with me? I mean, I know you have to clean up, but… please?"

"I'm not going anywhere, baby. I promise."

"Thank you. I'm dizzy." And scared. And hurting.

And the reporters were everywhere. They always were. He thought they were the worst part of it all.

"All you have to do is lie there. Just close your eyes and sleep. I've got you. You're safe." The words were ones Rye had said to him before, his giant always there for him.

Jeff held on, his heart thrumming in his chest so hard it felt like it wanted to break.

RYE DOZED for a couple of hours at Jeff's bedside before going out to find a nurse and get some information on Roach and Brandy. Neither of them was in intensive care, and they could go see them once visiting hours started. They'd leave Jeff in his bed, and she would arrange for an orderly to help move him.

Then he arranged for a twenty-four/seven guard on Jeff's door, Jude finally getting relieved. Rye was very clear: Nobody but doctors and nurses, with appropriate ID badges, were allowed in Jeff's room. The press was going insane, but he wasn't letting any of them near Jeff. Harassing everyone in the lobby was bad enough.

Finally, he returned to Jeff's side, pleased that Jeff was still sleeping. His baby needed the rest. Hell, *he* needed the rest; he was utterly exhausted.

Taking Jeff's good hand in his again, he let his eyes drift shut once more.

"I NEED to go pee. No! I am not going in a bedpan!" Jeff's voice was hysterical. "Please!"

The big male nurse was trying to keep him calm. "I can catheterize you now, if you'd like. It'll have to happen before they do surgery on your leg."

"Surgery? No. No, I need...."

Rye jerked out of his light doze, growling. "What's going on here?"

"Mr. January needs to urinate, but he's uncomfortable using a urine bottle, and he's not allowed up on that leg." One huge dark hand was held out to him. "Miguel Cervantes. I'm the day nurse."

"Hi, Miguel. I'm Rye. Let me talk to him, see if I can't help with the urine bottle. Someone's supposed to be coming this morning to take us down to see the other members of the band."

"You're scheduled for surgery at one. Dr. Patek is amazing."

"I spoke to a different nurse—she didn't say anything about surgery. Please, he needs to see Roach and Brandy." Rye had hold of Jeff's hand again, trying to keep him calm.

"Let me see what I can find out, okay? I'll be right back."

"Thanks." Rye focused back on Jeff. "Hey, you want me to help you with the urine bottle thing?"

"Just… carry me to the bathroom?"

"What have you got against the urine bottle?" He was not carrying Jeff anywhere; that poor leg didn't need any more jostling. "It's a bedpan."

Jeff looked at him like he was insane. "Yeah…."

Rye grabbed it. "It's not that bad, and then you'll feel better."

"I don't want to." Jeff was looking panicked.

"Why not, baby?" There had to be a reason.

Jeff shook his head and looked at his casted hand. "I can't hold it."

He grabbed the urine bottle and pulled back the covers, carefully lifting Jeff and putting the bottle into position.

Jeff squeezed his eyes shut, but nature couldn't be denied, and the nurse came in as he was finishing taking care of it.

"Okay, we're going to get you a wheelchair for your visit. I have to warn you: your friend, Mr. Roach, he's lost consciousness."

"LJ still wants to see him." Rye knew Jeff, knew his lover would fuss until he saw Roach for himself.

"I'll have an orderly come with a chair. It'll be a few minutes."

"Thank you." Then he turned his attention back to Jeff. "It's not going to be easy, seeing him."

Jeff wasn't in there, not totally, his eyes wide and bloodshot.

They were going to have to walk a tight balance between enough pills for the pain and feeding Jeff's addiction. It was a fucking good thing the rest of the tour was cancelled: this recovery was going to be a bitch. For the ones who recovered….

There was a soft knock on the door. "Boss? It's Willie."

"Come on in." He gave a smile to one of his best men who'd come on the tour with them, another retired cop.

"I brought the clothes you wanted. Stuff for you, stuff for LJ."

"You bring his sunglasses?"

"Yep. He'll be able to travel the halls incognito." Willie handed over the bag. "How is he?"

"He's going to recover."

Willie gave Jeff a long look and nodded. "Rumor has it the tour's done."

"Yeah. LJ's about to go into surgery for his leg, and he'll be recovering for a while. Then there's the rest of the band…." He shook his head. Hearing that Roach was unconscious now—and clearly not just sleeping—Rye wasn't sure Roach would ever leave the hospital. "They're making the announcement later today. Do me a favor: I want you and the boys to hang around for a couple days. I want someone with Roach and someone with Brandy while they're here, someone outside LJ's door too."

"You got it, boss."

"Thanks."

Willie clapped a hand on his shoulder, squeezed, and headed back out, cell phone already in his hand.

"Rye." The voice surprised him, although it shouldn't have, Donna hurrying over, looking like nothing more than a harried grandma. "I'm here to help."

Rye started offering her his hand, then changed his mind and went in for a hug.

He didn't linger, but he gave her a good squeeze, then stepped back from the bed a bit to give her room. "Hey, LJ. Look who's here." He hated not being able to just call Jeff, Jeff.

"Donna." Jeff stared. "Everything's fucked up."

Rye clenched his hands into fists to keep himself from wrapping them around Jeff.

"I know, kiddo, but we've got it under control, huh? And you're high as a kite."

"Uh-huh. I hurt."

"I know. I know. I'm here for the duration. Rye's here."

The orderly came in with the wheelchair.

"I'll lift you into it," Rye suggested before going to wash his hands with the gel soap by the door. He didn't want Jeff hurting any more than he needed to.

"You want some help?"

"Thanks, Donna. If you can just make sure I don't hit anything with his leg."

The orderly was holding the wheelchair in place for him. Between the casts and the bandages and the IVs, Jeff was a disaster waiting to happen.

Rye got his arms beneath Jeff's knees and shoulders and lifted him. Even with the casts, Jeff hardly weighed anything.

By the time they got Jeff settled with his drips on the pole attached to the wheelchair, Jeff was sweating and pale, utterly shaken.

"Give me his sunglasses and the ball cap from that bag, please."

Donna got them and passed them over. He stuck the hat on Jeff, then looked into his baby's eyes. "You need to come back here, just say the word."

"The cap hurts, Rye."

"Okay. Just the sunglasses, then, but keep your head down, okay?"

"Uh-huh. I just want to talk to Roach."

"Okay, then." He slid the sunglasses on Jeff's face, hoping like hell that Roach woke up.

They stopped at Brandy's room first, him and Jeff, Donna trailing quietly behind them, but her face was bandaged and she was out.

Jeff stared, head shaking. "That's not right."

"No, it's not. Are you sure you want to see Roach?"

"He's the reason I did this. He's the original band."

"Okay. I'll take you." Rye wheeled Jeff to Roach's room.

Roach was there, under all these bandages, and there was a hard-faced woman sitting in one of the chairs who Rye had to assume was Roach's wife. "LJ."

"Kathy. Why didn't someone tell me?"

"He knew it was so hard, kiddo, with the rehab. He didn't want to worry you. He's... he just wanted one more tour."

Rye put his hand on Jeff's shoulder, giving his lover support. "Is he—?"

"Dying. They don't know if he'll wake up."

Jeff nodded. "Can I talk to him?"

"Sure." She stood, got out of the way, and Rye rolled Jeff up. Roach didn't even look like himself anymore. The man was pale, still.

"You could have told me. I would have understood. I.... We could.... We... we did it. We were rock stars."

"You were." Rye wished there was something he could say, but he knew there wasn't. This sucked, big time.

Roach's hand twitched, and Jeff took it in his good one. "I'm sorry, huh? You aren't supposed to be sick."

Rye couldn't be sure, but it looked like Roach squeezed Jeff's hand. Jeff looked for a long time, then let go of Roach's hand and hung his head.

It fucking broke his heart.

Rye kept his hand on Jeff's shoulder, waiting for the word so he could take Jeff back to his room.

"The others? Bri and Scooter?" Jeff asked.

"They're fine. Not even a scratch." It amazed him, actually, that anyone had gotten out of that mess without serious injuries.

"Okay." Jeff was beginning to shake, to vibrate.

"I think we should go back to your room, b—man."

"Uh-huh. Donna, you take care of Kathy."

"Okay, honey. You got it. Good luck on your surgery."

"I need to go, Rye."

"I've got you." Rye backed them up out of the room, then made a beeline for the elevator to take Jeff back up to his room.

The media was everywhere now, ambushing them, and once they saw Jeff, the flashes started going off.

Rye protected his lover as much as he could and got them into the elevator, sighing in relief as the elevator doors closed the media out. Jeff was still, silent, so quiet.

Rye hated this. Hated it.

He got them back to Jeff's room, the nurse ready to start getting him prepped for surgery. Rye stood next to the bed, holding Jeff's hand and trying to stay out of the way. They pushed something into Jeff's IV "to relax him" and the tears started, sliding down Jeff's cheeks.

After the mad rush of getting him ready, they were left alone again, and Rye pressed his forehead against Jeff's, looking into those huge-pupiled eyes. "Don't cry, baby."

"I want to go home. I don't even know where I am."

"As soon as you're well enough to travel, we're going home. I promise, baby."

"If I die, I want to be cremated, and I want to be sprinkled somewhere beautiful."

"You're not going to die, Jeff." Rye wasn't going to let that happen. Not here, not now. Jeff was going to get things straightened out, and then he was going to... honestly, he was going to sleep for a month. And eat. Sleep and eat. Rye was looking forward to it, actually. He just wanted Jeff to be happy.

Jeff's eyelids drooped, the medication working.

Rye stroked the side of Jeff's face and whispered, "I love you." Then he dropped a soft kiss on Jeff's lips before straightening.

"Oh, you are so fired." Donna leaned against the wall and winked at him.

Rye felt his cheeks heat, but he straightened, refusing to be embarrassed.

"So, we have about ten million things to deal with, but you need to worry about getting cleaned up and getting some rest." Donna could be a drill sergeant when she wanted to be.

He looked down at himself, almost surprised to see he was still wearing the suit he'd been in last night, that he was covered in soot and other people's blood. "Willie brought me clothes. I'll use the bathroom here." Jeff had a private room, complete with the nicest hospital bathroom he'd ever seen. "Once he's in surgery."

"Fine, but you have to rest. You have to. You're going to have a stroke."

"Not as long as he needs me, I won't." He ran his hand over his face. "When is the announcement about the cancellation happening?"

"Today. I'll put out a press release about the injuries, and then, in a few days, cancel the rest of the tour."

"Will you look into the possibilities of him going out there as himself, doing his own songs? I'm not trying to go behind his back or anything, I'm just looking for a realistic view of a future without January that includes music for him. With all that happened, and Roach...." It might be the perfect time for Lord January to meet his demise.

"I'll let LJ tell me what he needs. I work for him, not the other way 'round."

"I'm not asking you to find him another job, just find out how feasible it is. He keeps telling me this is all he can do, but I keep telling him he has other options. All I'm asking is that you confirm if that's true or not."

"Sure. Sure, he's a kickass song writer. Always has been."

"Is anyone singing them? Or has he been stockpiling them?"

"He hasn't had me broker any in a while."

"He's been writing, though. A lot." Fucking good stuff too. And probably enough for an album. "You'll stick with him, yeah? Even if January is gone for good?"

Donna met his eyes, serious as a heart attack. "He's like a son to me."

An orderly appeared at the door. "Sir, we're here to take him down."

Rye nodded and stood. "Okay, we'll come down with you."

141

Rye and Donna fell in step behind the gurney. "I'm glad he has you. You'll stay and wait for the whole surgery?" He'd shower, change, then come down and join her in the waiting room, maybe close his eyes for a bit.

"The only reason I'd leave is if we lose Roach."

"Good deal."

Rye stayed until they took Jeff beyond the doors he was allowed to go through. Then he headed back to get cleaned up. He wanted to be ready when Jeff needed him.

CHAPTER ELEVEN

JEFF TRIED to swallow, but it hurt so bad, burned, like he was swallowing glass.

What the fuck?

What was going on?

Someone squeezed his hand. "Easy, baby. I'm here."

Jeff groaned, his voice gone.

"Shh. Shh. You don't have to say anything. Just squeeze my hand."

He held on, throat working, so thirsty. Something cold rubbed along his lips, then slipped between them. Oh, ice.

He pulled on the chip, the cold feeling so good.

"Better, huh?" Another ice chip was slipped between his lips.

Jeff nodded. Better. More. He focused on saying the word. "More."

"Hush, baby."

Another ice chip hit his tongue. "Rye." His Rye. His sweet giant. Okay. Okay, he was okay.

"Yeah. I'm here. You're good." A soft kiss pressed against his forehead.

He frowned and licked his dry lips again. Chuckling, Rye rubbed an ice chip across his lips, then into his mouth. "Pushy."

"Uh-huh. 'M I okay?"

"Yeah. They fixed your leg up. Between it and your hand, you're going to be in a lot of rehab. We'll get you through it, though." Before he could say anything else, Rye pushed another ice chip into his mouth.

Jeff needed to know how Roach was doing, how Brandy was doing, but he was so tired. He couldn't even care about his own injuries, not really.

"You've just come out of surgery. They said you did really well. Donna's working on getting you all transferred to a hospital back home."

"No. Home."

"Baby—"

"Home."

"Okay. I'll let Donna know that's what you want."

He nodded, and oh, that hurt.

Rye touched his cheek. "Easy, baby. Just breathe, okay?" Rye gave him yet more ice.

"Brandy wants a call when you're up for visitors, so she can come see you."

"Uh-huh." He closed his eyes, fading.

"There's no news on Roach."

Jeff squeezed Rye's hand in thanks.

"You want some music on or something? Maybe some TV?"

"Are you leaving?"

"No, I'm not going anywhere. I won't leave your side."

"Okay. Need you."

"And you've got me." Rye continued to stroke his cheek, fingers warm and gentle. "So no music or TV? You want to just sleep?"

"Uh-huh." He couldn't keep his eyes open.

"Okay, baby. You sleep. It's safe. I've got you." A soft kiss dropped onto his lips, barely touching.

Jeff let the drugs and the heaviness drag him down. Maybe he could stay there and never come out.

RYE WAS going to kill someone.

Possibly himself, just to keep him from killing anyone else. He was bored out of his mind. Jeff was bored, cranky, and hurting.

Brandy had been transferred to a hospital closer to home. Roach was still hanging on somehow, though he hadn't regained consciousness at all.

The doctors had made it clear the longer Jeff stayed in the hospital the better, so Rye and Donna had done their best. Rye was pretty sure they weren't going to be able to stall for much longer. He sure as hell didn't want to.

"I want to *go home!*" Jeff threw a glass of water at the window, the spray going everywhere.

Rye let an eyebrow go up. "Are you sure about that?"

Jeff glared at him. At least the paparazzi had let off.

"Come on, baby. I know you're bored. We could play some more checkers."

"Tell them I'm leaving. I'm getting on my bus."

"The bus is gone, baby. Donna's working on a plane." It was time.

"Now. Now. I need to go home." Jeff looked exhausted, raw, desperate.

Rye picked up his phone and hit Donna's number.

Donna picked up on the first ring. "What's up?"

"Is the plane ready? Because we are."

"Well, let's get on the doctors. It'll take hours even if they get started now."

"Okay. But today, yeah? We're going stir-crazy here."

"I'll get the plane ready—you get the doctors moving."

"It's a deal." He hung up and turned back to Jeff. "She's working on the plane. I'll get the doctors lined up to get you checked out."

"Okay. Okay, that's good. Now."

Leaning over, Rye pushed the button for the nurse. "Pushy, baby."

Jeff was skin and bones, gray, and that hair…. God, they'd be better off shaving it and starting over.

It would be something they could do to waste time. "Hey, baby. Once we get the being-released ball rolling, how about I cut your hair short all over?"

"I haven't had short hair since I was a teenager."

"It's kind of a mess, what with the shaved bits and all." Not to mention it hadn't had a proper wash since Jeff got to the hospital.

"Uh-huh. It smells."

"Yeah. I'll have the nurse bring me some scissors."

As if on cue, Miguel came in. "What do you need, man?"

"I want to go home. I need to. Talk to the doctor?" Jeff needed to go home.

Miguel glanced at him, and Rye just nodded. It was time. He'd promised himself when Jeff had finally had it, he would insist. Even if they had to go AMA.

"I'll holler at the attending, see what he says."

Rye put his hand on Jeff's shoulder. "It doesn't matter what he says. We're going home."

"Still, they like to believe they have a say."

Chuckling, he conceded that to Miguel. "We'd prefer to go with their blessing. Can we have a pair of scissors? His hair is a wreck."

"You want a barber brought in?"

He glanced at Jeff, though he was already shaking his head. The look on Jeff's face confirmed it for him. "No, just the scissors, please."

"Sure. No problem."

"I like him. He's cool." Jeff was rocking, back and forth, humming low.

"He's a good guy. You okay?"

"Aching. Fucking leg burns."

Rye leaned his forehead against Jeff's. "You want to meditate with me?"

"I don't know how."

"We can start by breathing together."

"I'm tired of everything."

He knew. He knew Jeff was restless and needing real sleep. "Close your eyes if you want, baby. Just close them and breathe with me, okay?"

Those long eyelashes closed. How had he not noticed them before? Long and dark.

"Now let's just breathe in. A nice, long breath."

Jeff sucked in a breath, the sound shuddering and raw.

"That's it, baby. Now let it out." He put his hand on Jeff's chest, giving him something to focus those breaths on. He was so tired of the hospital gowns, the weird smells, and he could only imagine how Jeff felt.

"In again... and out." He guided Jeff through more breaths, each one slow and long. The soft sounds were like music.

Rye found himself humming one of Jeff's songs that his baby had sung a lot back home. Oh. That was a smile. He kept humming, kept breathing, Jeff's chest rising and falling beneath his palm.

The door opened. "You wanted scissors, sir?"

"Leave them on the table, please."

"Sure. The doctor is coming in about an hour, and we'll start the check-out procedures."

"Thank you."

Rye waited until the door clicked shut, then focused Jeff back on his breathing. "In and out, Jeff. That's all that you need to worry about right now."

"In and out."

"That's right."

Jeff nodded, breathing for him.

God, he wanted to kiss his boy, wanted to climb into the bed and wrap around his lover and keep him safe.

Soon.

Soon, they'd be somewhere private, somewhere home.

They breathed okay for a while longer until Jeff blessedly fell asleep, and Rye backed off, started to pack their things up.

When Jeff woke, Rye would cut his hair and hopefully that would be enough time for the hospital to get them checked out.

He just needed his lover home. He would deal with everything else once they got there.

CHAPTER TWELVE

JEFF'S HEAD felt weird with his hair so short. After Rye had cut it, the nurse had come in with a razor and shaved it so it was even. Even. He snorted. Almost all gone. So now his head felt weird. Weird and light. He liked it. Of course, maybe that was the pain-killers. He had taken enough before the flight to make a hippo comatose.

The car went through the gate and pulled up in front of the mansion. Wow. It felt it'd been like forever.

Rye got out and came around to open his door. "You need help?"

He sat there, staring.

Donna stepped out. "Jeff?"

"Okay, come on." Rye picked him up, cradling him against the strong chest. "Let's get him upstairs to his bed."

"I'm going to go rest in my quarters, Rye. I'm exhausted." Donna gave him a tired smile. "I'll visit tomorrow?"

"Sounds good. Call first, eh?" Rye answered for him.

Jeff nodded. "Night, lady."

She patted his cheek and headed for the other side of the house as Rye carried him toward his rooms. He'd refused to accept a wheelchair or crutches, so thank God for Rye.

"Good to be home?"

"Uh-huh. I need a shower. My bed."

"Donna did her magic on the flight home and arranged a chair for the shower. A detachable showerhead. So you can sit and keep your leg and hand out of the water."

"Okay." Jeff thought he was going to just collapse, melt.

Rye carried him all the way up and into the bathroom, then sat him on the chair in his shower. Kneeling in front of him, Rye started to undress him.

"I'm going to cry, I think, or maybe throw up."

Rye continued taking off his clothes. "Are you hurting?"

"I don't know." He didn't belong in his own body.

"Okay. You just do what you need to do." Rye kissed his cheek, then stripped his own clothes off too.

Jeff's leg was propped up on the side of the tub, and his hand was wrapped.

"Ready for the water, baby?"

"Uh-huh." Jeff closed his eyes; the water on his nearly bald scalp felt so weird.

Rye slowly moved the showerhead, wetting his entire body but avoiding the casts. The feeling of the water on his skin was almost sexual.

"Can I ask a favor?"

"You know you can ask me anything, baby."

"Can you make me soup tomorrow?"

"I would love to make you a nice bowl of tomato soup."

"I would love that. It would be like being home." The tears came then, exhausted and hurting.

Rye let them fall, washing him with the soap that smelled like they were home, his fingers gentle but firm over all of his body. It was easy, simple, to let Rye touch him, love him for a minute.

Rye rinsed him just as thoroughly, and then the strong fingers worked soap into his scalp, careful not to tug or rub too hard on the shaved parts where they'd put in the stitches. They'd been removed a few days before they'd left the hospital, but his scalp still felt tender.

Still, it was amazing to feel like the hospital was being washed away from him, the scents and sensations of the place being replaced by Rye and home. There were going to be awful scars, terrible. He might even have a limp or lose motor control on his hand. It was possible. Of course, he wasn't sure he cared right then.

149

Rye kept spraying him with water, even after all the soap was gone. "Let me know when you want to come out."

"Now is fine. I just want to take a pain pill and go to sleep." Rye had taken charge of his pain pills. Which was probably a good thing. He might never wake up again otherwise, just get lost in them. It would be so easy.

"Sure—it's been a really long day."

After turning off the tap, Rye grabbed a towel and started drying him.

It occurred to Jeff that he probably should just take care of this on his own, should stop acting like an invalid, but he rested there, passive, quiet.

He let Rye pick him up again and carry him to the bed and then let Rye pass him a pain pill and a glass of water.

"You want me to join you?"

"Always." He needed Rye like breathing.

Rye slipped under the covers with him, carefully bringing him to rest with his head on Rye's chest. He hadn't been able to do more than hold Rye's hand in the hospital, and it felt like forever since he'd been surrounded by the warm, muscled body.

Jeff sighed, stretching and finding his spot, and then he was gone, sleeping hard.

Home.

RYE SLEPT through the night for the first time since they'd been on vacation.

So did Jeff, and he was awake well before Jeff.

It felt so damn good to be home.

So damn good.

Rye's stomach rumbled loudly, and he figured he should go make something for them to eat. Tomato soup because Jeff had asked for it. That was a good thing. He pulled on a pair of jeans and grabbed his phone, noticing a text from Brandon telling him to call. Hopefully the private investigator had some good news for him.

Downstairs, he got the tomatoes roasting and called Brandon.

"Hey, boss. Heard your primary had a hell of a time."

"Yeah. The whole venue went tits up."

"Well, my news isn't better."

"Christ. Well, just spit it out."

Had Jim relapsed? Or worse? Neither option was going to make Jeff feel any better.

"He's dead. He passed a few months ago, drug overdose. A... Donna Heard paid for his funeral expenses."

Son of a bitch.

Why hadn't she told Jeff? She knew he was asking. He bet she thought he would be better off not knowing. Rye didn't know. Maybe he was. He rubbed his face. "Man, that was not what I wanted to hear."

"No. Me either. I'm sorry."

"Yeah. Okay. Thanks for looking into that. Bill me, okay?"

"You got it. Is there anything I can do to help?"

"If anything comes up, I'll call. Take care of yourself, Brandon."

"You got it, man."

The phone went dead, and he stood there a second, eyes closed. Jesus Christ.

"Morning." Donna came from the backyard, book in hand. "Did you sleep okay?"

Rye turned and looked at her for a long moment before nodding. "Best night since we went on tour. You?"

She nodded. "I'm looking forward to getting home for a few days, but LJ's rooms for me are lovely."

"I know Jim is dead." He hadn't meant to confront her with it, but the words just came out.

She stopped, stared at him for a second, then nodded. "He is. They say it was an overdose. That he slipped."

"Jeff's been asking about him for months. Since before the tour started." He tried not to make it an accusation, because what exactly would he be accusing her of? Protecting Jeff?

151

"I know. I.... He believed in Jim. Honestly. Truly. I'm supposed to let him know the man wasn't strong enough? Especially when he was about to be tempted so badly?"

"I'm going to have to tell him." Jeff was going to find out sooner or later, and it would not only be better if it came from him, he wasn't going to let Jeff think he was lying.

"That's a mistake. What good could it possibly do?"

"Because I told him I would find out, and he's going to ask me. You think lying to him is a good thing?" Jeff trusted him. That was important to him. To them.

"Do you think a relapse is better? He died twice. Twice."

"He's stronger than you give him credit for, and the relapse is already on the table. They've been pumping him full of morphine and pain pills." He was worried Jeff wasn't going to be able to kick the pills.

"I just don't know what good it would do. It's over. The man is dead."

"I don't think it would do any good except prove to Jeff that I treat him like an adult, like an equal. That I'm not mollycoddling him." Rye shook his head. He didn't need to explain himself to her. He checked the tomatoes, deciding they were done.

"It's your job, to mollycoddle him, Rye. That's what I pay you for. To protect him."

"So you're saying I should lie to him when he asks me." He didn't think he could do that. Maybe if Jeff had just been another client.

But Jeff wasn't.

"Just say you don't know exactly what happened. I don't know. I was trying to save him some pain. That man was his friend."

Rye put the tomatoes in the pot with some vegetable stock and some garlic, salt, and pepper, turning the burner on to medium-high. Then grabbed the immersion blender. "We're just going to have to disagree on this point."

"That's fine." Donna headed off without another word.

Shaking his head, he put the blender in the pot and turned it on.

152

It only took him ten more minutes to get a couple of smoothies whizzed up and on a tray with both bowls of soup and two toast points each. Toast points. That would always remind him of Jeff and home now.

Grabbing the tray, he then headed upstairs.

Jeff was still sleeping, buried in the covers, so quiet. After setting the tray on the bedside table, Rye stripped off his jeans and climbed back in, pulling the covers far enough down to see Jeff's face.

It was so odd, the buzz-cut hair, the scars. It made Jeff's eyes look huge, though, amazing and dark. This man looked more like the Jeff he'd fallen for than the makeuped, contact-lensed vampire Jeff played as Lord January.

He looked like home.

Lying down, Rye curled up around Jeff, let his eyes close as he breathed Jeff in. He didn't want to tell Jeff about Jim. Hell, the man had had enough bad news.

Would it be lying if he just kept his mouth shut until Jeff asked? He knew it would. He knew there was nothing about any of this that was okay. He was just going to have to bite the bullet and tell him. He'd be there at least, to deal with any and all fallout.

Jeff's eyes slowly opened. "Roach is gone, isn't he?"

Jesus, could Jeff read him that well?

"Not Roach."

"Brandy? But she was getting better."

"No, no. It's Jim." Rye couldn't let Jeff go down his list of friends.

"What? How? What happened?"

He held on to Jeff. "Apparently, he overdosed."

Jeff stared at him, just stared, then curled up in the sheets, hiding himself away.

Rye wrapped back around Jeff. "I'm so sorry, baby. I know how important he was to you."

Jeff didn't answer, didn't say a word.

"I made you soup, baby. And a smoothie. Tomato soup. Strawberry smoothie. Your favorites." He wasn't letting Jeff fade away.

"I'm not hungry."

"You still have to eat."

"No. I'm not hungry. You eat it."

"You can't starve yourself, Jeff. I'm not going to let you slowly die."

Jeff wrapped himself tighter in the covers and hid, just a cocoon. Rye couldn't let that happen. He couldn't let Jeff hide away from life. He slowly unwrapped Jeff from the covers. Jeff fought him, curled into the pillows, good leg drawn up.

"I don't want to hurt you, baby, but I'm not letting you starve yourself." He wound up tossing the bedcovers and the pillows off the bed, leaving Jeff nowhere to hide.

"Leave me alone. Leave me the fuck alone."

"I can't."

"You have to." Jeff looked lost, devastated.

"No, baby. I can't. I love you, and I'm not letting this take you out." He pressed their foreheads together. "You can grieve, but you can't fade away."

Jeff started shaking, swallowing hard, over and over. Rye pulled his lover against him, offering Jeff all of his support. Jeff sobbed for long enough that Rye honestly considered giving him a Valium. They had a tiny prescription, for the trip home.

He kept rubbing Jeff's back, though, making sure his lover had his strength to lean on. To pull from. Finally, Jeff crashed again, breath hitching.

The worst thing was that Rye couldn't do anything to make it better. Like with Jeff's injuries. He hated feeling useless. He hated not being able to do anything while the man he loved hurt.

Damn it.

CHAPTER THIRTEEN

JEFF WASN'T going to wake up, wasn't going to think or eat or anything. He was going to sleep. He was going to sleep until he wasn't tired.

"Rye, I'm going to get him in to see a shrink. This is insane."

God, Donna. Just go home.

"A shrink is just going to prescribe him something, and he doesn't need that. He needs to grieve."

"This isn't reasonable."

"What do you want, Donna?" Rye asked her. "How exactly do you suggest he grieve?"

"Stop it. Go away. Everybody leave me alone."

Rye stood. "Maybe it's time for you to go, Donna."

"*Go away!*" Jeff shrieked. "*Leave me the fuck alone!*" He was going to scream until he died.

"You need to leave, Donna. I'll deal with this." Rye picked him up.

"*No! No!*" He let himself lose it, completely melting down, kicking with one leg, head tossing. Rye let him shout and yell and kick and bang on the solid chest. Sweat poured off him, and he really had to work at it, had to push hard for the energy to fight.

Finally, Jeff was utterly exhausted and couldn't fight another second, and Rye sat. Somehow they were on his bed, Rye cradling him. His throat hurt, his head hurt, and he couldn't breathe.

"It's going to be okay, baby, I promise."

He shook his head. He couldn't do this anymore. He couldn't. Jim had been the strongest guy he knew, the best. How could he do this?

"It is. I know you don't believe me, but it is. Anything you need, we'll get it for you." Rye began to rock him.

He let his eyes close, let himself be cradled, held.

"I've got you," Rye promised him.

"I told you to leave." He held on, though.

"No, you told Donna to leave."

"Okay." He could live with that. His throat was killing him.

"You want some ice cream, baby?"

Jeff nodded, then shook his head, then nodded again.

"That's a yes." Rye picked him up again and headed back downstairs.

He hid his face in the curve of Rye's throat, not so much as an ounce concerned about whether Rye had him.

They went into the kitchen, and Rye set him down onto a stool before gathering the things he needed. A bowl, a spoon, the ice cream out of the freezer.

Jeff's eyes felt gritty, swollen, so sore.

"Let's have this upstairs. Watch a movie."

"Okay." He looked at Rye, and it was so hard to breathe. "I'm sorry."

Rye shook his head. "You're allowed to be angry. You're allowed to be sad. And to scream, to push it all out." Handing him the big bowl of ice cream, Rye then picked him up again.

"Do the casts make me heavy?"

"It's going to take a bit more than two little casts to make you heavy, baby. You're back to all skin and bones, like when I first met you."

"Am I? I'm so tired."

"You are. It started on the tour."

Rye got them upstairs, setting him and his ice cream down on the bed. He nodded, waited for Rye to come to him, touch him. And Rye did, climbing into the bed and taking the bowl of ice cream from him.

Taking a huge amount on the spoon, Rye surprised him by taking that first bite himself. Jeff leaned hard, letting Rye support him, ease all the aches.

Rye's arm slid around him, and a kiss landed on the top of his head. The next spoonful Rye took was about half the size of that first one, and Rye brought it to Jeff's lips.

He took it and swallowed. Oh, it hurt and felt so good, all at once. He'd barely finished swallowing when Rye had another bite at his mouth. He loved how Rye loved to eat. His giant.

"Does it feel good on your throat?" Rye asked, teasing another bite in between his lips.

"Yes. Cold and creamy. Thank you."

"You're very welcome." Rye continued to share the ice cream between them, the cold such a contrast to Rye's warmth along his side.

With the ice cream in him, Jeff felt more present, more real. He wasn't sure if that was good or bad.

"Thank God we're home," murmured Rye. "I hated the smell of that place."

"The hospital?"

"Yeah." Rye hugged him close for a moment.

"I don't know what to do, Rye."

"About what?"

He chuckled softly, shook his head. "Everything."

"Oh, baby." Rye tilted his head and took a kiss, long and soft and easy. "You don't have to do anything about anything right now. You just keep breathing."

"That's it?"

"For now, yeah. You breathe. You eat the food I give you. Tomorrow we'll add something else."

"Tell me you don't hate me."

"I could never hate you. I love you."

"Okay." He had to believe; he didn't have a choice. He was too tired to argue.

"It's true." Rye kissed him again, then slipped another mouthful of ice cream in.

157

Jeff swallowed, the motion easier.

"What kind of movie do you feel like today?"

"Nothing scary."

"No. How about a comedy?"

"Yeah. Yeah, that works."

"Cool." Rye leaned over and grabbed Jeff's laptop, using it to set the movie up on the huge TV on the wall. Then the empty bowl was set aside, his body lined up against Rye's.

Jeff closed his eyes and breathed. In. Out. In. Out.

"I don't want a shrink in here, Rye."

"Then we don't call a shrink, baby."

"Okay."

"You gotta keep trying, though. One day at a time, but something every day."

"Trying?"

"To stay alive, to be one of the living."

He sighed. "I'm just tired."

"I know. But eating and starting to exercise again will help with that. I've got special plastic covers for your casts now, so we can go swimming."

"I don't know. I'm just wanting to sleep."

"We're watching a movie. No sleeping. There will be a quiz when it's over."

Jeff snorted, but it made him smile.

"I mean it." Rye was smiling too, though.

"Hush. Sleeping."

"Nope. Not 'til after the quiz after the movie."

Jeff shook his head. Nonsense. He wasn't having a quiz.

"Yeah. Lucky for you, though, you've got an in with the proctor."

He didn't want to laugh. He didn't want to be happy.

"Hey. You think Jim would have wanted you to stop living because he died?"

"I didn't think Jim would fuck up."

"He was only human, baby."

Jeff nodded. And Jim was better than him, stronger.

"You know you don't have to fuck up just because Jim did."

He would, though. It was inevitable.

"Come on, enjoy the movie."

"Yeah." He rested against Rye's chest. He was going to fuck this up, and he didn't even know what *this* was.

Rye kissed the top of his head, fingers sliding along Jeff's arm.

What was he going to do?

"ARE YOU ready to go, baby? The car is here."

Jeff shook his head, like the man had a choice. The casts needed to come off.

"No? You're showered, you're dressed—"

"Can't you take them off?"

"I'm a lot of things, baby, but a medical professional, I'm not. The car is right outside, let's go."

Jeff sighed, but they managed. Donna had gone home finally, and now they needed the next step to normal.

They'd managed a little bit of swimming, but without the casts, it would be so much easier. Also therapeutic, but Rye would be focusing on how much Jeff liked it. He needed his lover to wake up.

Rye led Jeff out to the car, and they settled in the back. He'd gotten used to sitting in the back with Jeff instead of doing the driving himself like he had coming back from that first outing. That felt like so long ago.

The photogs out front were starting to fade away, finally.

Jeff was quiet for the entire drive to the doctor and kept his head down as Rye escorted him up the elevator and into the waiting room.

They were shown into an exam room right away, the nurse promising them it wouldn't be long.

Rye paced around the little room, just getting a feel for it, before he sat. "You looking forward to getting them off?"

"I guess? They're heavy and hot."

"We'll be able to really start swimming once they're off. And you'll be able to get back into playing guitar."

"Yeah." Jeff was so still, like he was afraid to move, to think. He probably was. Rye would be happier with tears, with yelling. With proof of life. This stillness was, quite frankly, a little eerie.

The visit to the doctor was surprisingly uneventful, even if the one super-hairy emaciated leg was wickedly gross and, oh my God, stinky.

They had the number of a physical therapist to call and instructions to come back and check in again in three months, and that was that.

The doctor left, hurrying to his next patient, and Rye looked at Jeff. "Well... you ready to go home and take a real shower?"

"Uh-huh. I stink." Jeff stood up, steadying himself with his cane.

"It feel better, though?" Rye figured it had to.

"My hand feels just fine. My leg feels light."

"We'll get you working in the pool, see what other exercises the PT suggests."

"More doctors. I think I'll do okay on my own." His Jeff could be so stubborn.

"Physical therapists are not doctors. We can probably bring them to the house, meet them in the pool room, so they don't even need to see the rest of the house." They headed to the elevator, keeping it slow for Jeff.

Jeff got into the car, and Rye opened the sunroof. It was a beautiful day, and God knew that Jeff needed some vitamin D in the worst way.

"You want me to tell the driver to stop anywhere on the way home?"

"No. I'm tired."

"We could grab sundaes from the Dairy Queen on the way home. Strawberry sauce on 'em—"

"You're trying to fatten me up." That wasn't a no.

"Yep. Can't have you for dinner if you're all skin and bones."

160

Rye leaned forward and tapped Bobby's shoulder. "Take us through the Dairy Queen drive-thru on Waterloo, please." The press wasn't hounding them nearly as much now that the tour had been cancelled.

"Yes, sir."

Jeff yawned and curled into the seat, eyelids heavy. The lean face was turned up toward the sun, though, basking it in. There was no reason for Jeff not to get a tan now. No reason at all for Jeff to hold on to any of the trappings of Lord January. Rye ran his hand over the buzz cut, touching gently.

"I kind of like it, you know? It's coming in silver where the scars are."

He hadn't thought that Jeff had even noticed, to be honest. "It's unique, isn't it?"

"It's different." Jeff shrugged. "I like how it feels too."

"Good. That's good. I do too."

They pulled up into the drive-thru, and he told Bobby what they wanted, told the man to get something for himself as well, and passed over a twenty.

"Do you think I should put my piercings back in?"

"Do you want to put them back in?" He'd liked the piercings. They were something that had been for Jeff himself. Something real.

"Yeah. I miss them." Okay. Okay, two things that Jeff had an opinion about today. That was maybe a record.

"Then let's put them back in. I liked them too. I liked the way they felt when I touched you."

"Yeah?" That was a tentative look, a smile.

"Oh yeah. Even thinking about touching them—touching you like that again—gets me revved up a little." He'd been avoiding thinking like that while Jeff was recovering. The casts were off now, though.

"Perv."

Oh. Oh, was that a tease? Grinning, Rye's smile was wider and more natural than he could remember feeling in a long time. "Maybe."

The sundaes came back, and Jeff took a bite. That was all he took, but it was a bite.

Rye ate about a quarter of his own before he started cajoling Jeff to eat some more.

"I'm eating it."

"You're staring at it."

Jeff frowned. "Hush."

"You can hush me all you want, baby. You know it's not going to work." Was that a smile? He thought it was. "You looking forward to getting into the pool?"

"Yeah, yeah, I am. It was yucky with the bags and the casts."

"I know. It'll be fun again now. As will showers." Anything to do with water had involved a lot of work. Now they could be spontaneous. "Now," Rye added, "eat your ice cream."

"I had a bite."

"It's ice cream—you're supposed to devour it."

"Uh-huh." He ate another bite.

"Ice cream with strawberry sauce. Strawberry. I happen to know that's your favorite." He offered Jeff a spoonful of his own with caramel sauce.

Jeff wrinkled his nose, shook his head. "I don't like that."

"Then eat yours, baby."

Jeff managed a few more bites before they got home, and then he slid out of the car, juggling cane and ice cream.

Rye took the ice cream. "Careful. Last thing we want is to have to turn around and go to the hospital."

"Don't say that. I couldn't bear it."

He pulled Jeff to him and hugged him. "It's okay. You're fine."

"No, I'm not. I'm never going to be fine again." The words were low, surprising him.

"What are you talking about?" He put his arm around Jeff's shoulders, leading him carefully in.

"Nothing."

Right. Jeff really needed to wake himself up. "You need a shower. You can tell me what's going on in your head there." Rye went straight for the stairs and the bedroom.

Jeff took the stairs slowly, but on his own power.

"You made it all the way up on your own, that's pretty impressive."

"Yeah. Yeah, the muscles are weak."

"We'll build them back up again. The swimming is going to be amazing for that." He turned on the shower and started stripping.

Jeff stripped down too and then slipped into the water and started soaping up. Rye didn't take over the cleaning; it was a good sign that Jeff was taking the initiative. Jeff soaped himself up, leaning against the tile. Once Jeff was clean, Rye tugged him close, holding on.

"Hey." Jeff leaned right in, resting against him, loving on him.

"Hey." He tilted Jeff's head, kissing him.

His lover kissed him back. It wasn't erotic, just sweet. Steady.

Leaning their foreheads together when they were done, he looked into Jeff's eyes. "What's going on in that head of yours?"

"Nothing."

"Nonsense." Jeff hadn't thought of nothing in all the time Rye had known him. "Talk to me, Jeff."

"I'm just—"

"If you say tired, I'm going to holler." He raised a brow, waiting for Jeff to finish his sentence some way other than "tired."

"Sleepy?"

Butthead. "I'm going to spank you."

"You are not. Be nice."

"Some people think spankings are very nice."

"No one thinks they're nice. People think they're hot or kinky or whatever. Not nice."

"Some people are so kinky a spanking is nice."

Jeff chuckled, shook his head. "Come on, I want to sit down."

"Will you talk to me if we do?"

"Talk to you about what?"

Rye rolled his eyes. "About what? About what you're thinking."

"I'm thinking that you always think I'm thinking!"

"You're deflecting now." He dried Jeff off, enjoying the simple, familiar act.

"Am not."

"Yes, you are. I'm serious, baby. I want to know what's going on in your head."

"Nothing. Nothing is going on. I'm scared and tired and worried, and I don't know what to do next." Oh yeah, nothing was going on.

"I believe that you're scared and tired, but that's not nothing at all. That's something we can talk about."

"Okay. Okay, fine, but I need to sit down."

"You want to go downstairs and sit in the sun?" He led Jeff out of the bathroom.

"No. I'll sit in the bed."

"So you can go to sleep?"

"Eventually, yeah."

"We're talking first." Rye stacked the pillows against the headboard so they had somewhere comfy to sit.

Jeff wrapped up in the blankets, holding on to the edge.

Tugging Jeff into his arms, Rye held him close. "So at the risk of sounding like a broken record... talk to me."

"What do you want to talk about? I'm tired, I'm always tired."

"There's got to be more going on in that head of yours than 'I'm tired.'"

"Does there? I don't think so. It's all I can think about. I feel empty."

"Then maybe we need to fill you up."

"I don't think we can. I mean. I don't want to feel anything, not right now."

"Too bad." Jeff had been wallowing for long enough.

"What?"

"What, what? You're fading away, and I'm not going to let you just disappear into thin air."

"You don't get to choose that."

"I'm not letting you choose it."

"Just…. Just stop. Hush. For me."

"I can't, baby, you're too important to me."

Jeff smiled, but the expression still seemed sad.

"Tell me one good thing in your life right now," Rye suggested.

"You."

He smiled and leaned in, taking a kiss. Okay, that was an exceptional answer. "You win this round, Jeff Smart."

"I win all the rounds, you goofy man."

"Yeah, let's make sure you do."

Jeff curled up in his lap. "Do you ever want to go away?"

"I'd love to go away with you. Our trip to Iceland was amazing."

"We could go to the mountains…."

"Sure. Which ones?" He was easy: he wanted to be with Jeff, and he wanted Jeff to be happy.

"I don't know. Ones where we can stay for a while. With snow. Somewhere new. Quiet."

"I'll start looking into it, see what I can find. How long do you want to stay?"

"Can we stay all winter?" Jeff asked tentatively. He'd been horrified at first that the tour had been cancelled, but when Donna had explained they couldn't continue because of Roach, it seemed to have eased his burden, like it wasn't all on his shoulders right then.

"We can stay as long as you want. We'll find a place to rent." If they liked it, maybe they could live there permanently, sell this monstrous place.

"Okay." That was the first time Jeff had seemed interested in anything in days.

"Do you know how to ski?" Rye had been a couple of times and managed not to break anything. Jeff obviously couldn't go right away, but his leg would heal.

"No. I don't go outside."

"You didn't used to. You're going to start now."

"Maybe. I don't like the sun."

"You never have, or just since assuming the January role?"

Jeff shrugged and pulled the blankets around him tighter.

"Besides, when you're skiing, there's often no sun, and even if there is, you're bundled up pretty much from head to toe." He kissed Jeff's neck. "I'm not letting you fade away. I'm not." It was a promise.

"I just want to rest. I'm tired."

"You can for now. Tomorrow we'll talk about stuff some more, and you can have more to eat. One day at a time, isn't that how it goes?" He could look into a place in the mountains to rent once Jeff was asleep, get in touch with the PT.

"Yeah. One day." Jeff cocooned himself in, closed his eyes.

Rye pressed a kiss on Jeff's lips. "I love you, baby." And that was why he was going to keep pushing.

"Love you. Really."

"I know. But I like hearing it."

That earned him a smile. "Yeah. Yeah, me too."

"Then I'll have to just keep telling you."

"Okay. I can live with that."

"That's what I like to hear." Rye pulled Jeff against his body, holding on. The mountains, huh? He couldn't wait.

RYE WAS sleeping when Jeff woke up, and he found himself wandering, heading downstairs to the huge kitchen, to the room with the pool.

It was dark and quiet, and he slid into the water, letting it buoy him.

It felt good, being weightless, and without the current on, the water simply lapped gently at the edges.

He floated, eyes closed, face lax. He could just rest here forever with the water kissing his skin.

"What are you doing?" Rye sounded angry.

Jeff's eyes popped open. "Swimming?"

"By yourself! What if you got a cramp or something?" As naked as he was, Rye climbed into the pool with him.

"You taught me how to float." He backed away, just a little unnerved.

"I know, but I'm supposed to be with you here. Swimming alone is dangerous." Rye took a few breaths. "God, you scared me."

"I'm okay. I was just restless."

"You could have woken me."

"I'm not that big of an asshole."

"I would rather you wake me than go swimming by yourself."

"Are we fighting?"

"I don't know. Are you going to fight me on this?"

"Sort of. I'm a grown up. I wasn't being dangerous."

"Being in the water on your own is dangerous. I can't swim without you here too—this isn't one-sided."

"Oh." Well, that was, like, logical and shit. "Okay."

Rye chuckled. "Did you want us to have a big fight? I'm sure we can find something to argue about—"

"Shut up." He went back to floating.

Chuckling, Rye floated next to him. "I found a great place in Colorado in the mountains. It's available starting next month."

"What does it look like?" He wanted the right place.

"It looks like a chalet. All wood and big windows. It has an amazing view, a fireplace, a hot tub...."

He liked the idea of a fireplace, of a place to soak.

"There's a town nearby with all the amenities, so we can shop and ski or snowboard, stuff like that." Rye bumped him gently in the water. "I'll show you after we've eaten. There were a couple others as well, but this one was the best."

"It's the middle of the night. Are you hungry?"

"I could eat—you've got to be starving, though, because you haven't had anything since that ice cream."

"Not really. I think I've forgotten how to be hungry."

"That wouldn't surprise me. Gonna feed you anyway. Some soup, some crackers."

"Your soup?" None other was right.

"Of course."

"Okay. Okay, I could have that."

"Maybe some of that nice artisanal cheese melted on that yummy bread." Rye was always trying to feed him.

"I could try it, maybe."

"That would make me happy, baby."

Jeff floated for a few more minutes, then his stomach growled.

"Oh-ho. Someone is hungry."

"Maybe a little, yeah."

Smiling wide, Rye stood and held his head, mouth coming down on his. Jeff wanted this, wanted to enjoy it, experience it. "Mmm. Feels like forever since we've really done this." Rye moved him to the edge of the pool, pressing against him as the kisses continued.

"Uh-huh." He moaned, tongue slipping out to touch Rye's, caress it.

Rye pressed even closer, body hot, even in the cool water. Jeff wrapped his legs around Rye, and his cock rubbed on Rye's ripped belly. Rye's cock slid along his ass, hot and big.

"I.... Do you want, do you think?" Jeff asked.

"Oh, I don't have to think about it—I want you."

The words drew a grin. "Yeah?"

"Yes, baby. This should be proof." Rye rubbed against his ass.

He actually chuckled, hips rolling, rocking on Rye.

Rye deepened the kiss. "Want you."

"Yours." That was easy.

"Good." Rye lifted him out of the water.

He giggled for Rye. "Where are we going?"

"Somewhere we can make love. Water and lube don't make the best bedfellows."

"No?" His legs dangled a little as Rye lifted him.

"Nope."

Rye carried him to the kitchen, setting him on a tea towel on the counter.

"Rye?" He was going to make soup first?

"Yeah, baby?"

"This is the kitchen."

"Are you saying we can't make love in the kitchen?" Rye grabbed an apron and wrapped it around his waist.

"I haven't ever before."

"Then it's about time we did, huh?" Rye chuckled, the sound husky. "You want olive oil or corn oil for lube?"

"What?" Oh, he didn't know about that.

"Yeah, and we can use Saran Wrap for a condom." The corners of Rye's mouth twitched.

"Okay, you're fired."

"No? Glad would be better?"

Jeff started laughing, deep, hard sounds that felt weird and unnatural. Rye looked pleased as fuck, though. "Thank you, thank you very much," Rye said in a cheesy attempt at Elvis.

He grabbed for Rye, took a kiss. "Can we have soup and then go upstairs and make love?"

"I was planning the other way around—but your idea is better."

"I'm...." Hungry. He sort of really was. "I could have some soup."

"Excellent." Rye started working, putting the tomatoes on to roast, then cutting the bread thin, topping it with cheese, and putting that in the toaster oven. In two minutes he had a plate of bread with melted cheese and a glass of milk.

"You can start with that while we wait for the soup to be ready."

"You'll have some too, right?" He chose one, nibbling the corner of the cheese. Oh. Oh wow.

"I will." Rye grabbed a piece up and finished it in two bites. "Damn, that cheese is nice."

"Uh-huh." It was almost nutty. He liked that.

Rye kept coming back and grabbing bites of the melted cheese as he put together the soup.

Jeff had eaten one and a half of them when Rye was done with the soup, putting the bowls on a tray along with their refilled glasses of milk.

"Okay, let's go eat."

"Smells good." Jeff grabbed the plate with the remaining toast. They made their way upstairs and settled in the chairs by the little table instead of the bed. Rye lounged in his chair, unselfconscious about his nudity.

Jeff stood for a second, then put the plate down. "Can I sit in your lap?"

"Please." Rye patted his thighs.

"Cool." It was where he was warm and comfortable. The soup tasted amazing, and he drank deep, the heat filling his stomach.

Rye ate more slowly, watching him more than anything, a small smile on his lips.

Jeff relaxed back, humming over the sips.

Rye slid a hand along his skin, the touches gentle, just there.

"The soup is yummy." He'd finished the whole thing.

"If we ever need the money, I could bottle it." Rye put his bowl down and slid that hand up to Jeff's head, tugging him in for a kiss.

He opened, the kiss lazy, happy, and tinged with cream.

Shifting him, Rye got him seated with Jeff's legs straddling Rye's solid lap, their cocks squishing up together. Jeff was warm and happy for the first time in forever, it seemed. The kisses got deeper, Rye's cock hard against his now as everything ramped up.

His body responded, filling, feeling good. He reached between them and took them both in his hands.

"Mmm. Love your touch. So do." Rye spoke the words softly.

Jeff nodded, their noses rubbing together, sliding together as his hand kept working.

"I don't want to come like this," Rye told him. "I want to come inside you."

"Oh…." He rubbed their cheeks together.

"We do it like this, and you can ride me."

"Good exercise for my leg."

"Yep. Because we need the excuse." Rye was all smiles.

He chuckled again. "Multitasking."

"Mmm. This is the kind of multitasking I can get behind."

"Rye, you're not behind. Right this second, you're the cock in front."

Rye chuckled for him. "I'll be in your behind in a moment."

"I want that. I want to stretch."

"I will stretch you, I promise." Rye gave him a kiss. "We should get a couple plugs. Stretch you even when I'm not inside you."

"I… I used to…. That was a long time ago."

"Used to what, baby?" Rye rocked them together.

"Nothing. Touch me."

"Hate it when you censor yourself with me—you can tell me anything. Anything." Rye bit at Jeff's lower lip, fingers playing at his hole.

"I just used to… play and fuck myself, before the speed."

"Mmm. Now there's a sexy thought. We could visit the sex shop when we're out getting your piercings back."

"I'm not sexy anymore."

"Bullshit." Rye met his gaze head-on. "Those people who thought January was sex on legs might not think you are, but your lover—me—I think you're very sexy."

Jeff's cheeks lit on fire, and he ducked his head.

"It's true, and I want to do so many things to you."

"I just…. It's an old me."

"Being sexy is an old you?" Rye shook his head. "It's also a part of the new you. The you who has a lover. The you who is starting a new life right here, right now."

"Why are we talking?" Right here, right now. He liked that.

"Because the lube and condoms are over by the bed, and we're over here."

"Oh. Right. We have to move."

"We do." Rye picked him up. "We should get tested."

"You trust me?"

"I do. Do you trust me?"

"With my soul."

"Cool. Then we should get tested, so we can go bareback."

Everything with Rye was so easy, so straightforward. "Okay."

"We should have had the doctor take our blood while we were there."

"I wasn't ready. I was being unhappy."

"I'm glad you're ready now." Rye laid him down on the bed and grabbed the lube and condoms out of the drawer and put them down beside him.

"I can't guarantee I won't be sad again tomorrow."

"I can promise you that if you are, I'll let you be sad but will also try to make you happy." He picked up a condom and tore it open. "You ready to ride me, baby?"

"I am." Jeff reached over and rolled the rubber down Rye's fat cock.

"Pass me the lube. I'll slick you up."

The words were so easy, yet so erotic, and he handed Rye the lube. Rye tugged him so he was straddling the lovely abs, two of Rye's fingers sliding along his crack. He pressed back, took the touch in. Rye pushed his fingers deep, hitting Jeff's gland.

"Mmm…." He liked that. A lot.

Rye pushed against it again, then again.

"Good. Good, there. So good."

"We get a dildo, we can play with your gland for hours."

"Oh damn." He wasn't sure he was ready to need sex. To need Rye. Rye pushed against his gland again, then slid another finger into him, stretching them wide. He went up, kneeling tall. "Fuck."

Rye slid his free hand up along his belly, his chest.

"I'm scared of feeling so much."

"I won't hurt you."

"I know. I'm afraid I'll hurt me."

"You have to chance it."

"Please, don't stop."

"Only so you can ride me."

Jeff nodded and kept moving, riding.

Rye hit his gland a few more times before tugging his fingers away. "On me, now, Jeff."

"Uh-huh. Love that you call me Jeff."

"It's who you are."

Yeah. Yeah, it was. At least for now.

Rye got a hold of Jeff's hips and moved him into position as he held the thick cock. They moved together and the thick head slowly breached his hole. He groaned, his head thrown back, throat working.

"Fucking sexy lover." Rye's words were like a touch.

"Need you." He pulled up, sank down, just rode. Rye bucked up, pushed in deeper. *Oh, more*, Jeff thought. *Deeper, harder.*

Rye was on the same page, working with him to make it good. Jeff slammed down, riding hard, rocking a bit on every down stroke. Rye tweaked his right nipple, pinching hard. Oh. Jeff sucked in a deep breath, dizzy with it.

Pushing up hard, Rye twisted the other one. Jeff didn't even argue; he arched and leaned back into the pinch. Rye did it again, the sensations sharp and amazing. Jeff's body went tight, and he arched again, pushing into the touches.

Rye's thrusts became stronger, banging against his gland. Jeff's hands dropped onto Rye's chest, fingers curling in.

"Oh God. Love you." Rye bucked up against him.

"Love. Love." It was a song, and he started humming. Rye murmured, like a harmony. Jeff nodded, moving faster, the rhythm speeding. Rye's face was a study of pleasure, the blue eyes full of need. "Soon." He wanted.

Rye's hand dropped to Jeff's cock, tugging on it. "Okay, baby. Come on."

173

"Come on." He nodded. Oh please. Yes.

Squeezing his cockhead, Rye rubbed a thumb across Jeff's slit. Oh.

He shot hard, his body clenching against the pleasure.

"Fuck!" Rye bucked up into him a few more times before freezing. He held himself up, arms shaking, trembling. Rye shuddered through his orgasm, then let go of Jeff's cock, hands sliding up his back to his shoulders, and tugging him down.

Jeff slumped down, breathing hard, panting.

Rye stroked his spine, humming. "So good, baby. I love being inside you."

"Feels so good."

"You do." Rye kissed him gently before pulling out and dealing with the condom.

Jeff found himself dozing, and as soon as Rye came back to bed, he cuddled in, arranging himself so that he was comfortable.

"Movie?" Rye asked softly, pulling the covers up over them.

"Uh-huh. Sure." Dawn was coming, and he was full and warm, happy and well-fucked.

"I'm putting on the *Matrix*." They'd seen it a hundred times together, and it was funny how that made it better.

"Sounds good. Love you."

"Love you too, babe." Rye kissed the top of Jeff's head and cued up the movie, and Jeff was soon dozing lazily.

CHAPTER FOURTEEN

THEY STOPPED in Telluride to pick up groceries, then continued following the GPS to the rental outside of town.

It was fucking stunning—even better than the pictures—and Rye whistled as he pulled the car up the drive and killed the engine. "What do you think, babe?"

"Oh my God."

Jeff stepped out, eyes huge. He'd kept his hair clipped close to the scalp, which made those eyes look big as saucers.

Rye grinned happily. Yeah, the place was amazing and well worth an exclamation or two. Two stories, stone facing, a ton of windows, and a 360-degree view of the mountains.

"If you get bored of the view from the front, you can just move to a back room."

"Uh-huh."

Someone was speechless. He handed Jeff a couple of the grocery bags, grabbed the rest and their bags of stuff, and headed in. "Come on, babe." They'd picked up the key from the agent in Telluride. There would be no place to hide from the sun there—nothing but vitamin D and healing and life. Not only that, but there was a piano and Jeff had his guitar with him.

They were going to make love and make music and be. There were no cameras, no press, nothing to hide from. No fans, no worries. Just him and Jeff. He wanted Jeff to heal, to flourish. He was pretty sure that could happen there.

Jeff put his guitar down, then headed to the kitchen, dropped those bags off, and started exploring. It felt good, to see him excited. Rye put down the bags he was carrying and followed Jeff slowly, watching him explore.

There was a huge TV in the media room, a pool table, and then he headed up to the master bedroom. The master was stunning, with huge windows affording an amazing view. Jeff had a peaceful smile on his face, and he went to the window, then gasped.

"Hot tub? Outside?"

Rye stepped up behind Jeff, slid his arms around his lover. "Nice, huh?"

"It's amazing. Completely amazing." Jeff turned and offered his lips.

Rye took them, the kiss slowly becoming hot. Jeff tugged Rye's coat open, pushed it off his shoulders, and Rye blinked. Look at that, his lover, taking charge. He hadn't been sure it would ever happen, but this was a huge step forward in their relationship and, even more, in Jeff's recovery.

It hit the floor with a thud, and Rye grinned. "You want something?"

"Thought you'd be warm."

"You must be too, then." He returned the favor, pushing Jeff's jacket off.

"It's a good house. You did a good job."

"Thank you, baby. I thought you'd like it." It was why he'd taken it.

His shirt was opened at the neck, and then Jeff's lips brushed his skin there. Rye tilted his head back, letting Jeff have him. The love echoed through the caresses. Jeff's fingers touched his skin as Jeff undid his buttons. He stayed still, letting Jeff touch him, want him.

"Love your touch."

"I want you."

"I'm right here. I'm yours."

"I know."

His shirt was eased open, and Jeff sucked gently against his nipple. Wrapping his hand around Jeff's head, he kept him there for a moment. He could feel Jeff blinking slowly, eyelashes tickling him.

"Feels good." His voice had gone raspy from pleasure.

"Mmmhmm. Tastes good."

Rye slid his hands down Jeff's back, wrapping around the sweet ass and holding their bodies together as the breath began to pant out of him. God, he wanted. It felt like it had in Iceland: like they were free.

Jeff's fingers slid across his abs, and he tightened his muscles, making them dance for his lover. The soft moan slid across his nipple, tickling him.

That had him moaning, and he tightened his hold on Jeff's ass, pulling him in closer. His cock, hard in his jeans, pushed against Jeff's belly.

"Look at you, all raring to go." Jeff pressed one hand to his cock, stroking him.

"You're inspiring." Sexy as all get out, and all his. Only a crazy man wouldn't be hard.

"Can we try the bed out?"

"Yeah. We need to make sure it'll stand up to vigorous action."

"And hours of napping."

Uh-huh, except not. There was going to be loving, happiness, playing in the snow. Rye backed up toward the bed, taking Jeff's hands and encouraging him to work open Rye's jeans. Together, they stripped off clothes, all the layers that kept them from each other.

Then he rolled them down to lie side by side, giving them both easy access to all that skin. His fingers automatically traced the tiny scars on Jeff's back from memory. Jeff grinned for him and hummed softly.

"Happy?"

"Yeah. It's a neat house."

"Uh-huh." He nibbled on Jeff's lower lip.

Jeff pushed into his embrace, then kissed him, fucked his lips.

"Want you." Like Jeff wouldn't have figured it out already with the way his cock was pushing against Jeff's skin.

"Oh, good." There was a little snicker, a tease, and then Jeff rolled against him.

Rye rubbed and brought one hand up between them so he could pinch Jeff's nipples.

"Be nice."

Oh, now he knew this was nice. "I'm being very nice." He pinched again. "These should be pierced. When you get the other ones put back in."

Jeff shook his head, but grinned.

"Oh yeah. Then I could attach the nipple rings to the cock ring. Pretty gold chains—"

"Hush, you. I'm not kinky. I'm boring now."

"You could be kinky. I bet you'd thrive on kinky."

"Hush." Jeff kissed him hard, effectively shutting him up.

He let Jeff get away with it—after all, the subject would come back up, he was sure. Rye was looking forward to it, in fact.

His tongue played with Jeff's, his fingers lingering on those sweet nips, tugging and twisting them. Jeff moaned, panting into his kisses. Oh yeah, his baby liked it a little on the kinky side. Probably a lot on the kinky side.

That reminded him about Jeff's little tease, about before. He'd have to get Jeff to talk. Later. Much later.

Pushing forward with his hips, Rye rubbed their cocks together. God, he was loving this new Jeff, loving the way his lover was blossoming. He was going to fight with everything in his arsenal to keep this freedom for Jeff. He knew there were options, knew Donna was looking out for Jeff's best interests.

He wrapped his hand around Jeff's shorn head, tilted to deepen the kiss. Rolling them, he put Jeff beneath him, rolled their hips together.

Jeff brushed his fingers against the tip of Rye's cock.

"Oh fuck." A jolt of pleasure shot through him. When his lover did it again, his toes curled. "Oh God, baby. Don't tease. Please."

"Am I teasing? I'm not."

"Then I need more."

Jeff's fingers twined around the tip of his prick, twisting and squeezing. Rye humped, trying to push more of his cock into Jeff's hand. When his lover swooped down and sucked him in, he roared.

God, yes. Yes, please.

Rye tried not to thrust, but it was too damn good and his hips let loose. Jeff took him, wrapped those lips around the base of his cock, pulling all the way. "Jeff. Jeff. Baby. Oh God."

Jeff nudged his balls, rolled them.

Rye slid his cock along Jeff's tongue. The suction was fierce, keeping Rye in. "Feels so good, babe. Gonna make me come."

Jeff's answer was a long, low moan. It vibrated around his cock, making him jerk, making his balls draw up tight.

"Gonna make me come," he warned Jeff. All that earned him was harder suction. "Fuck!" He bucked, hips humping into Jeff's mouth. His entire body clenched, balls tight and hard. "Gonna!" It was all the warning he got out before he shot, pouring himself into Jeff's mouth.

Oh fuck. Fuck. He braced himself, tried to remember how to breathe through the pleasure. Wave after wave of pleasure moved through him, and when it was done, he lay bonelessly on the bed, breathing hard. Jeff's head rested on his belly, the short hairs tickling him.

He stroked Jeff's head, fingers rubbing. "Mmm. Thank you, baby."

Jeff nodded, rubbed his cheek against Rye's skin. "Was good."

"You might need to give me a minute to reciprocate." He wasn't sure his limbs were working yet.

"After a nap, Rye. I'm sleepy."

He chuckled. "So am I." He needed to get them under the blankets, in the warmth, but he was so sleepy. He grabbed the edge of the comforter and dragged it half over them. Good enough.

Petting Jeff's head, he murmured, "Love you," before drifting off.

JEFF SLEPT for hours, then woke up cold. He left Rye wrapped in the covers and found his clothes, headed downstairs to see if he could figure out the fireplace.

This place really was amazing, and he could hardly believe he and Rye were there, totally on their own.

The fireplace was natural gas and came with instructions, so he managed, curling up with a blanket.

He must have dozed off because the next thing he knew, there was a soft touch tickling his cheek and the smell of chocolate.

"Rye?" He snuggled in, smiled. "I turned the fire on."

"Yeah, it's cozy down here. I made hot chocolate. With mini marshmallows." Rye handed him the cup. Jeff stood and offered to let Rye sit. There was room for them both. After sitting, Rye tugged him down onto his lover's lap.

He settled in, sipping his cocoa. "Is it morning?" Life was so random these days.

"No, it's, like, nine o'clock. Now that we're settled here, we should try to get a schedule back. You do well with schedules."

He nodded. It was weird, living with nothing to anchor him. That was what Rye did, helped him be real.

"Did you see the pool yet?"

"No. I came down, started the fire, and fell right back to sleep."

Chuckling, Rye nuzzled his cheek. "It's just like the one back home. So we can swim."

"Oh yeah? I love swimming."

"I know." Rye pointed to his hot chocolate. "I also know you love those silly little marshmallows."

"I do. I know they're goofy, but they make me happy."

"And that makes me happy."

"It's good." Jeff hummed and sipped, the liquid heating him.

"Yeah." Rye leaned in and licked his lower lip. "It's really good."

"Is it going to snow again?" He'd never lived anywhere with snow.

"It'll snow a lot while we're here. I meant it about teaching you to ski. And snowboard and making snowmen and shit." Rye grinned and pressed closer. "Of course, we'll be snowed in a lot."

"We'll have enough food for you?"

"Oh, we'll keep an eye on the weather, make sure we go in and get supplies before we get snowed in."

"Okay. I trust you." He wasn't worried. He couldn't use if he was trapped in the snow.

"I know you do." Rye rubbed against him, taking the hot chocolate from his fingers and setting it on the coffee table. "I have your best interests at heart."

Jeff knew that. He believed it.

"There's a place in Denver I trust to get your piercings done." Rye tweaked one of his nipples. "We'll get these done at the same time."

"We will? I...." He'd loved getting the first piercings. Loved it.

"Something new for us."

He pondered the idea of new rings and caught himself humming.

Rye smiled, traced Jeff's lips with one finger. "You like the idea."

"I liked the rings. I used to like them, I mean."

"You keep trying to make like you aren't kinky anymore, and I have to admit, I'm not entirely buying it."

"I'm not." He didn't want to talk about it.

Rye shook his head. "Liar."

He shrugged. Maybe he was kinky. Maybe he wasn't.

"Are you worried about my reaction if you admit it?"

"That was another life. Hell, that was a lot of lives ago. That person isn't alive anymore."

"No, but you are. And it's safe to want things, baby."

"I think I'm just going to be boring right now."

"As long as you're not sleeping your life away."

He didn't answer. He hadn't decided yet.

Rye bit at Jeff's right nipple, teeth sharp.

"Hey!" He jerked, almost losing his seat.

Lapping and sucking, Rye soothed the hurt. Jeff's nipple ached, burned a little. Then Rye blew, the wet making his nipple cold. Jeff shivered, his skin seeming to tighten up. Lord, Rye made him feel things.

"I never got to reciprocate earlier." Rye moved to his other nipple, licking it with long drags of his tongue.

"I was sleepy."

Sucking in his nipple, Rye tugged on it.

Jeff arched, eyelids going heavy, but he wasn't sleepy now. Rye's teeth threatened, and then bit, but not as sharply as they had his other nipple. Or maybe he'd just been waiting for it this time. It still felt like electricity shot through him.

Humming, Rye increased the sensation. Jeff swore his nipples and cock were attached when Rye did that. His lips opened, and he panted. The burn was crazy, perfect.

Rye looked up, eyes meeting his, full of heat and need. He held the gaze, breath coming faster, heart rate speeding. Rye very deliberately leaned in, teeth wrapping around his nipple and then pressing into his flesh in another bite.

"Oh sweet fuck." He was going to come.

The bite turned back into suction, rougher this time, and each pull of Rye's mouth landed right in his balls. He wanted to jack himself off, but on the other hand, he didn't. Kissing his skin, Rye slowly moved down his chest toward his belly.

"No. No, please. Don't stop."

"I'm not stopping, baby."

"No. No, Rye. My nipples. Please."

Rye smiled and kissed his way back up to the right nipple, beginning to gnaw on it. Jeff arched and started rubbing, rocking against Rye.

"Definitely getting you nipple rings."

"Don't stop."

Rye licked. Twice. "Gonna tug and twist them."

"Rye!" He was going to scream.

Rye bit at just the tip. Jeff shot so hard his balls hurt, the world spun.

"Just from your nips. Oh, baby. So hot."

He nodded, head bobbing lazily on his shoulders. Rye shifted away and then came back with some Kleenex and wiped him clean. Jeff snuggled in, humming as he breathed against Rye's skin.

"That was sexy, baby. You are sexy." Rye's fingers slid on his skin, stroking idly.

"Can we have something to eat? Maybe some cheese?"

"Hungry. I like that. You want a cheese sandwich or cheese and crackers? Some hummus?"

"Cheese and crackers. Are there grapes?"

"Uh-huh." Rye stood, stretched.

Jeff grabbed the mugs and followed along, knees trembling. Rye nuzzled him, then sat him at the kitchen table, the chairs more comfortable than they looked. He curled into the chair and pulled his legs up under his chin. Rye put together a tray: cheese and crackers, grapes and strawberries.

"You're good at that. You could be a caterer." A giant bodyguard caterer.

Chuckling, Rye began putting together a pair of smoothies. "Me? A caterer? I'm only interested in feeding you."

"You could. You make plates nice."

"I don't think I'd enjoy having to make a lot of them, though."

"No?" Jeff couldn't help but wonder what he was going to do. Would he go back on tour? What would he do without Roach and Brandy? If he didn't, would Rye leave?

"I'll put it on the list of things I can do, though." It was quiet while Rye buzzed up the smoothies. Then they were added to the tray. "Okay. You want to eat by the fire? Oh! I bought the stuff we need for s'mores." Rye went back to the cupboards.

"I'll never eat this much." Rye was so excited, though.

"It's all nibble-as-you-go food—you can take as much time as you need eating." Rye added a bag of marshmallows, graham crackers, and a chocolate bar to the tray, along with skewers.

"I'll get the smoothies." Jeff sipped. Raspberry. It was brighter than the strawberry, a little tarter. Yum.

Rye leaned over and sucked on the straw of one. "They're good. The chair by the fire?"

"Yeah. It's big enough for two."

Rye put the tray down on the little table next to the chair, then sat, hands reaching for him. Jeff sat, relaxed, stupidly happy for the time being.

They took turns feeding each other. Little bits of cheese, a bite of cracker. Then a kiss, followed by the bright sweetness of some grapes. It was the best way to eat. Rye ate way more than he did, but that was okay, Rye was a giant. They finished most of the crackers and all the cheese.

Then Rye demonstrated the s'mores. "You cook the marshmallow over the fire. But first you need to get the graham crackers and the chocolate ready for the hot sugar."

"My mom made them in the microwave."

"They taste better over an open flame." Rye looked at him sideways. "You miss her? I mean, I know she hates what you do—did—but do you miss her from before that became a factor?"

"No. I don't miss anyone." Except Jim. And he would miss Roach, but Jim.... Jim was supposed to be better than him.

"I would miss you if I didn't get to see you anymore. Desperately."

"Do you think you'll get another job?"

"Are you firing me?"

"Never."

"Then I don't have to worry about whether or not I need another job."

"Oh, good." He didn't point out that Donna was Rye's boss, not him. He didn't care. He needed Rye to stay.

Rye gave him a look. "Can I tell you something? I'm not leaving you, job or no."

"Promise? Because... I love you, really."

Rye stared at him for a long moment, then put Jeff on his feet. Before he could say anything, Rye was down on one knee in front of him. "Will you marry me?"

184

"Rye?" Oh. Oh, man.

"I love you, and I want to be with you forever. So will you marry me?"

Jeff nodded. Someone wanted to marry him. Someone he loved too. "You mean it? Like for real?"

"I don't make shit up, baby, you know that. Come on. Don't leave me hanging here."

"Yes. Yes, love. Yes. I will."

Rye got up, lifting him up off the ground and kissing him.

Whoa. He was engaged.

Rye squeezed him. "I love you."

"You asked me to marry you."

"And you said yes."

"I did."

Rye grinned at him. "I bet they have jewelry shops in town."

"Do I get a ring?" He liked that idea.

"You do. Something unique. We could go down to city hall too. Investigate getting a license." Rye carried him upstairs.

"Here it'll be a civil union."

"You want to go somewhere that it can be a marriage?"

"We'll figure it out tomorrow."

"Yeah, tomorrow. Tonight we're busy."

They got to the bedroom, and Rye sat on the bed. Jeff settled into Rye's lap, offering him a kiss.

"Mmm." Rye was smiling again when their lips parted. "My husband-to-be."

"I've never been a husband before."

"Me neither, baby." Leaning back, Rye brought him down onto his favorite mattress ever.

They could figure it out, together. That sounded pretty damn good.

CHAPTER FIFTEEN

WELL, GOING ring shopping was out.

The snow was coming down like crazy, big flakes blown around by the wind. It didn't mean the day was a total wash, though.

"Hey, baby. We should go play in the snow."

Jeff was curled in a chair, staring at the snow, fascinated. "Huh?"

"We have snow pants and stuff. Let's go out and play."

"Snow pants?"

"To keep your lower half dry and warm." Rye went to their bags and started digging through them.

"You're silly." Still, Jeff was fascinated.

"Are you kidding? We could build a snowman. We could have a snowball fight. Hell, we can go sledding—I'm pretty sure there's a sled here somewhere."

"Is there enough snow for sledding?"

"I don't know. It's been at it a while. We'll have to see, huh?" He found the winter gear and tossed the boots toward the door, the snow pants and jacket in Jeff's direction.

"Seriously? We're going out in it?" That was a charming, excited little smile.

"Yes, seriously. You need help getting your gear on?"

"I guess. I mean, they're pants...."

"I usually prefer getting into your pants," Rye teased.

"They're blue."

How long had it been since Jeff wore colors? "Yep. And the jacket is crazy multicolored." It was a snowboarder jacket actually, but he thought the colors would suit his baby.

"It's pretty. You won't lose me, that's for sure."

"Yeah, a white outfit would be a mistake."

His own pants were red, and his jacket was just as colorful. He had mittens and hats and scarves too. There was a lot of paraphernalia.

"Is all this necessary?"

"Baby, snow is cold, and we're going to be out in it for a while." And his lover had zero reserves. No fat, no padding. Rye got his pants, boots, and jacket on before moving to help Jeff sort everything out.

"This is heavy." Jeff took a step. "And it squeaks."

"Yeah, yeah. You'll get used to it." He hoped. He put on Jeff's scarf and handed over the mitts. "Okay, we're ready."

They headed out, and Jeff looked up to the flakes, eyes lit up. "It's beautiful!"

"Yeah, it is." Rye raised his own head to the sky, opening his mouth and sticking out his tongue. He hadn't been sure if Mr. I Hate The Outdoors would come out, but the snow seemed to fascinate Jeff, making him spin and wander. Maybe the lack of sunshine helped. He trailed Jeff for a bit, then bent and grabbed a handful of snow. It packed easily, and he tossed the snowball at Jeff's back.

Jeff stepped forward, then spun around. "You threw snow at me!"

"Not just snow." He bent and gathered more snow, again packing it loosely before tossing it at Jeff.

Jeff's eyes went wide, and then a huge handful got scooped up. Rye put his hands on his hips, daring Jeff to throw the snowball— time to see how his baby's aim was. It hit him right in the chin, the icy puffball just exploding.

Gasping, he grabbed another handful himself and tossed it. Jeff twisted, and it missed him; the next one hit the center of his chest. Snickering, Rye gathered more snow, moving a few steps to the left as he lobbed his missile at Jeff, catching him on the shoulder.

"Meanie bodyguard!" Jeff moved quickly, zipping around him, and pegging him in the back of the head.

"You're the one making the head shots!" And taking it far more seriously than he'd expected; he needed to start moving.

Running off away from the house, Rye grabbed and tossed a couple of balls in quick succession.

Jeff laughed hard, following until he slipped, landing on his knees.

"You okay?" He jogged over to Jeff.

"Yeah. Yeah, just tripped." Jeff let him help him up, and Rye half expected a face full of snow but got a kiss instead.

Grinning, he kissed Jeff back. There was a lovely glow on Jeff's cheeks, his lover's lips cold. "Love you. This is…. It's magic, Rye."

"Yeah, it is, isn't it? You want to make snow angels next?"

"We have to take pictures!"

"Yeah, yeah. You want me to go get my phone, or should we do that next time?"

"We need the first ones!" The excited happiness in Jeff's voice made Rye's mouth dry.

"You got it. I'll be back in a second." Rye trotted back to the house, grabbed his phone, then rejoined his baby.

"So, we just fall back?"

"Yep. And then wave your arms and legs up and down."

"Okay. Make sure you get it." Jeff fell back, making angels. God, the cuteness.

Rye took a few pictures, then held his hand out for Jeff's. "I'll pull you up, so you don't ruin it." Jeff reached for him, looking so happy. He pulled Jeff up, lifting him out of his snow angel impression. "Look!" He snapped some more pictures.

"I did it! You next, my beautiful giant."

"Does that mean I'm making snow giants instead of snow angels?" God, he was having fun.

"Giant snow angels."

Chuckling, Rye found a clear patch and flung himself back.

"Yay! Now wave your arms!"

He did, his feet too, moving them through the snow. He felt like a kid again. Jeff took picture after picture, the man cackling like a loon. "Okay. Okay." Rye finally climbed out of the snow. "Snowman."

Jeff nodded. "Snowman, then cocoa."

"Oh yeah. I do believe that's the best part of playing in the snow." In fact, his lover was a little shivery already. Okay, they'd make a small snowman. "You roll the head, I'll get the bottom done."

"Okay." Jeff watched him a second, then started making a ball and rolling it.

He got a base settled, then began the next ball. Once it was done, he carried it over and set it on top of the base. "Yours?"

"Coming. You were fast." Jeff was breathing hard, tiring himself out.

"I'm ready to go in, but I wanted you to have your first snowman."

"What about arms and eyes?"

"We need to find a couple rocks and some sticks. A carrot for the nose."

"'Kay. I'll get the carrot?"

"And I'll get the sticks." He tried not to chuckle but couldn't contain it.

"And rocks. Don't forget the rocks."

"Yes, boss." He began looking, searching around the house for sticks and rocks. It took a bit, but he found the sticks. Jeff came out of the house and put the carrot nose and then two carrot vampire teeth on the snowman. Rye started giggling.

Jeff grinned at him, posed. "It's me, without the ink."

Rye tried to take a picture, but he was laughing too hard. Jeff looked so pleased, so tickled. Rye grabbed his lover, rolling them over and over in the snow.

"Cold. Cold, Rye!" Jeff was giggling hard, the words barely distinguishable. Rye ended up on the bottom, grinning up at Jeff. "I like snow."

"I can tell. And it's a good look on you." He brought their mouths together, enjoying the way the heat of Jeff's mouth and the cold of his lips merged. Jeff moaned for him, the sound pushing into his lips. They kissed until even the heat of their kiss couldn't keep him warm. "Okay. Inside."

"Uh. Uh-huh. Uh-huh."

"You're on top of me," Rye pointed out.

"Uh-huh." Jeff rolled up, then offered him a hand.

He took it, but got up under his own power and hustled them both inside. "That fire is going to feel damn good."

"Uh-huh." Jeff's teeth were chattering.

Rye stripped his lover down and put Jeff in front of the fire they'd lit earlier. "Stay put, and I'll get you that hot chocolate."

"Thank you. Thanks. That was so fun."

"It was." Still grinning, he went into the kitchen, quickly throwing a couple cups of milk into a pot and grabbing some brown sugar and some cocoa. It didn't take long for him to get a couple mugs of hot chocolate ready, and he tossed a boatload of mini marshmallows into Jeff's.

Jeff was dozing, bundled up near the fire. There had been a lot less of that in the last couple days than before they came here. And he'd totally worked Jeff out there. It was a good thing. Fresh air made you tired, anyway.

He'd let Jeff doze for fifteen minutes or so, until the hot chocolate cooled enough to drink. Slipping onto the couch, he took Jeff into his arms. God, he loved this man.

Jeff's eyes fluttered open. "Cocoa."

"You know it." They were going to have to buy more.

"Smells good."

"It is good. I almost brought some more s'mores stuff too but decided at the last minute not to."

"I just want this."

"Cool. So you enjoyed our morning in the snow, eh?"

"I did. That was so cool."

"The first of many. I liked watching you make snow angels the best."

Jeff grinned and nodded, looking more at peace than he'd ever seen. Rye kissed the tip of Jeff's nose and risked a sip of his hot chocolate. Life was pretty good.

JEFF LOVED it up here. Loved it. There was nothing but happy quiet and snow.

It took him a week before the guitar called to him, and he started writing, playing, lost in the sound for hours. He'd emerge from it to find Rye right there, watching him like he was the most fascinating thing in the world.

"Hey." His fingers were sore, his throat aching, but he was happy.

"Hey baby. You're amazing."

"Just messing around. I wasn't bothering you, was I?"

"If that's you just messing around, it's going to be unbelievably good when you really set your mind to it. And if you were bothering me, I could have moved to another room. I love watching you play, baby. You're transcendent."

"I was just writing some stuff." Jeff stood up, rolled his shoulders.

Rye stood as well, coming over and putting a hand on his shoulder. It was warm, good. "When are you going to admit that you've got a gift?"

"January had one. The band had something special." It was the first time he'd let himself think of the band since they'd come here. His mind still wanted to skitter away from those thoughts.

"January only had a gift because you do. And those songs... they're better than anything you did as January."

"Thank you." Rye was sweet.

"I mean it, baby. I'm not just blowing smoke up your ass."

He chuckled, the phrase tickling him. "Perv."

Rye hugged him. "That's me. Your own personal perv."

He hugged Rye back and then put his guitar away, careful.

"You want to go into town and see if we can find your ring?"

"Sure. No one will recognize me, right?"

"There's no way. You don't look anything like January. He's pale and pointed and fangy."

"And not nearly bald." He liked it, really, liked how it felt.

"Not bald, short-haired. It's totally different."

Jeff rubbed his hand over the stubble. "It is for me."

Rye chuckled. "I meant super-short and bald were different." Rye kissed the top of his head. "Come on. If anyone recognizes you, I'll protect you."

"My bodyguard."

"That's right." Rye wrapped him in a hug, pulling him up against the solid, big body. Jeff snuggled in and rested, just letting himself melt. "We'll lose the whole afternoon if we're not careful."

"Sorry." He didn't move, though.

Rye chuckled. "You want to just sit and cuddle?"

"No. No, it's cool. You're just so warm." And he was happy.

"We'll make sure you're well bundled up. We might think of getting a bunch of supplies in town—I saw there was a storm warning for tomorrow."

"That sounds good." He needed a hat and some paper.

"Cool. So we'll go." Rye kissed him, then stood, getting them moving.

Jeff dressed, put on his sunglasses, his heavy coat.

Rye put big puffy mitts on his hands, chuckling. "I look like a nerd."

"That's not a bad thing."

Rye pulled his toque down over his head and put on a pair of gloves, and they went out. The cold seeped in, sliding into his bones. Hustling Jeff into the car, Rye put the heat on, and it was soon pumping out hot air as they drove.

The road was clear, and they trundled into town, the fancy SUV bouncing along. Rye put on the radio, flipping around until he found some easy listening.

"You don't want death metal?" He had to tease. Had to.

Rye gave him a death metal glare. "We need to tape you and use that next time we're out driving."

"I'm sure I have January performances." He did enjoy teasing the bear.

"Not him. You. I want to hear you."

"We're the same person."

"No, you're not. He's a character you wear like a coat."

"He's more charismatic than I am. I don't miss the contacts."

"Your music is far better than his, baby. Far better."

Jeff loved how Rye loved him. Rye's hand slid over his leg, squeezed, and then he turned his attention back to the road. Jeff changed the channel until he found a classic rock station, and then he started singing. Rye started singing along. Rye's voice was low, fine, and he enjoyed listening. Jeff was almost disappointed when they got to the city center, parking in a little lot.

"So, what's the plan?"

"We go to the ring store. We go to the grocery store, and then, if the weather still looks good, I buy you dinner."

"And I need a soft hat and some paper."

"A soft hat? What kind of soft hat?"

"Just something for the house when my head is cold."

"Oh, I get it. Cool."

Rye got a parking slip and put it in the window, and then they were off, walking through the charming Main Street.

There were a dozen little shops, and Jeff amused himself window shopping, until he hit the toy store. He didn't even have to say anything; Rye just chuckled and went to the door, holding it open for him. He grinned and hurried in, bouncing a little.

Rye's soft laughter followed him, solid and happy. Oh, man. So many colors. Games. He loved games.

"You looking for anything in particular, Jeff?"

"It's all cool, huh? Do you like toys?"

"I guess? I haven't played with them in a long time. We could get a couple of board games to augment our backgammon board."

"Yeah? I'd love to." He could just take one of everything.

"Okay, whatever you want. If I don't know how to play it, you can teach me."

"We can teach each other."

"That sounds great, baby." Rye held his arms out. "Pile me up."

Jeff cracked up for him.

Grinning, Rye pointed out the board game section. There were a ton. He even recognized most of them. "Oh, Mousetrap. I remember that one from when I was a kid."

"Yeah? There's Life and Parcheesi. Who the hell names a game Parcheesi?"

"Some very cheesy guy."

Jeff barked out a snort, both surprised and tickled.

"We'll put it on the pile and find out if it's any good."

"Yeah. Yeah, that sounds good, Rye." Jeff couldn't stop smiling.

"Love making you laugh, baby." Rye's gaze was hot, and he had the feeling if they weren't in public, he'd have been pounced.

They bought cards and board games and a few wind-up toys. Then Rye picked up a monkey with really long arms, the hands at the end of them velcroed. "A hugging monkey. I love it." Rye put it on their pile.

"Can we get a saucer sled?"

"Yeah. We need a cart. Or to pile this stuff at the register."

"I don't think they're big enough for carts."

"Okay, pile it by the register it is." Rye went and dumped his armful of board games, before coming back with one of those little hand baskets.

"Now we can break the bank."

"Uh-huh. Crayons."

"Coloring books or construction paper?"

Rye picked up a couple books. "Look, they've got zoo animals and Bugs Bunny."

"Dude. Cool. They have the kaleidoscope ones too. Get those." Rye put a bunch of books and a pad of construction paper in the bag. "You like Lego?"

"I used to build the big kits in my bus."

"Oh, that's cool. Let's get some. I haven't played with it since I was little."

"Sure. There's Ninjas, Star Wars, buildings."

"Oh, let's go with the Ninjas!" There were about six different kits with the Ninjas, and he handed them all to Rye, who chuckled for him. He grabbed the R2-D2 one too, just because. Winter was long.

"Oh, if you're getting him, you have to get his lover too." Rye grabbed the C-3PO kit.

"Oh, dude. Too cool." Jeff felt… free.

"Yeah. And we can always come back. The realtor told me the place usually doesn't get snowed in for more than a few days at a time."

"Still…." The idea of long days playing with Rye appealed.

"Hey, I say we get everything we see that calls to us. It'll be fun."

"We're spoiled." They were. They were rotten.

"Uh-huh. You deserve it."

"For what?" What decent thing had he ever done?

"For getting better. For being with me."

"Oh." Okay, that was cool.

Rye kissed his nose. "What else tickles your fancy?"

"I think that's plenty. We'll play all winter long."

"And I know a lot of games that don't even need boards or dice or anything."

"Yeah? That's cool. I haven't enjoyed just hanging out with someone like I do with you."

"You're easy to be with." No one had ever said that to him. Ever. "Okay, let's go make that salesgirl's day."

"I hope she's on commission."

"Yeah, me too." Smiling, Rye put the rest of their stuff on the counter. "We're ready."

The saleslady stared. "Wow. Rock on, y'all."

Rye chuckled. "We're not into TV, and we've seen most of the movies we have."

She just grinned. "You boys just made my quarter."

195

"That's good, right?" Jeff smiled, and she tilted her head like she recognized him.

"It's fantastic. I'll even give you a discount—no taxes." She was still looking at him, like she was trying to work it out.

"Cool." *Please don't. I'm no one.*

"Hey, I thought we'd gotten that Millennium Falcon Lego kit. You want to go grab it, Jeff?"

"Yeah. Yeah, I'll get it." He flashed Rye a grateful look and headed over.

Rye chatted with the gal as she rang up their stuff, asking her about the shops and where the best place to get a nice warm, soft hat was. Jeff waited until almost all the stuff had been rung up, then brought the kit over.

"Do I.... Do I know you?"

Jeff shook his head. "I don't think so."

"We're new to the area," Rye told her, handing over a credit card. Jeff grabbed three of the bags and started carrying them out. Rye came out a few moments later. "It's okay, baby, she didn't actually recognize you, you just seemed familiar to her."

"I know. I just... I'm not ready."

"I honestly can't believe she recognized you as January. You look so different from him."

"Do I?" He looked at his reflection in the car window. Wow. He really did look different. Huge eyes, short hair, no fangy teeth. He wasn't nearly as pale as January either. He was just Jeff.

"Look at that cutie." Rye's face appeared next to his, his giant smiling.

"Just this guy."

"Well, I think he's completely adorable."

"That's probably good."

"It's definitely good." Rye kissed the top of his head and put the bags into the backseat.

"What next?"

"Groceries and your hat, then we'll see if we have time for a meal out."

"And rings. Don't forget that."

"Oh, I'd totally forgotten about those. What do we need rings for again?"

Jeff looked at Rye, then grinned. Tease.

"Groceries first. Just in case the weather gets bad earlier than predicted."

"That sounds reasonable. It's not like things will go bad." He hadn't been inside a grocery store in years.

"Yeah." Rye pointed out the grocery store, and they headed in. "Anything that looks good? Grab it."

"I—" *God. Overwhelming. Totally fucking overwhelming.*

"Baby? What's wrong?"

"I haven't…. This is big."

"Ah. Well, everything is organized by row, so we'll just start at one end and move along each row. You can do this."

"Sure. I'm not…." *Stupid.* Was he?

"I know, baby. It's huge, though, and you're used to food coming from the fridge or the cupboards in your kitchen." Rye gave him a wink.

Jeff nodded. It was so normal, so weird. They moved down the aisles, Rye adding stuff to the cart as they went. He didn't know what to add. All this food, everywhere.

"Don't worry, I'll get the fixings for lots of tomato soup and smoothies."

"Okay. And cheese with bread."

"And hummus and veggies. We'll get the standards along with special goodies."

"Okay. Okay. I like vegetables. And strawberries."

"I know. We'll do grapes too, and bacon and pancake mix and—oh, chips." Rye's excitement was bleeding into him, letting him relax and breathe. "You want fake bacon or are you good with the real stuff?"

"Can we try both?"

"Yeah, absolutely." Rye dumped some fake bacon into the cart with the real stuff. "Are you willing to try shrimp and steak and hotdogs?"

"There's no chicken lips in the hot dogs, right?" He wasn't eating that.

"They've got all natural, all beef ones here. Or pork ones, same deal. No bits and pieces and by-products."

"All natural. I like that."

"Yeah. We'll get some buns to go with it. Oh, check these out—frozen dough to make your own bread." Rye kept stacking things in their cart, filling it with everything under the sun. Jeff couldn't help laughing. Okay, this was fun, genuinely fucking fun.

They hit every single aisle, Rye sometimes asking him about stuff, but just as often simply tossing things into the cart. It blew his mind; Rye was definitely getting ready for a long winter. With him.

"Okay. Let's check out and go ring shopping."

"Yeah. Okay. And then home, huh?" He didn't want to eat in a restaurant.

"You don't want to eat out?"

"No. No, that seems stressful."

"No stress. We're on holiday."

"Yeah. Yeah, right." Real life was still waiting.

"Say it like you mean it, baby."

"I just…. Real life is out there. It would be so easy to pretend to really be here, you know?"

"No, I don't know. You really are here."

Jeff shrugged, unsure how to explain it. It didn't really matter anyway. Rye started putting their groceries on the belt, and he joined in, the cashier running it all over the thing that made it all beep.

"Do I need to pay?"

"I've got it." Rye handed over his credit card again.

"Okay." There was so much food.

"We won't have to go shopping again for days."

"Months."

Grinning, Rye nodded and started pushing the cart full of bagged groceries out to the car. "Probably." They loaded the car up, the damned thing full. "It's a good thing the rest of what we're going to buy is little."

"Uh-huh. The tires aren't going to hold."

Chuckling now, Rye took his hand. "They'll be fine."

"If you're sure, I believe you."

"I'm sure." They walked toward the jewelry store. "Do you want gold or silver?"

"What about a mix of the two twined together?"

Oh, that would be pretty. Interesting too.

"You like that?" Jeff asked him.

"I think I could, yeah."

"Well, let's see what we can get."

He nodded, and they headed in, the little store warm, inviting. They wandered for a moment, looking in the display cases. The salesman walked up. "Can I help you?"

"Please. We're looking for matching wedding bands." Rye put an arm around Jeff's shoulders.

"Oh? Congratulations!"

Jeff gave the guy a tentative grin. No haters. Good.

Rye smiled down at him, clearly thinking along the same lines. "Thank you. Do you do custom stuff?"

"We have a number of options, and we work with a number of local jewelers. Do you see something you like?"

"It's all very nice, but we were thinking of a band with white and yellow gold twined together."

"Oh? Something like this?" He showed them something big and clunky, and Jeff shook his head.

"No."

Rye took his hand and showed it to the jeweler. "Something more delicate that will look good on long, slender fingers."

"Let me think...." The salesman pursed his lips. "I think I should get your e-mail, and let's see if we can find something custom."

Rye looked at him and grinned. "Yeah, yeah, that works for us, doesn't it?"

"I think so. Something unique."

Rye took the pen and paper that the salesclerk handed over and wrote down his e-mail address. "We appreciate your willingness to accommodate us."

"Absolutely. Are you interested in stones?"

Jeff shook his head. "I don't think so. Rye?"

"No. We'd like it to be simple. Classy."

"Yeah. Exactly."

"I'll have our creative team put together a few sketches and e-mail them to you within the week. Is that soon enough?"

Rye nodded. "Yeah, that's fine. Thank you." They headed out, the snow beginning to fall. "That place the toy store lady said had nice hats is just around the corner. I think we've got time if we're quick."

"Okay. I don't need anything fancy. Just soft." He wasn't picky. Well, okay. He was totally picky, but he wanted a hat.

Rye led him to the place they'd been given directions to—it was a craft place, and it didn't take them long to find the knitted stuff. There was a cap made with the softest yarn he'd ever felt, ever. *Oh, that one.*

"That blue brings out your eyes." Rye smiled and touched his cheek.

"Is that cool? No one knows my eyes."

"It's very cool—they're beautiful eyes." The words warmed him, all the way through. Rye bought the hat and slid it onto Jeff's head as they went back out. Oh, this was going to be his new favorite thing. Rye put an arm around his shoulders, and they moved quickly back to the car through the falling snow.

"It's getting heavier." Jeff raised a hand, catching flakes on his palm.

"Yeah. Going straight home after the hat was the right choice."

"There's lots of food in the car. Lots." He hurried to the car, a little wigged out, ready to go home.

Rye's soft chuckles soothed him a little. "There is. We're going to be fine, baby. The roads are still clear, and I'm a safe driver."

"Uh-huh. I know."

Rye bundled him into the car, turning the heater up high.

"Home, home, home!" Jeff found a song he loved on the satellite radio.

Rye sang along with him as they drove, and as soon as they were out in the country again, it felt like they were already back in their own little white world. It was fascinating and wonderful and scary, all at the same time. But as long as he had Rye here with him, he figured he could survive it.

Chapter Sixteen

The storm raged and raged, and when they got up the next morning, it was still snowing and the lights were out.

Rye said a small thank-you for gas heating and gas stoves. What could have been a little scary was cozy instead. Burrowing deeper into the covers, he pulled Jeff close.

"It's okay, right?" Jeff was still mostly asleep.

"Uh-huh. We're just fine, baby." He stroked Jeff's side soothingly.

"The lights aren't on. They've been out since three."

"Why were you awake at three?"

"I don't know. I think the quiet. Maybe the total darkness."

He listened for a minute. "Wow, it is quiet. I mean, it's quiet here anyway, but now it's really quiet."

"Uh-huh."

Oh, how odd for Jeff. The man lived with noise.

"We're good, though. We've got heat, and a way to cook. And we can always throw the food out into the snow if it lasts too long."

"Yeah. Yeah, that's true, huh?" Jeff snuggled into him. "It's like we're all on our own."

"I know. The last two people on earth." He made *dun dun dun* noises.

As he'd hoped, Jeff giggled, going along with the joke. "Dude. There's no TV."

"That's okay, we have eight million games if we get bored of banging our brains out."

"Banging our brains out?"

"Boinking? Hot whoopee? Making love?" Jeff cackled, the sound merry, warm. "All of the above," Rye suggested, fingers beginning to move on Jeff's warm skin.

"I like this, being with you."

"It's my favorite thing." He felt Jeff smile against his skin. Tilting Jeff's head, he took a kiss, feeling an easy morning want turning into something more. Jeff stroked his chest, touching him gently, carefully.

"I won't break," he assured Jeff, pushing into the touches.

"Am I doing it wrong?"

"No, there is no wrong. I don't mind a harder touch, though."

"Okay."

Sweet baby. It amazed him, the mixture of cynicism and innocence. He took another kiss. He loved kissing Jeff. He could do it forever. Jeff reached up, fingers tangling in his hair, holding him. He knew Jeff loved their kisses too.

Sliding his thumbs back and forth across Jeff's nipples, he teased Jeff's tongue with his own.

"Love you...." Jeff hummed, so quiet.

"You too, baby. You're my heart."

Jeff's smile was settled, warm. Happy. Rye loved that he'd given this to Jeff. He wanted to give his lover more. Rolling onto Jeff, he deepened the kiss. Jeff wrapped around him, arms and legs holding on tight.

"I want you. I want to feel your tight body around my cock."

"Oh." Jeff gasped, groaned a bit.

"Uh-huh." He licked at Jeff's lips, then nuzzled along Jeff's throat, tongue sliding on hot skin. Jeff's chin lifted, throat working. Rye explored every inch, then found a spot, the perfect spot. Opening his mouth, he began sucking.

Soft, musical sounds filled the air, Jeff right there, soaring with him. He slapped at Jeff's skin with his tongue as he continued to suck. Jeff shifted under him and rubbed against him. His cock was hard, bumping against Jeff's.

"So warm. Warm."

"For you." He bit at the spot he'd pulled up.

"Uhn."

Oh, that was a good sound. So Rye did it again, rolling their hips as Jeff made the sound again.

"Want." His lover still sounded so surprised.

"Me too." He grabbed the lube from the bedside table. Jeff hummed and rocked, singing for him. Rocking in time with Jeff's music, he slicked his fingers up.

Dancing for him. Jeff was dancing for him.

Sliding a single finger into Jeff's hole, he encouraged the dance. Jeff's lips parted, tongue lapping his lips. Pushing deep, Rye found Jeff's gland. When he pegged it, Jeff sat up and gasped, hips rolling, once, twice.

"Easy," Rye murmured, encouraging Jeff to lie back down.

"Sorry. Sorry."

"No, no. That was an amazing reaction. I just don't want you to hurt yourself."

"Okay. That was big."

After easing Jeff down, Rye touched his gland again. Sliding a second finger in as well, he pegged the spot a little harder.

"Oh. Oh. Oh."

The little noises just kept coming. They were fucking intoxicating. He spread his fingers wide, twisted them together, then pushed in deep again.

"Rye!" The cry was sharp, wanton, and Rye wanted more. Twisting his fingers, he kept pushing, kept stimulating that sweet little gland. He wanted Jeff to fly.

Jeff kept moaning, kept riding his touch. Fuck, yes. Yes. That's what he wanted, that freedom, that need. With his free hand, he flicked Jeff's right nipple. They needed rings. Needed them. Then he could twist and tug and flick and make Jeff absolutely crazy. He wanted the rings back everywhere they used to be too, wanted to touch freely, to make them sing. He'd find a place they could go to once this snowstorm was over, when they'd cleared the roads.

In the meantime, Rye had fingers and teeth and could make those pretty little nipples sing. He leaned down, caught one in his teeth, and rolled it, side to side, sensitizing it. He kept finger-fucking Jeff while he did it, letting the sensations merge together.

"Rye. Rye, I… it's big."

"It's supposed to be." He licked the abused nipple, pressing hard with his tongue. Jeff's fingers tangled in his hair, tugging at him. He let Jeff tug him up so he could take a kiss, his tongue fucking Jeff's lips like his fingers were fucking Jeff's tight ass.

Jeff sucked his tongue, almost whining now. He had his baby needing. He'd wait until Jeff was begging, though. Breaking the kiss, he moved to bite at the unabused nipple, eager to give it extra color.

"No more biting—"

"You love it." It turned Jeff on.

"I love you." That wasn't a denial, and he bit at Jeff's jaw. Jeff arched, driving down on his fingers.

"Need it to be me." He pulled his fingers out and grabbed a condom, sliding it on. Then he slicked up his cock, getting it well lubed.

"Uh-huh." Jeff's body moved like Rye was still touching. He loved how sensual Jeff was, how alive and responsive. Jeff had blossomed for him. And Jeff had given him a reason to care.

He pressed his cock against Jeff's hole and pushed slowly in.

"My Rye…."

"All yours." He kept pushing in, filling Jeff up.

Jeff bore down, taking him in. His lover was so tight and felt so good around his cock. Jeff panted, lips parted, eyes focused on him.

Rye pulled partway out and shoved back in again, holding Jeff's gaze the entire time. He could see the need, the hunger in Jeff's eyes. Still watching his baby, he tweaked one of Jeff's nipples. The sweet ass gripped him like a fist.

"Love you." Thrusting, he pinched the other one.

"Love."

Jeff's head lifted up. Rye bit at Jeff's throat, letting his teeth drag and scrape. He could feel the way his sharper touches made

Jeff shudder. Hungry man. Jeff was learning to need, and Rye loved it. He bit down on Jeff's shoulder, his hips moving rhythmically.

"Rye. Rye, hurry." His boy was going to come without a touch to his cock. It made Rye punch in harder, faster, eager to push Jeff right over the edge. Jeff grabbed his shoulders, short nails digging in.

Rye brought their mouths together again, tongue-fucking Jeff's lips. Jeff's body milked him, muscles rippling against his cock.

"You make me fucking need, baby."

"Gonna—"

"Do it. Want you to come without a touch to your cock."

"Rye!" Jeff called out to him.

"Do it," he insisted.

Those amazing eyes went wide, and Jeff shot, seed spraying.

"Oh fuck." Between the smell and the way Jeff's ass was milking him, Rye was pulled into his own orgasm.

"Uh-huh—" Jeff couldn't even keep his eyes open.

"Love you, baby." He let Jeff take some of his weight, wanting to stay right there, just for a bit.

"Mmm. Love." Jeff yawned, snuggling in, making no move to get up.

Rye didn't see any reason not to have a nice long lie-in. He kissed Jeff's forehead and cuddled him in close.

"Best lights-out ever."

Rye chuckled. He couldn't agree more.

OKAY, THIS was creepy, and he wasn't getting out of bed until the lights came on and there was Internet. Jeff squeezed his eyes shut, staying buried under the covers, steadfastly ignoring the world.

Rye pulled the covers off him. "Come on, baby. The snow is smooth and beautiful. We need to make angels. We're going out to play, baby." Rye pinched his butt.

"No pinching!" He made a grab for the blankets.

"Then come play with me." Rye tossed the blankets over the end of the bed.

"Hey!" He scrambled for the edge of the bed, and Rye grabbed him, snatching him up.

"Better get dressed, or I'll toss you over my shoulder and we'll pretend to be polar bears."

"*No!*" This was almost fun.

Rye snickered and hefted him across one wide shoulder, heading down the stairs.

"Don't you take me out there without my coat! No!"

Instead of a snowbank, he was dumped onto the couch, his ass sliding on the leather. He grabbed a blanket and wrapped up tight.

"I thought we'd moved past the hiding-in-bed phase?" Rye sat with him, tugging him close.

"You gotta go with what's comfortable."

Snorting softly, Rye pulled him closer. "Like being January was comfortable."

"No. No, that never was. Never."

"Well, then. You don't have to go with what's comfortable. Besides, being with me isn't as uncomfortable as being January, I'm sure. It might be challenging sometimes, but—"

"You're saying many words...."

"You telling me to shut up?"

"No." He was saying that Rye didn't let him hide.

"Then what?"

Jeff shrugged, shook his head. He didn't know. He didn't know anything.

"Don't shut me out, baby." Rye stroked his cheek. "I want to know everything about you, about what you're thinking."

"No one wants that." No one but Rye.

"I do." Rye grinned. "Call me a sap, but I like the way that sounds."

He pushed into Rye's lap, settling. "Sap."

Rye kissed him, hands sliding on his skin. Damn this man, who could ease him, distract him, so easily. Holding his ass, Rye squeezed hard enough there would probably be bruises. Jeff wiggled, pushed into the touch.

"God, the things I want to do with you."

"Do with me?"

"Uh-huh." Rye squeezed his ass again, nails digging in this time. "I want to wake every one of your senses. Blow your mind."

"I thought you wanted to make snow angels." Blowing his mind sounded fun.

"I know it goes against my badass image, but I'm not going to actually throw you into the snow naked."

"Oh, thank you." He started giggling, so in love it hurt.

Rye just stared for a moment, then started to laugh too. "God, you are something special."

Jeff wrapped his arms around Rye's neck, held on tight.

"And I want you to believe that. You, not January, just you."

"At least I was bright enough to be January, huh?"

"You are smart and talented and good-looking, and there isn't anything you can't do."

"There's lots of stuff I suck at."

"Nobody is good at everything."

"Nope." That was true. Shit, nobody was anything at *everything*. Okay, that was stupid.

Rye traced Jeff's lips with his tongue. He moaned and opened, tongue touching Rye's. "God, you make me need more with every breath." That was good, right? Rye pulled him in closer, the heat of Rye's body keeping him warm.

"I miss the lights and the computer, huh?" Jeff said softly.

"Because they keep your mind busy?"

"Yeah. Because they're something."

"What are you keeping your mind busy from?"

"I don't know. Thinking, I guess."

Rye squeezed him. "About...."

"I don't know. Stuff?" Retiring. Living. Roach.

"You don't have to go through it alone, baby. Share?"

"I was thinking about the road, about touring, January."

Rye swallowed but didn't say anything. "What were you thinking about them?"

"Roach isn't going to get better, is he?"

"No, baby. He's not. The fact that he's not gone yet is a miracle."

"I can't do Lord January without him. He was the heart of the band."

"Do you even want to do Lord January anymore?"

"No. I hate it, but I have to work."

"What about the stuff you've been composing lately? It's gorgeous."

"It's okay." It didn't suck.

"So? Why can't you do that?"

"What if it doesn't make money? What if I can't afford Donna, you?"

"Well, I'm not sure you'd need to pay me once I'm your husband and all."

"Oh. Oh, that's good." Husband. His husband.

"I have a lot of money saved up. Do you?"

"I don't know. Maybe?" They'd have to ask Donna. Donna would know.

Rye winced. "You should know, baby."

"How could I? It's too complicated for me."

"Knowing how much money you have is too complicated?" Rye shook his head. "I know you're not stupid."

"No, but I don't even know where it comes from. None of it."

"From playing January."

"Right, but there's all these details." And he was a junkie. Donna handled it.

"That's crazy, baby. Hell, for all you know, you make more money writing songs than you did playing January."

Oh, wouldn't that be amazing? That would be perfect.

"Mmm, you like that idea."

"Sure I do. It would be like... magic." He was writing a lot these days.

"Then you talk to Donna. See if we can't make magic happen, hmm?"

"I could talk to Donna." He could. Well, once the lights came on.

"I think that's a great idea."

"Maybe, yeah. Maybe it is. Just to see."

"When we have power again, you can call her. Find out what's what." Rye grabbed his ass again. "Now, whatever will we do until the power come back?"

"I was planning on sleeping," Jeff teased.

Smiling happily, Rye leaned in and began to suck on his neck. Jeff leaned back, throat working as the little tingles turned to heat. Rye was already hard, thick cock pressing against him.

"You need." It surprised him, the way Rye wanted.

"Of course I do. You do it for me, baby. Deep in my soul."

"I like the sound of that. Deep in your soul."

"It's true." Rye stroked the spot he'd just sucked up.

"Deep...." His entire body started to heat.

"Yeah. Deep." Rye grabbed his ass again, fingers pressing hard as he pulled their lower bodies together.

It burned a bit, but it felt good, intense.

Like Rye was sensitizing every inch.

"Can't wait to get your piercings back in. Add the nipple rings."

"Mmmhmm." Jeff nodded, agreeing.

Rye's mouth took his again, the kiss hard, all consuming. It was so easy, to lick and taste and spread, tease Rye, touch.

His big lover moaned and groaned, pushing into each touch. Jeff tugged on one nipple, pulled a little bit. Moaning again, Rye licked his lips and mirrored the motion on Jeff's nipple.

Oh, he wanted more. He pulled a bit harder. Gasping, Rye tugged harder too—then twisted his nipple. A deep groan bubbled up in his chest, almost making him hiccup.

Moving to his other nipple, Rye tugged it as well. Jeff's fingers stuttered, stumbling over Rye's flesh. Leaning in, Rye took his right nipple in, sucking on it.

Jeff arched up, encouraging Rye to taste, to suck, to bite. Rye did, all three, sucking hard and biting even harder. Then Rye moved to work his other nipple just as hard.

"More," Jeff whispered.

Rye flicked his tongue across Jeff's nipple, then bit down, really hard. He cried out, shocked, stinging and so fucking turned on. Rye did it again, mouth hot and sharp.

"No. No more." *Don't stop. Fuck.*

"Your body is saying yes...." Rye moved to his other nipple and bit it really hard.

"No...." He pulled away, covering his nips, rubbing them.

Chuckling, Rye nodded. "Yeah, your mouth is saying no, but your body is saying yes. And you have me all twisted and turned around." Rye shifted, putting him down on the couch, rubbing against him.

"Uh-huh. I mean...." Jeff tugged Rye's cock, fingers circling the tip.

"Trying to distract me."

"Uh-huh." Absolutely. Rye's fingers went back to his nipples, pinching, tugging. "No more." Jeff couldn't stop his moans, though.

"Imagine them pierced, baby. Little rings to tug on."

"Love my rings...."

"Uh-huh. Gonna get 'em back. Gonna make you fly."

Jeff could believe that. He could. Rye was waking up more feelings than he ever expected.

Rye kept thrusting, moving their cocks together in the best way. Jeff wrapped both his hands around both of them, jacking them together. Nodding, Rye went back to his nipples, licking and biting at them again. God, this was magic. Perfectly magical.

Growling around his nipple, Rye made it vibrate, the sensation going straight to Jeff's prick.

"Oh...." His hands squeezed tighter, jerking hard. That made Rye bite down again, teeth sharp. "Rye!" He was going to come.

Humming, Rye sent more vibrations from his nipples to his cock. Jeff let go, shooting so hard his bones rattled.

"Jeff!" Rye called out his name, shouting and adding more heat between them.

The sensation went on and on, spinning through him. Rye's kisses made it even better. Those hands worked him like magic, played him. He didn't even get soft. How was that possible?

"I don't go more than once."

"So what's this?" Rye rubbed the tip of his cock.

"You. It's you."

"No, baby. This is your cock." Rye's eyes twinkled.

"Butthead." The urge to giggle was almost unbearable.

Rye laughed softly and squeezed Jeff's prick. His balls drew up tight, aching. Running his thumb across the top of Jeff's prick, working his slit, Rye was trying to make him lose his fucking mind.

"You're going to come again for me."

"I.... Again?" His hips couldn't stop moving.

"Oh yeah. I know you can feel it." Rye just kept touching, pushing, the sensations undeniable. Two fingers pushed into his hole, stretching him, the pressure almost rough. That little sting of pain made it all the better.

"More." Jeff needed it to go on and on.

Rye found his gland, pegging it as Rye teased his slit with the other hand. The two zings joined, merged together. His teeth sank into his bottom lip. That was when Rye bit down on his left nipple.

"Rye!" Spunk pushed from his balls, spraying between them. It left him shaken, sweaty.

Rye let his nipple go, moving to kiss him, tongue pushing lazily into his mouth. Jeff whimpered, head shaking side to side. Rye's fingers slid away, the hand on his cock letting go as Rye settled next to him.

"Mmm. God, you're sexy. You really are."

"I...." He blinked, licked his lips.

Snuggling in, Rye smiled against his neck. "I love you, Jeff."

"Love. Love. My giant."

Rye chuckled. "All yours. Every inch."

That thought made him grin, and he felt wicked.

"Someone's thinking very naughty thoughts." The look in Rye's eyes was naughty too.

"Me? I'm innocent as the driven snow—"

"Driven into the ground and mixed up with gravel, you mean."

Jeff swatted Rye's arm playfully. "Hush, you!"

Rye kissed the skin just beneath his ear. "It's okay, baby, you're perfect just like you are."

"Stop it."

"Stop what? Kissing you?" Rye licked the same spot he'd kissed.

"No. No, not that."

"Then what? Telling you how I feel about you? I love you, just the way you are."

"That's so cool."

"Then why on earth would I stop it? Why would you want me to?"

"I don't know. I guess it's silly."

"Do you believe me when I tell you how great you are?"

"I believe that you think I am."

Rye growled. "Baby, you're awesome." Rye bumped their foreheads together.

"Ow." He cracked up and grabbed Rye's ears. "Be nice."

"I'm *trying* to be nice." Rye's lips touched his for a moment.

Jeff rubbed their noses together. "I wish…."

"What do you wish, baby?"

"That this could be our life."

"It is our life, Jeff."

"No. No, I mean, our real life."

"Well, why can't it be?"

"Because we're just doing it for now." Right? This wasn't theirs—this peace, this house, this life.

"Our life can be anything we want it to be, Jeff. And we're going to get married and be together for always. We'll always have this." Rye held on to him and pulled him close.

Jeff held on, wanted to believe it.

"I'm not going anywhere, baby. Not ever."

"Not ever?"

"Not ever." Rye kissed him, like he was sealing the vow.

Jeff held on, happier than he'd ever been. Ever. He hoped, if he held on tight enough, he'd get to keep it.

213

CHAPTER SEVENTEEN

THE POWER was off for over a day, but they survived it just fine, and Rye had to chuckle at Jeff's cheer when everything came back up again.

They plugged their phones in, Jeff's beeping immediately to let him know he had voice messages. Jeff listened, taking notes on his laptop, and then suddenly Jeff stopped, put his phone down, and headed to the bathroom.

That was strange.

Frowning, Rye followed him and knocked on the door. "Baby?" The water started, and he thought he heard crying. "I'm coming in, Jeff." He opened the door and went in, worry like an electrical wire.

Jeff was on the bottom of the tub, curled up, sobbing.

He climbed right in, not even bothering to take off his clothes, and picked his lover up. "What happened?"

"He's gone. He's gone, and I missed it."

"Baby, who—oh. Roach?" He squeezed Jeff tight.

Jeff sobbed, just cried like his heart was broken.

Rye didn't know what to say except "I'm sorry," and he said it again and again, whispering it into Jeff's skin.

"He was a good guy. He made me famous, taught me about music."

"I know, baby. It sucks that he's gone."

"I should have been there."

"Was he awake at all? At the end?" Rye asked, keeping his voice gentle.

"No. No, Donna said he just slipped away. Two days ago."

"Then it wouldn't have made a difference if you were there."

Two days. When the power had gone out.

"No, but still...." Those red eyes stared at him. "My head hurts."

"I bet it does. Your heart too, eh?" He stroked Jeff's cheeks, knowing his lover had to go through this. Much as he wanted to— and man, did he want to—he couldn't take this for Jeff.

"Uh-huh. Everything. You have your clothes on."

"Yeah, well, you're more important to me than them."

"Still, you've got to be uncomfortable, and I need aspirin."

"Yeah, yeah. Be all logical and shit." Rye turned the water off and started stripping out of his admittedly disgusting clothes.

Jeff handed him a towel and wrapped one around himself, heading for the big bed.

He grabbed the aspirin from the cabinet over the sink and followed Jeff out. "Hey, let's go sit down by the fire." No more hiding in bed.

"I want to lie down."

"We can curl together on the couch."

"You don't like the bed?" Jeff pulled on a huge sweater and a pair of pants.

"I don't like you hiding in it."

"I...." Jeff stared at him.

Rye opened his arms. "Come here."

Jeff ran to him immediately. After picking Jeff up, Rye headed downstairs. Jeff's face was in his throat, breath warm and soft. He put Jeff down on the couch and turned to light the fire. Jeff pulled all the blankets around, making them a nest.

He settled in with his lover, tugging Jeff close. "Do you want to talk about it?"

"He was.... He found me. He invented LJ."

"He was your friend." Even if Rye thought being LJ was the worst idea ever. "It's good to mourn, natural."

"What is going to happen now? The band is going to be nothing."

215

"It's time to let the band go, baby." It was selfish of him to be glad about that, he knew it.

Jeff began to cry again, tears sliding down the lean cheeks. Rye let him cry, holding his baby and stroking his hand along Jeff's back. The tears came and went, then returned, and they stayed together.

"I have you," Rye whispered, holding on.

"I don't want to be a performer anymore, Rye. I'm so tired."

"Then don't, baby." He knew Jeff didn't believe it yet, but it really was that easy.

"Okay." Jeff's eyes closed. "My head hurts so bad."

He fished the bottle of aspirin out of his pants pocket and handed two over. They'd forgotten them earlier. Jeff took them dry, making Rye wince. Gross.

Rye tugged Jeff close again, kissed the top of his head. "You don't have to perform anymore, baby, honestly. You're an amazing songwriter."

Jeff pulled the blankets around them tighter.

"You can mourn, but I'm not letting you hide from our life together."

"I just want to be here with you."

"That works for me, baby."

"Good. Can... can there be soup later?"

"I've got tomatoes, so yes, there can be. I can even do grilled cheese sandwiches." He would do anything for Jeff. Absolutely anything.

"Later. Just soup."

"Anything you want."

"Soup. You. Holding. I hurt."

"I know. I won't let you hurt alone, though."

"Do you think Roach cared about me? And Jim? Did they like me?"

"Yeah, I do think so. I think that's why he didn't tell you about the cancer—he didn't want you to worry about him. And Jim... the man was your sponsor, of course he liked you. You can't have that kind of relationship if you don't like a person." Rye knew how hard it was for someone who was a celebrity to have true friends. It had been especially hard for Jeff because of the persona LJ had been.

"I swear, you'd better not die on me. Not for years and years and years, and then we'll go together, at the very same second."

Rye nodded. "That works for me, baby." He held Jeff tight— he wasn't going to let anything get his baby, ever.

"Cool." Jeff sighed. "Good."

"Do you need to call Donna?"

"Probably, but I don't want to, not yet."

"Okay. Are we going to the funeral?"

"There's not going to be one. He didn't want one."

"Okay." Did it make him awful that he was glad about that?

"I don't want to go anyway. He's dead."

"Yeah." Rye squeezed Jeff tight, wishing he had some magic thing to say to make it all better. Jeff cuddled in, held on. Maybe he was, just by being here. Which he always would be, so they were good.

JEFF CALLED Donna, pacing and watching the snow fall.

"LJ. How are you?"

"I quit. I'm going to write. Just write. I want to sell the big house, and I want this one. I want my life here."

"Okay."

He blinked. "Okay?"

"Well, honey, if you take away the costs of running the LJ empire, you're actually making more writing."

"Okay. You'll still be—" His friend. His manager. His soul. "—Donna?"

"As long as you don't expect me to come see you when it's snowing."

"No. No, you have to take a snowmobile out to the main road." It was amazing.

"Seriously? And you're choosing to live there?" Donna didn't get it. At all. She was an LA lady, through and through.

"Uh-huh. It's—" Real. It was a real place where he was just Jeff, just a guy. "—a good place."

"And you're happy, honey?"

"Yes. I need this—the quiet, the solitude." Rye. He needed Rye.

"As long as you're happy and doing what you want, I'm on board. You still with the giant?"

"He asked me to marry him."

A sharp gasp came down the line. "Oh, honey, I'm so happy for you. Unless you said no, in which case he's fired."

"We're ordering rings. Gold and silver together."

"Congratulations. Really."

Jeff grinned. "It's like a new life, Donna. Like a new start."

"That's great, L—" Donna cut herself off, chuckling softly. "So what do you want me to call you now?"

"Jeff. I'd like to just be plain old Jeff Smart, please."

"You got it, Jeff." It sounded right, hearing Donna call him that. Call him by his real name.

"Can you help with the house and stuff? All the details?"

"Of course, I can. You leave it in my hands. Once it's sold, you want to buy the place you're renting now?"

"I do. We do. It's amazing. Even if there's enough snow you have to use a snowmobile!"

Donna snickered, then sobered again. "You want me to let everyone know you won't be using their services anymore? Like Janie?"

"I... I'm sorry. I'm really sorry."

"Honey, it's the nature of the beast. One day you're the driver of the biggest star out there, the next day you're doing airport runs for rich kids. No one is going to blame you for not being LJ anymore. Especially under the circumstances."

"I just—" Being Lord January was going to kill him.

"You just what, honey? The only person who you have a responsibility to is yourself."

"I still…. They're good people. I can't do it anymore."

218

"And you don't have to." Donna sighed. "Honey, go tell your man what you're feeling. He'll help."

"I love you." It seemed important to say that these days.

"I love you too, Jeff." Donna sounded like she might be tearing up.

"It's going to be okay, right?" He was feeling panicked, and Rye's huge hands landed on his shoulders. They massaged him, the heat of Rye's body a wall behind him, supporting him.

"Of course it's going to be all right, Jeff. We're going to keep making money, you and me."

"Okay, you're not mad at me?" He couldn't bear that. No way.

"For what, honey?" Donna sounded honestly surprised by his question.

"I don't know...."

Donna's chuckle was soft. "Is Rye there?"

"Uh-huh."

"Go hug him. Call me later."

Rye kissed the top of his head, the silent support sure, steady. There, just like it always was. Always.

Jeff hung up the phone and then turned to hold on, heart pounding furiously. He'd done it.

Rye's arms wrapped around him, pulling him even closer. "You're shaking."

"I did it, Rye."

"What did you do, baby?"

"I quit. I told Donna to sell the house."

"Really? You've officially hung up the LJ mantle?"

Jeff nodded, swallowing hard, panicking a little.

Rye pulled back to meet his eyes, that smile huge. "That's great, Jeff. It really is. Will she keep representing you as a songwriter?"

"Uh-huh." He was going to throw up.

"Cool. That's really, really wonderful. And you're selling the house in LA? So we're going to stay here? With the snow and silence and the beautiful mountains?"

219

"Uh-huh." He looked into Rye's eyes. "I'm wigged out."

Rye nodded. "It's a huge change, I get that. I have your back, though."

"That's what Donna said. Can we get in the hot tub? Hold each other?"

"Only if we can roll in the snow afterward." Rye's eyes twinkled at him.

"You're a sick, sick man." Funny, though… and his.

"No way! It's a real thing. It's supposed to be invigorating."

"No."

"No you don't believe me, or no you won't do it?"

Jeff couldn't stop his smile. "Just no."

"Damn. Okay, we don't have to do it. This time. One day, though." Rye picked him up and moved toward the hot tub. "We are going to forgo swimming trunks, though."

"Okay. This time." He wrapped around Rye, held on tight. "Love you."

"I love you too, baby. More than anything."

"Good, because I need you."

"Yeah, you do. Probably almost as much as I need you."

Jeff didn't know about that, but that was okay. They were building something—something real. Something good. Jeff looked at Rye and twined their fingers together. "Love, can we try the bacon sandwiches tonight?"

He was feeling like he could be brave.

Often referred to as "Space Cowboy" and "Gangsta of Love" while still striving for the moniker of "Maurice," SEAN MICHAEL spends his days surfing, smutting, organizing his immense gourd collection and fantasizing about one day retiring on a small secluded island peopled entirely by horseshoe crabs. While collecting vast amounts of vintage gay pulp novels and mood rings, Sean whiles away the hours between dropping the f-bomb and pursuing the *Kama Sutra* by channeling the long-lost spirit of John Wayne and singing along with the soundtrack to *Chicago*.

A long-time writer of complicated haiku, currently Sean is attempting to learn the advanced arts of plate spinning and soap carving sex toys.

Barring any of that? He'll stick with writing his stories, thanks, and rubbing pretty bodies together to see if they spark.

Website: http://www.seanmichaelwrites.com
Blog: http://seanmichaelwrites.blogspot.ca/
Facebook: https://www.facebook.com/SeanMichaelWrites
Twitter: @seanmichael09

Cupcakes

By Sean Michael

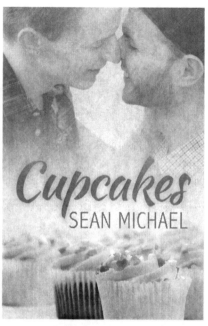

Allen Jameson had it all—the perfect house, the perfect partner, the perfect life—until his partner, Gary, died suddenly, leaving him alone in the real world, where life isn't so pretty and people make mistakes. Now Allen is the owner of Sweet 'n' Sassy Cupcake Shop, a cute boutique downtown, where he invents delicious flavors like strawberry and French meringue. Between working long hours and making special orders, Allen barely has time to think.

Then a hunky contractor walks into his shop looking for a treat. Allen and Byron Bannigan are total opposites, but they're perfect together—salty and sweet like Allen's signature peanut butter and chocolate ganache cupcakes. But as Allen struggles to juggle his business and his boyfriend, he learns he can only handle so much. He may have to choose between the cupcakes in his store and the cupcake in his bed.

http://www.dreamspinnerpress.com

DIRTY Dining

EM LYNLEY

CPSIA information can be obtained at www.ICGtesting.com
Printed in the USA
LVOW10s1451230415

435824LV00019B/585/P